FATAL Opposition

TRACEE LYDIA GARNER

FATAL OPPOSITION
© Copyright 2017 by Tracee Lydia Garner
www.Teegarner.com

Published by Tracee Lydia Garner
ISBN: 978-0998109961

All rights reserved. No part of this publication may be reproduced, distributed, or transmitted in any form or by any means, including photocopying, recording, or other electronic or mechanical methods, without the prior written permission of the author.

This is a work of fiction. Names, characters, businesses, places, events and incidents are either the products of the author's imagination or used in a fictitious manner. Any resemblance to actual persons, living or dead, or actual events is purely coincidental.

© Editing by Best Words Editing, LLC

Printed in the USA.

Cover Design and Interior Format
© KILLION GROUP INC.

ACKNOWLEDGEMENTS

Thank you, Amber Leima, my editor and friend. Thank you for being with me through the entire Parker Brothers series. Onward to our next family saga!

December 2017

Tanya,
Please enjoy my story and thank you for entering my Goodreads giveaway.
Best to you,
Tracee

1
I Thee Bored

JAMES PARKER YAWNED FOR THE fourth time that evening. This wedding reception wasn't like the bachelor parties he'd been used to attending back in his college days, and that was not a good thing. The most exciting thing that had happened to him so far was playing counselor for his friend and fellow football player Braxton Denton, who seemed increasingly inebriated, regarding his problems with women. The game highlights on the big screen across the room were the only other entertainment available, and the whole situation had James certifiably bored out of his mind.

Truth be told, he should have been studying. There was plenty of information he needed to review for a series of upcoming meetings, as well as checking he had the right attire for his new home in Virginia. Goodness knows he needed to be well-dressed for the interviews his coaches had apparently lined up now that they were in the off season. His lack of a definite contract so late into the season was playing on his mind. Beyond that, he was growing tired of playing counselor to his friend and just wanted to leave.

Lifting his glass, James took another sip of iced tea and tried not to wince. The drink needed more sugar if it was going to come even close to the kind his adoptive mother, Georgia Parker, used to make. This bitter, too-lemony-tart version would have to do. He set the glass down on the bar with distaste.

James couldn't just sneak off to find a nice warm bed in

one of the hotel's many rooms, though, because he'd somehow been tapped – again - as the designated driver for the loud knuckleheads around him. The more sloshed he watched everyone get, the more crowded James knew his truck was going to be. Irritated, he picked up his phone and searched to see if there were any on-demand transit services in the area. Maybe, he thought, he could just grab a hotel room for the night until everyone was accounted for, then mete out coffee and showers to the sore-headed ones in the morning before then, and only then, handing them back their keys.

There was a time when James hadn't been the responsible one, but things change. He had witnessed tragedy and he had grown up. Fast.

"Jay, I think we can work it out."

"Yeah?" James was pulled back to listening with half an ear to the dragging conversation: an old standard with his pal Braxton, about love. He fumbled for his usual response. "Definitely try. I mean, you're getting older, time to settle down."

"What's that, Jay? Now I'm old? What the heck, man?" James could almost see Braxton's hackles raise.

"No man, come on…" James rolled his eyes at the drunken state of his teammate. The booze explained this tendency to get insulted easy and early.

James took a deep breath and looked around the lounge area. Today's wedding had been nice enough, but now it was over. His friend Carl had gotten married to his longtime girlfriend Blakely. Now the happy couple were likely upstairs changing outfits while everyone else danced, stuffed their faces and waited for their reappearance.

Yes, he thought, it was official: he was stuck there, with nothing to do but babysit two idiots that were still reigning supreme in bachelorhood. From his vantage point, their situation looked pretty depressing. He himself hadn't gotten married either, but unlike them, he told himself, he finally had his priorities straight for once. He would get married, went his mantra, and he swore he was ready to do so now. He was done with a life of partying and drinking. For the most perfect examples of a loving marriage and family, all he had to do was look around his own family: first and foremost at his adoptive parents, now deceased, who'd taken him in as a baby. Now that they were gone, he had his brother Cole and his wife Allontis to look to.

James was on good terms with Adrian, his eldest brother, but his relationships with Dexter and Cole were especially close. The fifth brother, Deon, was in jail. If Cole, who'd been a bachelor just a few short years ago, and Dexter, whose wife had died tragically after having been unfaithful to him, could find it in themselves to love again in spite of everything, then James believed that someone could love him too. His faith taught him that married life was sacred, and settling down appealed to James on many levels. Now, just to find the right person.

He could find love, he was sure; but of late, he hadn't been all that inspired to look. He certainly couldn't in the company of his current comrades. He eyed his drunk friend again, annoyed at being forced to play chaperone. Braxton's eyes were open, but his face rested atop his glass, half full of brown liquid. The end to James's night couldn't come quickly enough.

James smiled as he mentally dismissed his current companions and turned his thoughts to his brothers and their love interests. James had only known Leedra Henderson since that past Christmas, and the first thing he'd learned about her was that she baked a lot. Each time their paths had crossed, she'd filled him with coffee cake, muffins and warm banana bread. More importantly, though, she made Dexter and his daughter Kira happy, and she and James had soon become fast friends. She seemed the perfect foil to both Dexter's quiet nature and Kira's preteen tendency to over-dramatize just about everything.

James took a deep breath. He loved his family and missed them all very much. Being on the road so often for games was taxing, and he was happy that his schedule would allow him to spend time at home reconnecting with them for a few months over the summer before training camp started back up. He was looking forward to the start of a whole new chapter with his new team. Present company excluded, that is, he mused wryly.

When cheers rang out, James stood up with everyone else and looked to the entrance of the ballroom. The crowd of revelers rushed to greet the newlyweds as a mellow song came on for their first dance.

He was happy they'd finally arrived: that meant he wouldn't have to stick around much longer. A toast, a father-daughter dance, another few rounds of drinks for Brax no doubt, then he was home free. The couple would depart for some tropical island honeymoon and that meant James could exit too, with his rowdy brood of adult children in tow. He sat back on the barstool, counting the minutes.

"I'm'a call 'er."

Braxton had finally managed to sit up straight, but the red-rimmed eyes betrayed his condition. James eyed him wearily. "Look, uh, why don't you wait until you're sober before you do that? You might say something you regret."

"Om boy, that'sha good idea. You're smart, friend."

James rolled his eyes.

"How can I gets sobered fasser?" Brax slurred.

"Um, sleep usually I guess, but this stuff, Braxton, won't help," James responded, sliding the glass out of his friend's reach despite his protests. "Bartender?" He caught the server's eye and motioned him over. "Coffee for this one - and please, no more alcohol, okay?"

Though the bartender nodded, James saw the mischief in the man's eyes, as if to say: "Sure thing, but that's what hotel rooms are for." James sighed. Drink responsibly was just a catchphrase. Encourage endlessly was the real tag line. James nodded his thanks when the server set a mug of steaming black java before Braxton and surreptitiously emptied the highball glass into the bar sink.

Standing to look out over the dance floor to check whether

they had reached an acceptable juncture to leave, James noticed an attractive woman enter with her phone to her ear. He followed her with his eyes as she sat down at the other bar on the opposite side of the large ballroom. James waited to see if someone else would join her, because surely someone would.

There was a familiarity to her, but he couldn't place where he might know her from. Musing a little, James looked back at his phone. He tapped a series of icons to pull up a recent broadcast: not interested in what was being said, only searching through the faces that appeared on the screen. One beautiful face he sought in particular. He had to figure out if that was her or not. Intrigued, he looked back across the room and found the woman, still alone, was still on the phone. Although he was now sure they didn't know each other, it seemed a perfect time for him to introduce himself.

2

Birthday Bust

CASHELL BRUER HAD ARRIVED AT the hotel on time - which was more than could be said for her friend. While listening to the usual list of excuses over the phone, she took a moment to look around and appreciate the expansive bar: not for the numerous bottles of this and that lining the back, but because it was simply a beautiful spot. And it was nearly empty. A few pool tables were dotted around nearby, but tonight she was content just to sit back and observe. Since she wasn't partying and dancing with her girlfriends now that she'd been stood up, she would just have a relaxing drink and think about the long list of stuff she needed to do for next week's upcoming assignment.

She made herself pay attention to her dear friend's hasty apologies, distractedly making the occasional sympathetic noise. She smiled at the bartender, all in black with a smart bowtie, who was waiting patiently for her to finish her conversation. "Virgin strawberry daiquiri" she mouthed and he nodded, leaving to mix her rather uninspiring favorite.

So much for getting turn't up - wasn't that what the young folks said? Man, she felt old. Cashell didn't even drink usually, but if she and her friends had been out together she might at least have ordered one alcoholic beverage.

"Girl, look – don't worry about it," she sighed into the phone, doing her best to make her friend feel better: something she seemed to do too often in both her professional and private lives. "Please. Be real. Anyway, I'm here now and I'm all dolled up, so we'll see what fine trouble I can get myself into, huh? I'll just, uh, get a drink and maybe I'll spend the night - treat myself, ya know?"

After a pause: "Yes, I know it's expensive, but you only turn thirty-three once. You missed my thirtieth, remember? - and this was supposed to be a do-over... not to make you feel bad or anything," she added, a little dramatically. "Well, we'll get this done, one day. Perhaps I'll just show up with a party pack to go. We can cut up in the basement while the kids are asleep. How's that sound?" She smiled, trying to keep an upbeat tone in her voice. Sounds like I'm saving the day yet again, she thought. After a few more moments of her friend's profuse apologies gushing into her ear, Cashell reassured her a final time that she wasn't hurt and bid her farewell to end the call at long last.

Debating whether to leave when she'd only just arrived, Cashell tossed her phone glumly onto the barstool beside her purse. So much for a girl's night out. What a bust! she thought, crestfallen that her fun plans for the night would buckle in the absence of her best friend. Your only friend, a nasty little voice corrected. She reminded herself that it must be hard to come out on the town when you had a family and little children to take care of, trying in vain to muster some sympathy for her friend's situation. All the planning and advance notice in the world could never mitigate when duty called.

Family: now there was something she knew nothing about. She had a family, certainly - a mother, a father and an older brother - but a family of her own, a son, daughter, husband... she didn't know anything about those things at all. All her relationships so far had been painfully short, not to mention so very few and far between.

She crossed her legs as she sat on the stool, trying to get comfortable. Who sat on these things, anyway? Her derriere was too big to find any real comfort. She looked down at her sparkling shoes. She'd purchased them just for a night like this, imagining that she'd be dancing with her girlfriends and maybe even finding an eligible guy to dance the night away with, just for her birthday. She wasn't prone to stalking fancy hotels and parties just for the heck of it. She was usually quite conservative and a bit of a homebody. Most nights found her at home with a book, reading or watching the news. Her birthday, on the other hand, was surely supposed to be a little more fun.

Despite the downward turn of her thoughts, Cashell took a moment to thank God and count her blessings. She was of sound mind – for the most part, anyway. She wasn't in the hospital for her birthday, not this year at least, and she was gainfully employed. She smiled, rocking a little to the music for the first time now that she'd put everything into proper perspective.

When the server approached with her overpriced Slurpee, she thanked him before looking askance at it. "Um, do you have any actual strawberries you can put in here?" Might as well get her money's worth.

The bartender rolled his eyes but nodded and left, returning a moment later with a plate of four strawberries, sliced and drizzled with some kind of thick ruby syrup.

"Thank you," she said, genuinely elated. "It's the simple pleasures in life, like real strawberries, that mean a lot," she added, smiling.

Well, this may not be a birthday party exactly, but she was alive and well and determined to have a fun night. So far, the dizzy height of fun had come in the form of strawberries with a side of red liquid sugar. What could she possibly have to look forward to next? Maybe a bowl of ice cream with chocolate syrup? Be still my heart. She shrugged, turning on the stool and almost tumbling off: a signature move. She sighed, but managed to keep her butt in the seat as she looked out across the room. Maybe she'd just cut her losses and head home.

The hotel was really quite exquisite, she noted, with beautiful sky views above and an abundance of lights around casting pretty blues and purples on the sofas, the low tables and the chrome of the barstools. The pale natural light of the moon that filtered in through the large skylight overhead created plenty of shadows: dark corners and nooks perfect for lounging and sipping your choice of drink - or maybe some heavy petting with a really cute guy, Cashell mused... if she were into that sort of thing, that is, and if she was eighteen years old and attending her senior prom. She grinned wryly at the inventions of her wandering mind.

The bar where she was seated was long, and the nearby lounge looked inviting. There was another bar on the opposite side of the cavernous room, pretty much a mirror image of the one she was sitting at, with its own bartender. At the other bar, she noticed, there was only a small group of men seated off to the side, sipping drinks, talking and playing pool.

All at once, a group of people burst in through the far doors in a human train, dancing and giggling around the room's maze of dark corners and running past her in fits of giddy laughter, stumbling over their own feet. Before long, the bar where she sat was filled with deafening music as more people flocked in to join them. After a minute or two of wondering what on earth was going on, she noticed a woman in a beautiful white dress and a man, obviously the groom, spinning her around. The group of revelers made a circle around them and they danced, oblivious to anyone but each other.

The bartender set another slushy drink in front of her and indicated the top with a smile. To her delight, there were fresh strawberries in the drink this time around, right on top for her to see. She smiled at him with thanks.

"We have two weddings here tonight: one here and one upstairs," the bartender informed her, noticing the direction of her gaze. "We have another lounge if it's too loud in here for you, Ma'am - did you want me to show you where it was? You'd have it to yourself."

Just what I want: to be alone... not, Cashell thought silently, meeting the waiter's questioning stare. She hoped she didn't spy pity in his eyes. Aloud, she responded: "Think they'll mind if I just sit and watch for a bit?" She liked the music, even though the booming of it would likely deafen her.

"Wedding crasher, are you? I wouldn't have pegged you as the type," the waiter quipped, with a twinkle in his eye. "Well, they haven't even looked your way - they're likely all pretty drunk. The party's already been going a minute. Watch all you want, hon. I'm sure there's a single person in there somewhere to dance with, if you were to shimmy your way into what looks like the Soul Train Line over there." The waiter chuckled at his own wit and moved away toward the other end of the bar.

Shimmy her way in? That seemed silly... but Cashell did love dancing, and she enjoyed the romance she could see in the couple's eyes: the happiness of their special day and the way they interacted with one another, joyfully oblivious to whoever else was around.

You really shouldn't have subjected yourself to any of this, the nasty little voice chided her. It was true. Watching the fun just focused her mind even more sharply on the fact that for most of her life, illness had kept her from these very sorts of things. She motioned to the bartender once more.

"Can I have some water please?"

When a man set his drink down at her end of the bar, Cashell looked over and her throat went dry. The simple glass of water she'd just ordered couldn't arrive fast enough. The man smiled at her and took a seat on the barstool next to her purse.

"You want more iced tea, boss?" the bartender said, making his way back up the bar.

"No way, Stephen - your iced tea sucks!"

Cashell observed the two, momentarily shocked and even annoyed at the bluntness and lack of respect this new guy showed the bartender. She held her daiquiri closer to her mouth as she watched Stephen – that was the bartender's name, apparently - merely shrug his shoulders and give a sardonic laugh.

"Well, our iced tea's better than your slide technique when

you're running the ball on that field, Tinkerbell."

Cashell's eyes flicked over to catch the stranger's reaction. The two men looked threateningly at each other for just a beat... before they joined in laughter together. They exchanged a fist-bump and all seemed right with the world once more. Men.

Cashell followed football, but she really didn't recognize this man or know what position he might play. He did play, though, obviously. He was tall, even when he sat down, and "running the ball", as the bartender had commented, meant he threw it - or he was supposed to. That much she knew. She couldn't stop herself from checking out the rest of him. Even clad in a form-fitting tuxedo, he didn't appear to be overly muscular, but he filled out his dress shirt nicely and she could tell that powerful arms were underneath: the fabric was taut all around his biceps. He had a large, fit torso with no belly fat whatsoever, and large hands. She couldn't help but inspect all his features more closely to see if she could place him on a local team. She couldn't.

"Hello, beautiful." Her heart stopped.

"Hello," she said, giving a shy smile. He'd clearly been checking her out too. She silently braced herself for a cheesy follow-up line.

"I'm James Parker."

Just a full name: not the kind of thing she'd expected. She nodded, wondering if that name should ring a bell. She looked away and then back at him as if some new awareness might dawn on her, but none did.

"Cashell." She held her hand out tentatively and he took it. His grip was strong and firm; he shook her hand, lingered and she was the one who pulled away.

"Bruer, right?"

Startled, she looked at him more closely, her defenses instantly going up. Suddenly hesitant, she set her drink aside in what she hoped was a casual way, wondering what the man before her was all about - besides good looking, besides tall

dark and handsome, and besides knowing her last name.
"I've seen you on television. I'm Dexter Parker's brother.

3
Fun!

"OH!" CASHELL IMMEDIATELY RELAXED. "Of course. I, uh, helped your brother... well, I helped him when his wife was in the accident, and then later, when Evie – I mean, Leedra - came back into town. How are they doing?"

"They're good."

"Did they get married yet?"

"I don't think it will be long. I'm sure you'll get an invite in the mail any day now," James smiled.

"Oh, I doubt it. They seem like the small, intimate wedding type: few guests, close friends and family only, that sort of thing. I may be a token invite if they do, but nothing more, you know?" She brushed off the idea of attending. She'd always loved weddings, though, ever since watching them from her hospital bed on Days of Our Lives.

Growing up around too many romantic novels, she had always wanted to witness any and all the nuptials she could, right before her very eyes. Silly childhood interest as it was, it got old quick when you didn't ever seem to be the one walking down the aisle to meet your own knight in shining armor.

"You helped them through not one but two rough patches," James reminded her. "I think they all think a lot of you. You in love with Dexter or something?" he added jauntily.

She looked at him sharply and shook her head. Truth be told, everyone is a bit in love with Dexter, she thought ruefully. He was a great person. But no - she wasn't really in love with him. She was in love with the idea of being in a relationship, a lasting reciprocal arrangement; and that's what men like Dexter, and likely Cole, inspired. Unconditional love for the ones that were lucky enough to be on the receiving end.

Now, as she regarded the man across from her – whom she kept telling herself was too young and naive for her to be talking to at all – she found herself looking at his arms and neck. A tattoo peeked up over his collar: it was barely visible, but what must have been the top of it was there. He had a sparkle in his eyes and a beautiful smile, with a wide mouth and lush full lips.

She looked down. "I'm not in love with any Parker brother. From what I've seen, Cole and Dexter are good upstanding people and I've grown to care about them. That's all. I don't drool over men who are attached. And, frankly, I don't appreciate the insinuation to the contrary," she replied coolly.

Feeling that she'd handled that situation quite smoothly, Cashell took a long sip of her drink – and promptly sucked up a rogue piece of strawberry. She set the drink down as she spluttered and coughed. Instantly, James moved closer to her, thumped her back gently and, with quick fingers, took the straw from her frozen drink, put it in her water and handed it to her. She gulped it greedily.

Even with her windpipe cleared, her body still tingled with new awareness and all kinds of sensations. He rubbed her back in a circular motion she was surprised by the way it made her feel. She swiveled on her seat just a bit so he was forced to stop.

"Thank you." Her voice came out groggy, raspy. She cleared her throat again and set the water back on the bar. Of all the people to have a medical issue in front of, this man was not the one. Mortified, she averted her eyes. She hadn't realized she'd gulped most of her water in her nervousness until James walked around the bar, took her glass and pressed the right button on the soda gun to refill it. He set it back in front of her.

"You know your way around a bar," she commented. "Should I be worried?"

James smiled. "Nah. I have my bartending license, so I've filled in for Cole at his restaurant in NYC a couple summers. Came in handy in college… 'til I discovered extracurricular activities."

"Impresses the ladies, I'm sure," she said, rolling her eyes. She was on to him. Playa!

"Sports," he said, correcting her, his face serious if not a little wounded.

She nodded, surprised. "Oh. I'm sorry, I… Thank you." What could she say? She'd been coughing, he had made an effort to comfort her, and now here she was insulting him.

Determined to keep quiet for a few moments, she sipped pensively until all seemed well with her throat once more: she could talk normally again at last. "So, the brothers. There's Adrian, then you, right?"

"Yep, then Deon, Cole, Dexter. Five," he said, counting them off on his fingers. "Deon's in jail, so I guess he sort of doesn't count for now. Then there's me. I was the last one to be adopted. Adoptive parents can only rehabilitate so many, so four successes out of five ain't bad." James shrugged. "Now your turn. Why are you here all alone?"

Cashell contemplated what to say, but nothing phony came to mind. "I, uh – well, it's my birthday," she eventually confessed.

She watched as his stare became serious. She turned away: she didn't like this new scrutiny. The last thing she wanted was for him to feel sorry for her. Cashell watched the people on the dance floor. The crowd, jovial and riotous before, had thinned out considerably. The wedding party was gone. Now there were only a handful of couples left and the hips on those bodies seemed relaxed. Their embraces were close and they seemed to sway way too intimately for such a public place. She felt the blush creep up her neck at the sight mixed with the very suggestive lyrics of the contemporary song.

When Cashell turned back around, she averted her eyes. James looked out, saw the same thing and his eyes widened.

She wanted to laugh, but that might invite awkward conversation about what they were both witnessing.

Testing her voice, she cleared her throat again before speaking. "Um, do you know the couple that got married here tonight?" Her head jerked back to indicate the couples without turning for a second look.

"Distantly," he replied. "I got kind of volunteered – volun-told, haha – to be a designated driver for whoever is left and doesn't have a reservation to stay the night. Likely to include those two knuckleheads over there." He nodded in the direction of the men at the pool table. "Lucky me."

The movements of the men in question and the sudden raised voices clearly indicated that a simple game of pool had gotten drunkenly out of hand. James shrugged. "Hope I don't have to break up a fight tonight, too." As they continued to regard the group of men, a small knot of women wearing the team's jerseys and too-tight jeans joined the pool players. James rolled his eyes and cast a glance heavenward. "My time here likely just got extended." He turned toward the bar in resignation, sipping his soda.

"Are those guys your new teammates?" Cashell said.

"Almost. The John Hancock hasn't been put on the dotted line yet."

She nodded. "What are you waiting for, then?"

James shrugged, and she wondered if he was surprised she asked.

"Negotiations, a better agent, all of the above." He said after a few minutes. "I'll probably sign next week."

James realized with some surprise that, throughout the evening, he'd discussed all sort of details about his personal and professional situation to someone he'd only just met. He took a deep breath. There'd be plenty of time to figure out his contract issues. He could even get hold of the right lawyer to assist him, if he would just buckle down and read the contract.

Truth be told, he was glad for the reprieve from football while he integrated himself back into the local area. This was where he grew up: the nation's capital, where things were familiar, where his true family was, and he'd been relieved to get back to them. He still struggled to identify with a true home base, due to the fact that he didn't know his biological family, but his ideals about what constituted home and family and what it really meant to belong somewhere were gradually changing. He knew that might always be a struggle, no matter where he lived.

"I was in the Carolinas for about six years, mostly for college, then got drafted to the state team. We went to the Super Bowl and lost; then I told my agent that if an opportunity opened up here, I'd take it - regardless of anything else working out, regardless of pay. Getting back here was more important than anything else."

James had always wanted to be back there, and recently the timing had finally presented itself for him to come home. There wasn't as much pressure now that he'd played some ball over the last four years. After all that had happened in Carolina, he could honestly say the only thing he felt was gratitude to escape from that area and that situation relatively unscathed. This was an opportunity for a new start, a new chapter, and he was trying to embrace it.

Determined to live in the moment, James looked back at his beautiful companion. He wanted to shift the subject away from his family issues, which was easy when he devoted his full attention to her.

"You certainly didn't come here to be trapped at the bar listening to some random passerby's musings about his fledgling career," he began. "You look really pretty tonight. It's your birthday, so where's your man hiding at?"

He was graced with another smile, but behind her eyes, he sensed something else. Pain? Disappointment? He wasn't sure. Surely someone as pretty as her, a career woman no less, had it all going on. Maybe her date was running late. He looked at his watch.

"My girlfriends were going to meet me here, but, uh, they both have families," she replied. "Their kids go to the same school and both caught some kind of bug... you know how it goes."

"That's messed up, especially on your birthday."

James looked at her, his eyebrows raised. "Let's see now - what can we do to turn this thing around? We should at least try, shouldn't we? You came to the hotel, you're all on fleek, looking fine... hmm. What do you ladies normally like to do?" He crossed his arms and studied her as she shifted in her seat, unsure whether to be flattered or embarrassed by his attention.

"It's – it's fine. I was gonna go home, I start a new assignment next week - I should start reading up on my background reports," she stammered, suddenly shy.

"Not on your birthday, Cashell - really?" James returned. "Tell me: what did you want to do here? I know how important just chit-chatting with your girl friends can be, but you had to have more than just that planned for your big night?"

Cashell relented. "I wanted to go dancing."

"No way! And they say women are complicated. Shoot, that's easy. And this is the perfect place." James smiled as he eased off the stool, moved closer to her and held out his hand.

He was unprepared when she slid down from the barstool. He was tall, at six feet four inches, but she was... not. He dwarfed her short stature by more than a foot. Her heels gave her some height, but she was the cutest little short thing he'd ever seen.

"Television makes you look way taller," he said, looking down at her in playful disbelief.

"Gee, thanks," she snapped.

"No, I just mean - "

"I'm short. I already know this."

She looked up at him and placed her hands on her hips, looking so fierce that he actually moved back before smiling down at her, not meaning to hurt her feelings. "Something tells me you are short but formidable," James offered.

"That's nicer I guess. Thank you."

He sensed her reticence, but she was smiling up at him. That was a good sign: thank goodness she wasn't easily offended. She grabbed her purse from the stool and took his hand.

James didn't have to lead her far, and she heard the music before they got there. The doors of the nearby room swung open to reveal what looked like a hundred or so people dancing in the dark, with strobe lights highlighting all kinds of bodies all intertwined, bumping and grinding in tune to the music blasting from the speakers. James moved forward, still holding Cashell's hand. They paused long enough for her to secure her bag across her body, then they hit the dance floor together.

If she was nervous, so was he, but he'd brought her there and now he had to make good on his impromptu spontaneity. Hesitant, feeling rusty, old, outdated as far as this scene was concerned, and possibly in a little over his head, James determinedly closed the distance between them, put his arms loosely around her and swayed, tentatively at first, until she begin to move more vigorously with the beat. By the end of the song, they danced as if there were no one else there but the two of them.

4
Not Fun!

AS THEY LEFT THE DANCE floor a few songs later for a drink break, Cashell continued to watch all the people around her. Everyone seemed to have endless energy for partying and dancing nonstop. James led her through the crowd to the bar and ordered her a cherry Coke. She realized with some surprise that he hadn't asked her about whether she was drinking anything stronger, and he ordered a Sprite for himself. He passed her the Coke before taking a sip of his own soft drink.

James certainly was in shape, she noted in admiration. He didn't ever seem to sweat; or if he did, dancing wasn't enough to get it going. There was more light closer to the bar, and she was glad because it meant she could see him better. His eyes were lighter than they first seemed, almost amber-brown. He had large ears and a wide nose, and his hair was thick and bushy.

A Parker brother, she thought incredulously. Of all the people to meet that night... Cashell hadn't even remembered there were any more guys in this family. While she'd never met James, she'd have thought she might have recognized him, perhaps from family pictures hung around the Parker home. If she had, she thought as she looked at him, she'd have been sure to put more effort into arranging a meeting.

As James had mentioned, Cashell had had cause to visit the Parker family home some time ago while representing Dexter, James's brother, as a media consultant following his wife's mysterious death. Subsequently, Cashell had assisted the family once again when Leedra - now Dexter's fiancé – had turned out to be a missing person featuring in a complex cold case from twenty-five years ago, finally solved when Leedra reappeared in the States after years at sea. It had all been complex but interesting work, Cashell reflected fondly.

In helping Dexter, Cashell had come to learn a lot about the family, but she'd never actually met James Parker before. He was the last and youngest brother and, so far, completely different from the rest as far as spontaneity and humor were concerned. There were some other differences, too. While Dexter, a doctor, was just outright handsome, James was a dangerous-looking sort. He held mischief in his eyes and looked as if he liked to joke around a lot.

Cashell's earlier feelings of being abandoned on such an important day had taken a dramatic upturn and she noted with pleasure that she was actually having fun for once. She tried not to dwell on the fact that eventually, after tonight, her birthday would be over and she'd be back at her all-consuming job, managing crises for people who couldn't seem to keep their high profiles out of love triangles, scandalous allegations, mysteries and countless other personal and professional dramas that hurt their families as well as their careers. Just next week, she'd be working for a contractor for one of these sorts of cases: one that she didn't yet have complete details about. In an effort to avoid her work consuming her life entirely, she was scaling back individual clients.

"What are you thinking about?" Cashell's eyes flicked back to James as he questioned her.

"Just, uh, work." She blushed. "I'm trying not to, but it just finds its way into my brain."

"You got a good-looking man doing his best to entertain you and you're thinking about work? Darn it, I'm losing my charm."

Cashell laughed. Spontaneously, she touched his arm, which felt warm and solid under her cool fingers. His show of arrogance made her smile. He didn't even seem as if he meant it that way – just silly enough to make her laugh.

"You're quite charming and I'm having fun. Thank you so much."

James nodded. "So, what else was on the agenda for tonight?"

Cashell felt his gaze intensify and, setting her drink aside, she snatched up a cocktail napkin and dabbed away the beads of perspiration he must have seen on her upper lip and forehead. Despite the fact that it was still early in the winter season, the room was warm, and the number of bodies in the place just increased the temperature that much more. Truth be told, that wasn't the only reason her body temperature was rising, but she wouldn't mention anything about the other cause. She was having a wonderful time, and she would not let anything ruin it for her.

"Let's see," she said, thinking about what her erstwhile girlfriends might be doing for her – or making her do – at this stage in the evening if they were here. "I suppose one of my friends would be giving me some sort of dare. And maybe one of them would have brought cake." She looked around for the bartender. "Do you think they have a menu here? I could order some chocolate cake for myself, to take home."

James laughed. "Take it home? You could just share it with me! What am I anyway, chopped liver?"

Out of the blue, he leaned across the bar and whispered something to the female server. The woman smiled at him initially, but once he finished talking she turned a colder, less friendly stare toward Cashell. Cashell could see her all but hissing and drawing her claws.

"What did you ask her?" she asked with some apprehension.

"I'll tell you in a minute."

"You're mysterious, James Parker."

"Am I?"

"Yes."

"You like it?"

She detected the hope in his question.

"Very much," she said, a little coyly. Was he flirting? Was

she? She moved her hands, snapped her fingers and tapped her toes to the music. She closed her eyes again, savoring the night — because all too soon it would be over and done with for good.

"You're thinking about work again? Man, now my ego really hurts."

"I'm not. I was thinking about… well, my life. You get a bit nostalgic around your birthday. Another year… you know?"

James shrugged.

"You don't know," Cashell corrected herself. "You're like, what, twenty-five?"

"Somewhere around there," he smiled.

She nodded. The fact that he didn't volunteer his age probably meant he was even younger than she'd guessed.

"I'm thirty-three," she declared.

James staggered back in mock horror, laughing. "What a death sentence. Goodness gracious. Let me find your aide so she can wheel your old butt back home and get your oxygen tank." He snickered, but stopped when he saw she wasn't laughing with him. "Sorry, Cashell. I was kidding, really. All right, close your eyes." Cashell saw the woman bartender doing something out of the corner of her eye. After a moment's hesitation, she closed her eyes as he'd requested.

She heard some things around, but it was impossible to discern anything amidst the music's loud volume until he whispered in her ear that she could open them again. When she did, to her delight, he was holding a huge piece of chocolate cake before her, with a very large mound of ice cream beside it. A lit candle glowed on the top.

"I would sing you Happy Birthday, but this music has made me tone deaf," James said.

She laughed, unable to believe her eyes. Nostalgia was all well and good, she thought in a bit of panic, but crying at this moment would be the worst possible response to his thoughtfulness. Even as she felt the tears prick at her eyes, she managed to blink them away along with her welling emotion.

"This is the best birthday ever," she managed to say.

James handed her a spoon, but before she could remove the candle he pulled the plate from her eager fingers.

"What happened to the wish? You have to make a wish first – like duh! For realsies!"

"I..." Cashell was thoughtful. She suddenly realized that she didn't actually know what she wished for. None of the wishes of old had come true, so eventually she'd just stopped hoping. She loved chocolate cake and she loved ice cream, though, and this portion was very generous. The chocolate layers seemed to beckon to her seductively. Just like when they'd been dancing, she wished heartily that her nerves would let her breathe for just a few moments: that her doubting-Thomas issues would disperse and just for once let her stop thinking ahead, missing the wonderful time that was right under her nose.

"I don't believe in wishing so much. I..."

"Then say the prayer that's been on your heart a while."

She nodded, her eyes riveted to his as he nudged the plate closer to her. She was a little taken aback that he was so willing to supply a faith-based alternative so boldly to someone he had only just met, as opposed to the standard operating procedure of the wish. She began to wonder if he prayed for real.

"Okay," she said with determination. "I can do that."

She closed her eyes tight, prayed her most heartfelt prayer harder than she ever had before, and blew out the candle with a single, simple puff. She hoped beyond hope that this prayer on this particular birthday would come true by the time her next birthday rolled around.

When she opened her eyes, James was still there. So far so good! She laughed out loud at her silly way of thinking. Between cake, ice cream and loud music, this was the best birthday of her life.

———◆———

A while later, James scraped up the last of the cake and ice cream with his spoon and popped it into his mouth. Cashell had eventually cried uncle and asked him to finish the treat. He couldn't believe it himself, but he was actually having as much fun as she was.

As he and Cashell moved to the dance floor one last time, an alarm sounded in another part of the building. He heard it in the distance, echoing around the halls. His hands tightened protectively on her as people around them gradually realized that there was an emergency. The shrill sound of the alarm seemed to grow closer moment by moment.

"I think we're gonna have to evacuate," he said, speaking close to her ear. A second later, there was a loud scream from the kitchen and a man ran out with the sleeve of his jacket on fire. There was a large explosion and it felt as if the entire hotel shook.

In a flash, James was on the move, pulling Cashell along with him. He went straight to the man with his arm ablaze, whipped off his jacket and deftly smothered the flames. Smoke rose.

When the shaking and booming of the explosion subsided, everyone who wasn't too scared to move started yelling and tumbling in a mess toward the door. Unfazed, James continued helping the man, who regarded him with stunned amazement. Now that his arm was no longer on fire, he clearly wasn't planning to wait around. He managed to utter some mumbled thanks before joining the stampede toward the doors, limping and cradling his injured arm.

James hurried back to Cashell, who was looking up at him as wide-eyed as if he'd just taken out some sort of criminal.

"Are you okay? I won't leave you," James reassured her. He followed her eyes. "The guy seemed okay," he added. "He was on his feet, he was moving, he was obviously well enough to exit on his own."

"Okay but, uh, that was really brave, James."

James shrugged. "Let's get to the stairwell. The elevator probably won't be in working order." He took her hand.

"It won't?"

James shrugged. "We can check."

They made it to the stairwell and James grabbed her protectively once again as someone in a much greater hurry than they pushed past, bumping Cashell closer to him.

"Cashell, look at me," James said with fresh concern. "Do you usually sweat so much?"

Cashell shook her head. "N-no, I... I'm just winded, from dancing so much, then all this excitement."

Cashell was pitched forward again as another explosion rocked the hotel floor. People around them screamed and started to run.

"What's happening?"

"Fire, fire! Terrorist attack!" someone yelled, and now more people hurtled toward them, crushing to get to the stairwell exit as if they had only just realized they were in danger. James held Cashell tightly to shield her from the jostling of people, whose fear had overridden their common sense that an orderly exit would be safer than this chaotic movement of bodies. They were all drunk, no doubt, and he felt a burst of anger. James didn't think it was a terrorist attack: not that he knew what one would look like, but he supposed they would have heard gun shots or something. Still more people bumped into each other and a few fell down. He prayed no one was trampled in the chaos. He pulled out his phone to check for any automatic alerts around their location. None.

"What does it say?"

James dipped an eyebrow, searching further through the news feed. "Nothing yet to indicate this is a terror attack," he replied. The stairwell door was jammed with a crowd of people that wouldn't fit through it. Another major catastrophe might even be at hand if people didn't stop their panicked rush. James's frustration grew. "Look - we're gonna take the back stairwell," he said over his shoulder to Cashell, pulling her away from the throng.

When they reached the elevator, he studied a map mounted

next to the industrial metal fire doors. "This way," he said decisively, grabbing her hand again to pull her urgently away from the chaos and down the hall. He had to push against the crowd, but was finally able to reach another stairway in an adjacent hall that had no people around it at all.

"Are you sure?"

"You can trust me," James replied decisively. "I won't leave you, no matter what - okay?"

Cashell silently shook her head. The fear on her face told James there was more of a problem than met the eye. This wasn't the expected reaction of someone that could just walk down the stairs to evacuate a building. There were a lot of stairs, but surely it was nothing major? He felt that he had to be missing something. Gently, he led her down the first flight and the second, until her steps faltered and she sat down abruptly on the steps.

"Are you okay?"

She nodded. "I'm okay. I just – uh - " She grasped her wrist, fingering what had looked to James like a normal pretty bracelet. As she moved it, he finally noticed the tag and the raised red lettering. "James, I - I have a heart condition."

Understanding at last, James took her face in his hands. "Aren't you lucky you're stuck with me, then?" he said without hesitation. "I'll make sure you get downstairs fine, okay? You have many more birthdays ahead of you."

If Cashell was surprised by his conviction, she didn't argue.

"We'll take our time. We'll walk slowly, carefully, so you don't fall. When you need a little break, I'll carry you."

"You can't carry me down all these flights of stairs, James," she protested incredulously.

He smiled. "Not fast, no; but if you make it part of the way down, I will carry you the rest of the way."

"I'll be all right, I just - uh, I can't go fast."

He could see she was embarrassed admitting that, yet the only thing on his mind was establishing just how extensive her heart condition was. Had Dexter ever mentioned it before?

She seemed fine, beyond fine, and perfectly fit at first glance. All he said in response was: "You underestimate me."

She started off rather quickly, but stopped halfway and sat down - not because she was winded, but to discard her shoes.

"Better?" James asked.

She nodded, but remained sitting on the step. "Sorry, but my pantyhose are slippery - I'll have to take them off too, so I can move a little faster without slipping."

He nodded and averted his eyes as she shimmied quickly out of her pantyhose. She stuffed the hosiery into the pocket of her dress and looked wistfully at her jettisoned shoes. "I love those shoes... but I mean, if it comes down to my life or the shoes, I choose life – I guess." She grimaced.

James smiled. "That's a girl. You don't want me thinking you're the superficial type, right?" He seriously doubted she was.

She managed a tight smile and James offered her his arm again. They continued down the stairs. Moving together, they kept a steady pace until they were over halfway down.

James was thoughtful as he took the stairs, careful not to rush her and hoping he'd reassured her. The dancing had likely winded her, and he was still puzzling over the new mystery of her heart condition.

The stairwell was quiet and cold, but the silence was a welcome change from the earlier chaos. In this new quiet, her breathing seemed extra loud in his ear - and extra strained, as he listened more intently. She leaned more and more on him for support. When they eventually made it down, he resolved to take her to the hospital. He would stick by her, no matter what. Suddenly, James felt an unexpected and overwhelming responsibility for her safety.

"James?"

Her labored voice, now barely a whisper, snapped James out of his reverie. "Yeah?" James stopped moving to look down at her. She was leaning on him almost completely now and he viewed her with concern.

"I just want to tell you that sometimes I faint."

"What – when? Like, pass out, you mean?" He always thought of himself as calm, but this latest revelation had him flustered.

She started moving again, and he went with her. He took the steps one at a time with her at his side, his long strides having to contract to match her short ones. "Yeah," she continued. "Like, I faint sometimes... I feel like that's what might happen once we get to the bottom. I just want you to be prepared. It happens. I'm not scared, it's just that fainting spells sometimes happen when I'm winded. Okay?"

"Um - okay." Prepared... how exactly was he supposed to prepare for something like that? James couldn't tell if what she was telling him made her feel just as nervous. Was she informing him or reassuring herself?

"I'm just telling you because I don't want you to be nervous, okay? If an ambulance comes, you can show them my bracelet. It has medical codes on it that only they would know."

James nodded absently. "Okay. Look, this is the fourth floor. We're almost there."

He wasn't encouraged by her small smile. She did give a nod, though, and at this point he'd take any sign she gave as something positive. Then, out of nowhere, she spoke up.

"Despite our present situation," she whispered, "I just want you to know that I had so much fun tonight. Hey - we made it!" she smiled, hugely relieved to be near the exit. "Oh my goodness, we made it. You sure know how to show a girl some fun. Now I can get some air."

James grinned from ear to ear and turned to look at the most beautiful eyes he had ever seen. He gave her a spontaneous hug – after what had admittedly been an amazing night, he regretfully imagined that this was goodbye.

"I hate that my heart always has to interfere with my activities," Cashell sighed.

"We're fine, Cashell. You made it! Now we can get you rested and look for a doctor, just to get you checked out."

James leaned down, preparing to brush his lips against hers. She smiled dreamily and so did he, but suddenly she looked panicked, almost apologetic, and placed a hand over her heart. It was then that she fainted.

5
Work Relations Revelations

JAMES ENTERED THE ASHBURN OFFICES on the campus of the Washington Rebels team park and walked to the conference room. He had just completed his official signing with the team. He still couldn't quite believe he'd have the opportunity to play at home: his real home. The DC metro area was his real home, no matter what his birth certificate said. This was where he'd been raised.

At this stage in his career, while this process was certainly exciting to James, it was also just another day. He had opted for a low-key signing: business only, no press. He'd been through this rigmarole once already in his career and he knew the novelty wore off quickly, so it was best not to entertain the jumped-up fanfare until he could get out on the field. He had a healthy degree of humility about these occasions and he kept that front and center in his brain. He had a second chance now, and he planned to honor the do-over opportunity God had given him.

Despite the low-key front he tried to maintain, the contract might as well have been on fire in his hand. He was ready to tell someone. He felt really good. He'd likely call his brothers – and Allontis, naturally – as soon as he could get out of this final meeting. He was home, and his North Carolina past was benched.

James had just learned of this impromptu meeting last week. He could only guess that perhaps it was standard operating procedure here. Surely it was too early in the process for any discussions that he should be nervous about? He turned the corner of the carpeted hall, where pictures of all the local football greats lined the walls. It was quiet. Generally, players scattered like flies in the off season. At this point, most were already in vacation mode: all the more apparent here, considering it was only March, and the celebratory spirit had been in ample evidence at the wedding Friday night. Today's visit to the campus was only his second one so far. The place was nice: everything was in pristine condition, and sparkling clean.

James grasped the handle of the mahogany door and when he entered, he stopped in his tracks. Two people he could do without seeing stood before him: two people he had no interest in spending any time with beyond the occasions when they were all in uniform and working together on the field to defeat their mutual opposition. He'd made up his mind about Alex Cuban and Trent Jessup just the other night: after their drunken brawling and bawdy behavior with the rest of the group, he'd decided he wouldn't be socializing with them unless he absolutely had to. From now on, they weren't friends – just coworkers.

The room was large, but the big table took up most of the space. Televisions were mounted on all four walls, and a credenza with water stood next to a fridge packed with Gatorade. He noticed that the others already had drinks in hand, but decided not to get one for himself. He didn't know yet what this meeting was about, so he had no plans to make himself at home. Not yet.

"What the heck happened to you the other night?" Alex sneered.

James took a seat at the long conference table a careful two seats away from his teammates.

"What do you mean?" James replied. He knew what they were talking about.

"You left us high and dry," Trent lamented.

"Yeah, thanks a lot, J – some team player you are!" Alex said, echoing Trent's frustration.

James rolled his eyes. He didn't know them well enough to be sure when they were joking and when they were serious. Since he'd only known them a short time, he decided they were probably joking. That would have to do until he could read them better. He liked them all right, he supposed, but he just didn't tend to 'hang out' with anyone anymore. That was a hard type of person to be, especially considering both his age and his profession. The things he enjoyed didn't fit the stereotype of the single, eligible, multi-million-dollar-earning football bachelor.

He shrugged off their stares of incredulity. "You guys, I'm sure you've heard of a little company called Uber. They can give you a ride, you know." James gave a short laugh, his brain busy recreating the night when he'd been rescued by beauty. Despite the chaotic turn the end of night had taken, he'd trade a lot for some more time with Cashell Bruer. Any day of the week.

"I was ready to go and then the fire broke out and I couldn't find you guys," he responded. "I took the emergency exit stairs down to my truck and just left." That was mostly true, he told himself.

"Saw you with the women at the party and figured you'd made some love connection," Trent chimed in, raising an eyebrow.

Truly, James wished he'd met Cashell sooner in the evening. If only all hell hadn't broken loose, he could have had more uninterrupted time with her - plus she wouldn't have fainted on her very special day. On top of all that, he'd never actually managed to give her that kiss.

Although things had ended poorly, James was happy: he felt that he'd lucked out with how he'd spent his evening. Cashell's heart condition had unnerved him at first. When they'd gotten downstairs and she'd fainted, he'd carried her outside to one of the many ambulances on the scene and gotten her checked out. To his great relief, the oxygen and monitoring the EMTs gave her had revived her and she'd slowly woken up, gracing him with a beautiful smile. Relief had surged through him and he would have kissed her if her brother hadn't arrived, thanked him briefly and whisked her away.

James knew he would never forget the feeling of her weight in his arms, yet he reflected that he knew nothing about her at all, really. Despite the crazy night having taken place two whole days ago, he could not manage to get Ms. Bruer out of his mind.

He didn't catch what his new teammates had just said, and he really didn't care. Regardless, whatever it was would have to wait, because all eyes now turned to the door as the general manager entered, flanked by the assistant and head coaches. Solemnly, each of the men took their places around the conference table.

"Good morning, gentlemen," growled the team's manager. "I wish it was a better morning, but it looks as though the antics of last Friday night bear testament to exactly why your images need improving. Wouldn't you agree, Mr. Jessup? - Mr. Cuban? - Mr. Parker?"

As soon as they'd entered, James had sat up straight; now he realized with a cold shock that he was included in these remarks. He had no idea what they were talking about.

"Anyone want to tell me what occurred Friday night? Or should I just infer?"

James looked at Trent and Alex, waiting for their responses. "What's he talking about?" he blurted.

Trent and Alex both began talking at once and the coach spoke again, putting up a hand.

"You are very lucky that the ink is dry on all your new paperwork, otherwise I guess this might've been cause to terminate your contracts before they'd even started."

"Look, coach, uh - things got out of hand," Trent began uneasily. "I guess we got a little rowdy. The bride and groom had left, then the girls from the team came and did some sort of bachelorette thing – you know..."

"Yes, we've heard about the 'girls from the team' - who,

mind you, were wearing team-licensed outfits at the time." The coach looked severe. "They are in their own meeting, being addressed separately. Unless attending an official team event, you don't wear team paraphernalia. I thought I'd print out the team book and give you all a second copy, just in case you are somehow still unaware of our policies and procedures."

James caught the spiral bound book as it glided across the smooth veneer of the table and stared at the cover before looking up incredulously. The others had caught their books in the same manner.

"Sir," James started. "Bill, look, I left early. I don't even know what you guys are talking about."

He was having some trouble following along, but he certainly wasn't about to be lumped into something that didn't concern him. He hadn't been with them for the latter part of the evening, and had definitely not been present when whatever they had done caused all that chaos to ensue. He didn't even know enough to be sure they were the guilty parties in any of it.

"Well, then surveillance will clear you, Mr. Parker, as soon as we get our hands on it."

"There's surveillance?" Trent yelped.

"Of course, Jessup," the manager continued icily. "And, speaking of which, you need to start conducting yourself as if there is a camera circling above your head at all times. I want you all to know that if this comes back to bite us, your contracts will be terminated. Do I make myself clear?"

"Excuse me." James spoke up even though he felt like no one was listening to him at all. "Just so we're clear, I was at the bar having a drink with... with a friend I'd met. If Trent and Alex started something, I was not involved. I was trying to find my way out of the building, like any sane person would have. Everyone was running, we were all tripping over each other - it was complete ridiculousness. People could have had gotten hurt. I have no idea what these clowns were up to at the time."

"Convenient, isn't it?" snarled the coach, suddenly irate. "Like I said, we'll wait to view the surveillance footage."

"You have my word. I wasn't there." James tried to keep the anger out of his voice. He was sitting up straight and he'd scooted to the edge of his seat. He couldn't believe this. On day one, he was already in the red zone. His fingers tapped the table. He was experiencing a mild case of déjà vu… but he was done with that life, that particular time in his life, which had been littered with silly and life-alteringly bad judgment calls. No one in this room knew what he'd been through in college, all thanks to a bunch of screw-ups just like the two adolescents in the musclebound adult bodies beside him. Just what he needed – and he hadn't even got things going yet…

It was even more obvious now that he had to steer clear of these guys, and he'd start doing that today. He'd let them know he wouldn't be 'hanging out' with them any longer, as soon as this ridiculousness was over. He tried to tune back in to what the management team was saying to him.

"Well, if you are as above-board as you say, then our new public relations firm will have an easy time with you, won't they?" Bill was finishing.

"Huh?" James was wrongfooted.

"The team from Bruer & Associates will be here any minute. You all are to tell them about every public-relations incident you've ever had, both long past and more recent. We'll get her team's input on handling any situations. She's an old hand at dealing with this sort of thing. She'll be polishing your respective images and taking stock to see who needs a total rework of their personal life. Before they arrive, let me make it clear: I want no more 'situations' in the first place. Do you all understand?"

"Wait – what did you say the firm's name was?"

James looked toward the door just as it swung open and, as if in slow motion, none other than Cashell Bruer entered the room. She and her assistants shook the hands of the coach, assistant coach and general manager, making hushed small talk and greeting one another. James's mouth formed an O as he watched Cashell wrap up her salutations and take her place confidently at the head of the table.

6

Meet Ms. Who?

CASHELL STOOD AT THE FRONT. It was an old power play, simply to show that she felt in charge and would command the room. However, having seen James there, she was now certifiably unsure she would be commanding much of anything. She placed her bag on the floor and her portfolio on the table before taking a seat, smiling at all the men around her.

She hated coming in on the tail end of something, and by the looks on the faces of the men present it was clear that she and her team had walked in on a very volatile situation. She hoped the stony silence had nothing to do with her presence or the reason she was there. If she wanted them to leave with any particular impression of her, it was that she was an ally and not their enemy.

"You're late, Brax."

At the manager's words, Cashell followed his eyes to the door as another player breezed in. He was clad in jeans and a muscle shirt, his eyes obscured by mirror shades. He didn't say a word as he moseyed in and took a seat.

"I told you to dress appropriately," the manager barked.

"It's fine," Cashell interjected. "Gentlemen, I just want you all to feel comfortable. I'm simply here to ensure that the image of the league - and of your individual personas - are made more… family-friendly. I want to see if we can get ahead of any further news that might be a detriment the organization, before the information gets out on its own. Do keep in mind that I'm working for the team on a limited contract, so you won't have to put up with us long at all." She gestured to her associates with a disarming smile.

"But the contract can be renewed," the manager cut in.

"Of course, Bill. I just wanted to let the guys know that I won't be hanging around here interfering in their lives forever," Cashell explained reassuringly. "This is a campaign of sorts, with actual time limits and endings. Put up with us for a little while and I guarantee I'll make you look good." She winked at Bill - and noticed James lower his eyebrows as she did so.

Cashell hadn't known he'd be there until she'd read over all the information about her new contract job, the day after the fateful evening at the hotel. As soon as she entered the room and saw James, her heart beat a little faster. Still, she managed to don her poker face and smoothly pretended not to know him at all. She hoped that whatever he thought about her now, he would be able to understand why this situation had come to pass. She could tell he was not happy. She'd explain everything to him later, if only he would give her the chance to do so.

She was also hopeful that emphasizing the brevity of her stay would help her win over some minds and perhaps even score her a few moments of steady eye contact. James was looking at her right now, but for the most part he'd pulled out his phone and ignored her altogether. The mention of her brief stay, she realized, had actually done nothing to win anyone over.

"So we're clear, gentleman. Ms. Bruer's company is here for us - as a league and an organization," Bill intoned grandly. "She is not here to cater to any one individual, or to clean up episodes of crap hitting the proverbial fan - whether you toss that crap individually or whether you get together with your homeys to pitch it collectively. Not for anyone. Now, what she will do is work on getting each of you some positive coverage as we move into the season with a completely new roster of folks. I say again: she will not spend an undue amount of time sweeping your personal junk under the carpet. Understood?"

The players grumbled, but it was something: Cashell suspected that an agreement had been reached at last. That was as much as she could hope for at this early stage. Bill glared at them all.

"Go ahead, Ms. Bruer."

"Thanks, Bill. So, first off, can you all introduce yourselves?"

Cashell was surprised and annoyed when Bill spoke up once again.

"We have Trent Jessup, wide receiver; Alex Cuban, runningback; and Parker and Brax over here are QBs." He was clearly used to treating his players as if their mouths didn't work. It was clear she'd also have to work on him.

"Thanks again. I'm Cashell Bruer, as Bill might have mentioned. My team consists of Shannon, our social media guru; and Brandon, our new intern."

Cashell went on to explain her team's role in more detail, and go over some finer points of the interview she would soon be setting up for them. She cut out some of her spiel about her background. It was becoming clear that, given Bill's dominant nature plus his evident anger over whatever had occurred before she'd even arrived, she would do better to win them over on an individual basis. She needed just a little time to work her charm. This meeting would be over before long, she told herself.

"I really appreciate everyone's time. I'll contact you this week." She stood and moved around the table to shake each of their hands. Trent seemed fine: aloof, yet at least cordial. As he smiled, she swiftly pegged him as the teenager sort: barely any facial hair, slim, with a diamond earring in each ear. When she shook Brax's hand, his shades only revealed a beveled version of herself: she could not make out what his eyes were saying. He was beefy and large, towering over her slight frame. His body language wasn't so mysterious, however: he held her hand and smiled down at her a little too long – that is, until James patted his chest. Brax looked over at him, startled, and let go. If he thought James's behavior odd, no-one said anything. Though she dreaded shaking James's hand, she did so hastily, all but high-fiving him in her effort to make as little contact as possible.

James's eyes met hers. "Ms. Bruer, I'm the only one here under complete error."

Unsure what to say, Cashell didn't utter a word in response. She felt him move his hand in closer, trying to capture her own in a more appropriate shake, but she deftly escaped it.

"Time will tell, won't it Parker?" Bill interjected.

James's heated look wasn't lost on her. Though she wanted to tell him she didn't believe him to be a troublemaker, right then wasn't exactly the time to show her bias. That much should be obvious, she thought with some frustration. Instead, determined to finish strong, Cashell gritted her teeth as she made her way back to her seat. She wouldn't acknowledge Bill's comment either way.

"Great. It is very nice to meet everyone. It's going to be a great summer and I look forward to working with each of you."

James's mute stares were no match for her own evasion technique. She'd work with him on that as soon as the opportunity arose.

The men stood and filed out without any more talk. She'd never been so glad to see anyone leave a room, but their departure did mean she now had to deal with Bill. She hoped she'd get some clarification on exactly what he was looking for, because his requirements seemed to go deeper than he had initially told her. She drew breath to address the irritable manager, but before she could get a word out Bill spoke first.

"The eye needs to be kept most closely on Brax and Parker. If anyone is up to no good, we'll cut them first."

Cashell did a double take. Bill had spoken right across her. She eyed him with thinly-veiled annoyance as he continued:

"Ms. Bruer, you work first for us. That's the most important thing you need to understand."

"Excuse me?"

"I'll try to put this as simply as I can for you, Ms. Bruer. Whatever there is to be found, we're counting on you to ensure it's all discreetly disposed of before the game opener at the end of the summer."

7
The Family Hour

BACK AT HIS NEW HOUSE, James walked slowly out of the room he'd been working on. He was examining the place as he went, making mental notes about all that needed to be done to bring it all up to a standard he was satisfied with and give it that homey, moved-in feeling.

He felt a little guilty for not seeking Cashell out after the meeting was over the other day. Considering the fact that he was new on the team - and being as how his numbers and abilities on the field didn't seem to be speaking for him - he figured that now he knew where he stood in the management's view of things generally speaking, it was best just to lay low. To steer clear of any further controversy, his plan was to avoid talking to or engaging with Cashell on company property.

Almost a week had already gone by since that meeting, and his anger and annoyance over it seemed to ebb and flow. Anger that in all their conversation at the hotel she hadn't once mentioned she'd be working for the Washington Rebels - and annoyance at himself, for thinking that for some reason she'd owed him more information than she'd shared.

He hadn't exactly told her what team he'd played for either, he mused. True, the local news channels had reported as recently as January that he was looking at property in Northern Virginia, even airing a short piece when he'd closed - but that didn't automatically mean Cashell was thus following every move of his career. Or following his career, period. After all, he'd just signed his contract the very day she'd shown up at that meeting. Cashell was likely busy framing the story of the team's newest acquisition, transmitting the information to all the media outlets.

It wasn't about her, he reminded himself. It was the fact that despite considering himself to be a good dude of integrity and character, today had been a harsh reality check: someone was always there to remind you that there's still more to prove. The truth was that he had been truly relieved to see her standing at the head of the table, regardless of what had brought her there.

He was glad she was all right.

The night when she'd sat up from her fainting spell on the narrow stretcher of the ambulance, he'd stayed with her until she called her brother. Just as they were exchanging brief and awkward pleasantries, she had been whisked from the scene by her concerned sibling.

A few days after the meeting, James had given Trent and Alex a lecture in the parking lot as they headed out to their cars. He wanted to make sure they were fully aware of the danger their actions had put everyone in – whatever those actions had been. He still couldn't quite believe it, but it was becoming clear that rescuing Cashell from her own birthday bust had saved him from a much bigger mess.

When Cashell had entered the room, he'd forgotten what he was thinking about - and it was evident that everyone else had noticed her, too. Especially Braxton, he recalled, who'd lingered over that handshake a little too long for James's liking. James was annoyed at the thoughts that marched through his mind, but it was undeniable that Cashell's fitted suit with its cinched blazer had just hugged her in all the right places. Despite what he'd witnessed the other night, with her vulnerability in his hands, that Monday morning he had met a commanding woman who exhibited both confidence and charisma.

"Aaaaah!"

James dropped the hammer in agony as he pounded his own thumb instead of the nail.

Squeezing his injured thumb and examining the damage,

he was startled and even more annoyed when the doorbell rang. He checked his watch and stuck the offending digit in his mouth as he walked over to answer the door. When he opened it, he was surprised to see his brother Cole standing on his new doorstep.

As usual, one look told James he had already somehow failed. His brother's look was always intimidating: scrutinizing, assessing, then dismissing.

"I knew you'd forget," Cole sighed as he brushed past. A big bundle of blankets nestled in his arms and two groggy little girls trotted hot on his heels.

"Hi, Uncle JJ."

"Hey Uncle J."

"Hey," James said, kicking himself for not having been ready. Cole was right, of course: he had completely forgotten. He closed the door, lest his bare feet freeze, and turned around turned to greet his favorite girls, each one kissing both sides of his cheek before wandering sleepily into the living room and finding a couch on which to flop themselves down.

"What's up? - uh, why are they so tired?" he asked. Not that James was complaining. In fact, if they slept for a few more hours, he could maybe even get some groceries ordered and delivered. He prayed his fridge might at least appear passably full. It really wasn't, and he knew Cole would be checking it out at any moment. James eyed his brother, the pain from his thumb completely forgotten.

"Uh, look Cole, I didn't forget exactly. I just... had a busy week," he finished lamely.

"Yeah? You want to talk about it?"

James shrugged his shoulders. Cole had enough on his plate, with a new baby, two kids and two restaurants to manage. Somehow, over the last few years, the two brothers had lost the connection they once shared.

Your fault, a voice reminded him. He knew it. It was his fault. Focusing on his career and trying to avoid his family never did him any good. He just wanted to find a place he belonged. For that reason, he'd recently become interested in knowing who his real parents were. He hadn't gotten far, but he was still in the process of digging, and all that effort had meant he'd hardly seen his adoptive brothers at all. James thrust his hands deeper into his pockets.

"I'm still Cole, okay?" his brother said softly. James nodded, evading his brother's kind and searching eyes. He knew that he was the one who had some growing up to do. After four years in college and two in the NFL, he had moved into this home in an effort to reconnect with his family. Bridging the gap was obviously a little harder than he imagined. It would certainly require way more effort on his part than he'd guessed.

"Place is coming along," Cole remarked, pacing around the partially finished rooms. "It feels more like a home now. Hey, you've made quite a few purchases since you first moved in. Living room looks complete," Cole said, carefully setting down the blanketed bundle. The covers fell away and James was surprised to see little Jacoby emerge, awake and alert. The child looked around but stayed close to Cole's leg, taking everything in.

"Hey, Jacoby."

"Hi."

James smiled at his nephew. When he eventually got comfortable, Jacoby - who was all of three years old - took off for the living room in search of Hannah and Kira. James watched him go, amazed at how big he was getting, as Cole continued his self-guided tour.

"I see you got some pots and pans so you can cook. That's good. You got food?" When Cole got to the fridge and opened it, he whistled. James came to look over his shoulder.

"Milk's out of date."

James winced, then shrugged. "I thought I'd take them shopping for things they like," he offered, in a sudden flash of inspiration.

"You want to take two preteens and a three-year-old boy

shopping?" Cole repeated incredulously. "They're not stationary infants any more, Jimbo. All of them are prone to wander – oh, and please, whatever you do, don't take them to any mall with a Forever Twenty-One."

James grinned. "Okay. I know we'll be, uh, fine."

"Your only saving grace is that Hannah keeps an eagle eye on Jacoby whenever we're not there until she's sure she can trust the adults," Cole continued. "She won't stop watching over him unless Allontis, Leedra or myself is there."

"Really? Everyone really likes Leedra, huh?"

"She's very special, considering all that's happened."James shrugged. Although he'd met Leedra a few times now, he hadn't gotten to know her that well. He'd liked her instantly, but he wished he'd been around more when times had been really tough – like recently.

"Do you need any money?"

James looked at his brother sharply and shook his head. He found it funny that anyone would ask a man with a $2.4 million contract in the works if he needed money.

"I know you're between jobs," Cole added with a twinkle in his eye. He and James laughed at the same time.

"I signed this week," James returned, trying to sound casual.

"Yeah? Why didn't we get an invite? That's a big deal! Congratulations. I'm proud of you, Jimbo. Momma G and David would be too."

James nodded, surprised at the emotion he felt. "Yeah. It was just a small signing. I didn't want the attention." Cole gave him an affectionate punch on the arm, then lowered his voice discreetly.

"Have you, uh, found your Momma yet?"

James shook his head. Cole was the only person that knew he had started the search for his biological parents. While that took money, it didn't take that much considering. James had more than enough. He knew his brother was just looking out for him. It was nice of Cole, James supposed, but it felt weird. He was hyper-aware of the fact that Momma G and David had given him everything. After they'd died, his brothers had been there just the same, helping with everything from paying for the rest of his schooling to ensuring he had a place to live while away at school and being there for him when he'd first been drafted. Now that he was a man of independent means, he intended to be more self-sufficient.

"The only things I've really purchased are this house and the truck." James left out the part about how much it was adding up to fixing up the damaged rooms of this beautiful but drafty McMansion. He wasn't materialistic, he told himself. He still had a chunk of change left – plus he'd just signed the contract and it wouldn't be long before he had the signing bonus and the first increments. "I'm good." Financially, he was better than good.

"What will you make for dinner the next few days?" Cole said, changing the subject.

"Pizzas!" One of the girl's voices drifted in from the living room.

"Pizza! Yeah, great. Sounds good!" the other echoed.

"Don't let them eat pizza every day, okay?" Cole clarified to James with a wink.

James smiled, "I won't."

Cole grinned, then became more serious. "Now - back to the subject of your mom."

Despite having evaded the earlier question, James knew somehow they'd circle back. "The investigator said that, uh, she may be in a nursing facility down there."

To tell the truth, James hadn't yet read the full report from the firm he'd hired to find his family. It was sitting unopened in his email inbox, with several attachments dangling seductively. As much as he had been eager to know, he was now putting it off. If he was honest with himself, he was fearful that it would turn out to be bad news – or, maybe even worse, just another dead-end installment in what seemed like a series of let-downs. A part of him dreaded opening up a can of worms.

"Interesting. So you just moved all the way up here but she

may be back down there, the place you just left?"

"I left to get back home," James replied.

"Well, welcome back."

"Thanks." For some reason he found his brother pulling him into a hug. Even though it was brief and included a manly pat on the back, James's eyes stung again from the emotions it brought up.

"How's the girl situation?"

"What?" James dipped a brow at his brother's question, caught completely off-guard. "There is no girl situation."

"Okay, okay, don't be hostile," Cole smiled, putting up his hands in mock surrender as James walked him out. After this last line of questioning, James was no longer too sorry that Cole was leaving.

Cole checked over the car, ensuring he didn't forget anything that the kids would need. He reached in to unbuckle the car seat and handed the bulky contraption to James. "Hannah knows how to put it in, in case you don't."

James nodded, trying not to feel too insulted at his brother's ribbing, and took the plastic seat. He retraced his steps to his new front door, waving his brother goodbye as his car pulled out of the wide driveway. He was looking forward to spending time with his nieces and nephew – partly because having them at his house for an entire week might finally get his mind off the other stuff that was going on in his life. Cole's searching questions only seemed to stir up feelings James wasn't used to having. These feelings centered in large part around his mother, and what he saw as his own cowardly evasion of really searching for her. Cole's questioning stirred up another sore subject, too: James's relationship status. No love interest, no girlfriend, no family. Unbeknownst to Cole, James had thought about this topic more often than he cared to admit to in recent weeks. These thoughts had only intensified after he'd met Cashell Bruer.

No: this week, James would focus on his family, and with any luck he could move on from thinking about her. He and

Cashell would have plenty of meetings coming up later in the summer, and James - despite desperately wanting to know more about her - was not necessarily looking forward to any of them. And there, he thought wryly: just when he'd thought he'd found something to take his mind off her, there she was again.

8
Locked Out

IT WAS REALLY DIFFICULT TO get hold of someone who was busy assuming the worst about you. After weeks of having her emails and phone calls dodged, Cashell decided to pay James Parker a visit in person. This one wasn't something she would just leave to her intern to set up. Aside from the fact that she wanted to approach things in a more personal and friendly manner with all the players across this board, this was different. This was James: the man that had not only shown her an awesome time on her birthday, but had proceeded to stay by her side down more than twenty flights of stairs, even as complete pandemonium swirled all around them. She'd already met with the other three men, anyway: James was last on her list.

Cashell hoped this particular meeting would be more productive than the others had been. The other players had all been a little put off by her forward and proactive approach, but they had warmed up a little once she'd explained her goal of helping them tell their stories to the interested public. Unfortunately, she pointed out, crafting one's own story wasn't as easy as it used to be, and she was on hand to help navigate the tricky waters of modern-day media in all its forms. Despite their initial obtuseness, Trent and Alex eventually seemed amenable to her assistance; but Braxton Denton was still more interested in flirting and messing around than in working with her as a professional. Despite her best efforts to make it clear, he still hadn't figured out that she was there for the job and nothing more.

Sliding into the driver's seat of her car, Cashell encountered a more practical and immediate problem. The thing wouldn't start. She stared at the glowing yellow 'check engine' light in front of her, wondering with exasperation what in the world the problem could be this time. She couldn't explain anything to James properly if she couldn't get to his house.

Getting out of her little black Volkswagen Beetle once again, Cashell managed to pop the hood and frowned down at her engine. She wasn't sure what she had expected to see under there, but those mazes on the backs of cereal boxes looked easier. She'd likely have better luck with them than with trying to figure out what was wrong with her car.

Contemplating possible reasons for the malfunction, Cashell noted that there seemed to be nothing wrong with the only three things she knew anything about: gas, batteries and tire issues. She'd just gotten a new battery, that much she knew… and that was where her automotive expertise ended.

Frustrated, Cashell glanced up at the ominous gray clouds. What looked like the finest little dots of snow were starting to fall. Perfect. "Are you serious? It's the end of March, people – really?" she said out loud. As if to mock her, the very next flake that fell seemed fatter and rounder than the last. Pursing her lips, she took a deep breath, closed the engine and marched back around to her car door. She grasped the cold door handle and pulled… but it didn't budge. With a sinking feeling, she realized that it was locked – and all her belongings, including her cell phone, were inside.

Starting to panic, she looked around her. Nothing, not even a welcoming chimney rising from a distant house, was in sight. She pulled her flimsy coat tighter around her. She rapped on the window pointlessly and winced: it felt like she'd cracked one of her knuckles. "As competent an image as I project, alas ladies and gentleman, it's all a ruse. I'm incompetent. Thank you very much, take a bow, have a seat," she said aloud, and she would have given herself a chuckle if only she didn't feel so alone and sad.

James felt like his arms were going to fall off. He heaved the last of the groceries into the house. Surveying the piles of items, he spied his two accomplices, hard at work. The tops of their heads were barely visible over the mounds of bags and jugs of juice that crowded the countertop.

There were challenges involved in watching a child whose big brother was a chef. One of these was that a trip to the store was not so much a commonplace chore as an epic adventure in palette and consumer choice. Hannah knew every food there was, and her determined gaze always seemed to travel up past the cheaper generic store-brand products to the ritzy, expensive name brands. She knew the best-tasting version of everything: bread, peanut butter, biscuits, milk, eggs, cheese, maraschino cherries, nuts, ice cream, even sprinkles. For goodness sake, James thought - who knew there were so many kinds of sprinkles?

"You guys are killing me! I've never seen so much food," James joked, cheery despite the trauma his wallet had just been through. He really was ecstatic to have this time together with the kids.

So far that morning, they'd eaten breakfast, played games and set up the kids' rooms with all their stuff - and when they'd looked up, more than half the day was already gone. They'd taken the trip to the store after making a comprehensive list, but this quickly became obsolete when they got to the store. The additional thirty random items not on the list were testament to that fact.

Little Hannah stood up and smacked her forehead with her palm. "Ah! I forgot the detergent. Do you have any detergent?"

"What?" James stopped putting things away and held the refrigerator door open to stare at her, swallowing the urge to laugh out loud at her quaintly adult gesture. "Uh, why do you need detergent, sweetie?" he asked.

Hannah rolled her eyes dramatically. "What else do you do with detergent? Wash clothes."

James didn't mention that he could, in fact, think of other things - he had a number of friends with colorful lifestyles. "I, uh, think I've got some, but uh…"

"She likes to wash clothes. She does it to help Lonnie out," Kira informed him.

"Your Aunt Lonnie? Okay…" Wow.

"You really do talk to much," Hannah chided Kira.

"It's Uncle James!" Kira protested.

"And so what?" Hannah put her small hands fiercely on her hips.

James stood and watched this exchange. He'd never once heard them bicker before. "Yes, I'm Uncle James, but I'm a really good listener and I'll always be here for both of you," he soothed. "You guys can tell me anything - you know that, right?"

He got a small nod from each girl before they both resumed unloading the bags in silence. James decided to press for more information. "So, uh, Hannah, do you mean that Lonnie's needed some extra help lately? Has she been sick - other than just the, uh, normal stuff after having the baby, I mean?"

"Well, like right after, she was. It was weird. She went all… weird. Leedra helps a lot too," Kira piped up.

"Okay, but um, Kira, let Hannah talk. If I ask her a question, it's not an invitation for you to answer for her, understood?"

The girl nodded, somewhat abashed.

So much for fun and games. There was something unusual going on with how the girls were behaving, and it was evident there was something up with the wider family at home that he had no clue about. Surely Cole would have said something.

The once-little girls before him weren't little any more, he noted. They were growing up.

"Can someone find the ice cream so it doesn't melt?"

Hannah moved to find the ice cream and handed it to James, who put the rest of the items away and set up a kitchen work station for the girls. As was their tradition, they would help him make whatever their choice of meal was for the night.

Characteristically, Kira was the first to break the silence. "What is there to do here, anyway?" she asked without preamble. "I heard this county is famous for wine, but that's no good to Hannah and me. Hey, why did you move from North Carolina? I liked visiting you down there."

James smiled, ignoring the testiness in Kira's voice as she nonetheless fired off her barrage of questions. His ever-dramatic niece was just mad because of his recent chastisement, but he knew he'd be back in her good graces before long. Truth be told, he hadn't completely decided on the entertainment piece of their week-long adventure just yet, but he had a few ideas in mind.

He decided just to take her questions one at a time. "First of all, I moved back here to be closer to the likes of you three." He gave Kira a playful poke in her belly, which earned a yelping laugh, and he hugged and squeezed Hannah to win back a few more points. "To answer your second question," he continued, putting on a phony deep gameshow-announcer voice, "here in beautiful, picturesque Loudoun County we have ziplining, indoor skydiving, a waterpark, a kids gym and even a trampoline park." As the girls' eyes lit up with excitement, James felt with pride that he'd scored still more uncle points. Win.

"I bought you guys a tent," he continued, warming to his theme. "We have a place called Algonquin Park, but maybe we'll just camp out at the back of the house to start with. We can make some s'mores. We could go to the park for a night, once we've had some practice."

"You do know there's a blizzard coming, right?" Hannah said with another eye roll.

Debbie Downer. James shrugged his shoulders, trying not to seem too surprised or disappointed. Honestly, he had not planned for snow when he'd arranged their visit. It was March, after all, but while he knew the chances of snow weren't completely over, a blizzard this late in the season was just an annoying fluke. This was Virginia, though, and here up north it was never too late for winter's last frigid hoorah. Thank goodness for movie streaming and DVDs, James thought. With any luck, Allontis and Cole would have packed some for the girls as a precautionary measure in case of inclement weather.

"So what?" James countered, dismissing his nieces' obvious expectation that they would be stuck indoors bored for the duration of their visit. He rolled his eyes dramatically back at them. "Well, maybe we'll get enough snow to build a snowman. Maybe we'll have a competition. Jacoby and me against the likes of you two. What do you say?"

"Oh, it's on!" Kira exclaimed, instantly forgetting her cool-girl exterior. "I think that will be fun. We don't do that at home much, and we haven't had enough the last couple of years anyway – plus, I didn't have any other kids to play with before Hannah came along."

James grinned as he continued to put away the last of the items that the girls had helpfully pulled out of all their grocery bags. He hoped what Kira said was a subtle peace offering to Hannah – who, meanwhile, had given Jacoby a banana that she'd cut up for him all by herself. The baby of the family was otherwise entertained at this particular moment, though, immersed in watching a cartoon on the kids' tablet Cole had sent along with them. A small string of drool dangled from his bottom lip. Witnessing the child's obvious contentment, James wished he could freeze-frame this moment. He wanted to hug little Jacoby close and tell him not to grow up too fast.

"Listen, you guys, I'm gonna go pull the truck in and get the mail, then we're having pizza or sloppy Joes."

"Are our presents in the truck?" Hannah said hopefully.

"Hmm, I don't know. The mailbox here is a little too small for big presents." With a hearty wink, James held up his hands to indicate a large box. Yes, he was often known to be late with the presents, but the girls knew he always had something for them when they visited. Their visits were their Christmases-once-removed. Rather than rush through gift exchanges on the few days they were off school over the festive season, with James so often playing either at home or away during the holidays, he and the girls usually had their own mini Christmas during some other week at a different time of the year, when they celebrated his gifts to them. The tradition had started when Hannah had come into Cole's life and he'd learned that she was his sister.

"Big presents?" Hannah gasped in awe, and the girls high fived each other with excited giggles before going back to preparing items for dinner.

"Girls, keep an eye on Jacoby - I'll be right back. Remember, no knife usage without me in the room, OK?" The girls, seemingly friends again, nodded as James headed back out to the garage to carry out his regular evening routine. First he checked the garage door, ensuring he'd remembered to close it properly. He locked the side door so no one could sneak in (or out) during the night, and he walked the perimeter of his property as he did every evening to stretch his legs and to ensure all was well.

As he walked, admiring his new house from the outside, James thought about his adoptive father. David had taught him a lot of things about care, tending, fixing and mending a home. Unlike most other material possessions, James's house was symbolic to him: something he could be proud of, something he could care for and call his own. Almost like... a family?

James shivered at his own thoughts, the cold air seeping into his bones. He looked up at the darkening gray sky and then back at his yard. He couldn't believe how much snow had accumulated in such a short amount of time.

At the mailbox, some of the accumulated snow tumbled off as he opened the little door and took out the fatly wadded wedge of mail. He didn't check his mail every day because there wasn't normally much to check, beyond the latest sports catalogs and flyers advertising home lawn care and maintenance tools. James scanned quickly past all the various pieces of new-homeowner junk mail and was just preparing to toss the whole stack into the recycling container when his eye fell on a familiar logo: a globe with a lighthouse's beam shining across it, captioned "Search The World". It was the emblem for the investigation company he'd hired almost a year ago.

James paused, the envelope in his hand. He'd already had the email, so why, he wondered, would the firm also send a follow-up letter? He took a deep breath, but then thought better of opening it after all. Not right now. He let the other mail fan back down to cover the letter, to wait for a time when he could deal with it properly. Later. It was the only piece there which might be of any importance, anyway.

As he moved back up the front path to the house, James noticed the two packages sitting by the front door. His mind was now in deep thought about his birth parents. Were both still living? Who were they? - what did they do? Questions began to weigh heavily on his mind. James wondered whether he should wait until his company left at the end of the week, or whether he should open the envelope later tonight while everyone slept. The possible urgency of the information contained within it, the timing... but before he could finish his thought, his toe caught what felt like a massive lump on the ground as he approached his front door. The mail stack flew from his fingers and scattered papers and letters across the porch as he put out his hands reflexively to break his fall.

Righting himself, he descended the steps again with some annoyance to inspect the offending lump that had tripped him. He didn't remember leaving any boxes out here on the front path. As he brushed off the dusting of snow, a bright red coat became visible. Alarmed, he moved more quickly, hauling what he now realized was a person upright into a sitting position. He didn't need to brush the snow from her eyelashes to recognize her and his heart sank, wondering why on earth she was out here. Did she know she was this close to his house?

"Cashell?" he whispered, before gathering her into his arms

as if she weighed nothing at all and carrying her hastily into the safety of his warm home.

9
Angels in the Snow

IN THE LIVING ROOM, HIS mail forgotten, James tapped Cashell's face gently. All three of the kids had gathered around the sofa, where'd he placed her to see what was wrong. The snow stuck to her like a fine mist and her lips were dry and cracked, but at least they were not blue.

"Cashell!" James said again as he pulled her face closer to his ear. For the first time, he felt her faint breath tickle his cheek with a wash of relief.

"It's Cashell?" Kira exclaimed. "Oh man. I'ma get Daddy on the phone right now."

"Yes, get Daddy - I mean, your Dad… get Dexter on the phone," James agreed, his heart sinking. He wished his doctor brother was there right now, helping him when he had no clue what to do, rather than being an inconvenient seventy miles away. Even though Kira was around a doctor all the time, she was a kid, so for all her preternatural capability she couldn't bring him that much reassurance. He was on his knees next to Cashell, holding her frozen hand in his own.

"We should get her into some dry clothes, ideally some warm blankets. Let me see if Dad is available," Kira said calmly as she held the phone to her ear.

"Right," James stuttered. Again: wow.

Kira walked to the window while waiting for Dexter to pick up and gazed down the long winding street. "That must be her Beetle out there. I can just see it, right down at the end of the road. If so, judging by the snow on it, she's probably been out there for a long time," she observed.

James's eyes bulged, realizing that Cashell must indeed have been out there for the better part of the day. It looked like she'd left her car and gone trekking to find some help.

"Daddy?" Kira had made contact with Dexter and immediately put him on speakerphone.

"What's the matter, baby?" James heard the tinny reply.

"Daddy, Cashell is here. She passed out in the snow at Uncle James's house. He just found her. We think she's been out there for more than a couple of hours: her car must've broken down. Her pulse is registering, but it's faint; and she's breathing, also faint."

James looked incredulously at his niece. If she wanted to be a doctor like her dad when she grew up, he noted with amazement that she was much further along already than he could ever have imagined.

"Well, remember that she faints a lot," came Dexter's steady voice.

"Yes, Daddy."

"If she walked far in the cold, sweetie, she could have gotten winded," Dexter's reassuring low voice continued over the phone. "She can't walk long distances. You need to warm her up. Not artificial heat, no electric blankets or anything like that, but try massaging her feet. Remove any cold or wet boots or socks, get closer to the fire, tell James to start a fire – hey, what is he doing right now, anyway?"

"He's removing her wet coat and some snow... snow is spilling out of her jacket, Daddy."

"Tell him to check her head: maybe she hit her head or something on the way down. Maybe she's concussed."

James was doing everything that Dexter said. His fingers felt around Cashell's hairline, noticing how soft it was, and made their way down further to trace the outline of her ear. At last, he felt a raised bump on the back of her head. He indicated it to his niece.

She moaned. James had never been so happy to hear a sound in his life.

"Daddy, she's moaning. She has a bump on her head."

"Is it bleeding?"

James pulled his clean fingers away and showed Kira.

"No, Daddy."

"If she's moaning that's a good sign," Dexter's voice replied. "She should be fine - just try to keep her awake if she comes to, although her inclination may be to sleep and she may have a headache. Now then, are you sure she just fell? She wasn't hit by a passing car or anything like that, was she? I'm ..."

James was slightly annoyed when Kira left the room, taking the rest of whatever her father was saying with her. Mostly, though, he was just thankful Cashell was all right: that she made any sound at all, even if it was one of pain, just to reassure him she would be okay. It didn't, however, give him any other answers to the many questions that ran through his head. For starters: what had she been doing out there in the middle of a blizzard? Why did the two of them keep running into each other? And why did this particular beauty keep ending up quite literally in his arms?

James looked over when Kira returned - she was no longer on the phone with her father.

"Uncle JJ, Daddy's going to send some instructions to your phone so you can print them out and follow them, okay? He said if she's moaning, she should be okay, but to keep her warm and comfortable and to make sure she goes to the doctor in the morning. He'll call back in a while to see how things are going."

The young girl paused and regarded her uncle with tenderness. "She's gonna be okay, James."

James did a double take, wondering if Nurse Kira would be staying the night and also when the young niece who'd been so testy and pouty just hours ago would return in her place.

"Why don't you start the fire and we will lay on her legs to warm her up faster?" Kira suggested.

James nodded, stunned at how childlike and helpless he felt. He couldn't believe any of it. Even little Hannah had blankets in her arms, though, and the two girls were looking at him expectantly, as if to say 'get a move on.' He moved from Cashell's side and did as they suggested.

As the girls piled on the blankets, Jacoby rushed in with a giggle, thinking it some sort of game. Hannah's arm shot out to warn him and he stopped.

"Sorry bud, this isn't a game. Thanks, Hannah," James said, getting up. He placed the heavy grate back in front of the old fireplace. They were using it for the first time since he'd had it inspected: a service he said a silent prayer of thanks that he'd gotten done, considering how much he needed the fire right then. He watched the embers kindle the paper underneath two chunky logs and went back to holding Cashell in his arms. She was still really cold, which worried him. He lifted her again and scooted them both closer to the fire, setting her gently on the floor. He sat at her back and massaged her arms and hands, saying silly things, mostly all the questions he had about her visit there to see him. The girls put the remaining blankets and pillows closer around them and James removed the last of her outer layers, finally reaching the last layer: a shirt that he found was cool to the touch but, thankfully, dry.

When they were all settled in the living room, James was only slightly on edge: a big improvement. He wanted to ask if Kira knew anything about Cashell's heart condition from meeting her before, but decided not to, just in case Cashell could hear everything they were saying. From what he'd said on the phone, it was clear that Dexter was familiar with Cashell's health history.

Instead of probing further, James simply said: "Let me see the phone with your dad's instructions, Kay Kay." Kira got up and passed him the phone from the far end of the table.

James tried to remember anything he could about the times he'd suffered a concussion himself: not much, obviously, given the nature of the injury. The first things he read on the list of symptoms his brother had sent were: a desperate need to sleep, headache, but don't give any drugs until patient has been up and conscious for at least twenty-four hours. Possible disorientation. Because heart is an issue, fainting spells of several minutes' duration not uncommon, but cold may have adverse effect on stress to the heart, prolonging fainting. Ensure no frostbite...

James reread the short note, wishing his brother had made complete sentences instead of this inscrutable doctor-style list format. Knowing him, Dexter had likely dictated it rapid-fire into his phone and then sent it off without checking it over, in an effort to get the information transmitted to James as quickly as possible. Even though the speed was appreciated, the memo was clearly written to be read by other experienced doctors who would instantly understand its garbled content. James wasn't a doctor at all, he reflected wryly: not by any stretch of the imagination.

"How long do you think she'd been out there?" Kira sat at the end of Cashell's petite body, rubbing her legs and feet.

"I don't know, sweetie."

"She's gonna be fine," Kira said confidently. "Are you guys friends? Did you hire her for your football career?"

"No. I mean, yeah, we're friends, but she actually got a job with the league. She has to do some interviews for the team – me and all the other players."

"Daddy said to talk to her," Kira reminded him.

James looked down at Cashell, suddenly bashful. Now that he was being asked to talk to her on demand, by his niece of all people, he had no words. In any case, worry was currently silencing his lips, sidelining the feelings he'd privately been developing for her. Now he was just concerned about her, a fact that put all his usual chatter out of the window.

"I should have brought my stethoscope," Kira mused.

"You have a stethoscope, sweetie?"

"Of course. Dad bought me a 3M Cardiology 4. 27 inches. It's hot pink," Kira smiled. James was privately amazed that Dexter had bought his daughter a genuine, functional piece of medical equipment. It seemed too expensive for a child - and who knew they made them in different colors, too?

"But her pulse sounds fine, it's good and strong," Kira continued. "Uncle James, Hannah and I really can stay by ourselves and take care of Jacoby if you want to take her to the hospital. I promise we'll be okay."

James had been mentally preparing for a visit to the hospital with three kids in tow. He looked down at Cashell, still having no clue what to say or to do. Kira sat quietly, staring into the fire; Jacoby played with his cars, not bothering anyone. Brushing a stray hair from Cashell's brow, he murmured aloud: "Why are you here, Angel in the Snow?"

"To tell you something."

James jumped, surprised that she'd responded. "Cashell?"

Her eyes had flickered open.

"Ooh. Head hurts, cold… I wanted to tell you something but…" she sighed, then sneezed.

Three sets of 'bless you's echoed simultaneously in the air.

"You gotta wake up and talk to me, okay?" James said urgently, thankful she had talked even if she made no sense. At the word "cold", James pulled her closer and rubbed his right hand up and down her arm. He clasped her hands and fingers in his own, enclosing them, willing the brutal chill away. He pulled the blanket closer up to her chin.

"Tired…"

"We're out of blankets," Hannah said, returning to the living room from her quilt-based recon mission around James's house. James sighed. 'More blankets' would need to be added to the ever-lengthening list of things he still needed to purchase.

"Thanks," he said to Hannah. He was grateful when she sat down quietly and didn't ask or say much more of anything.

"I know you're tired, Cashell, but open your eyes and look at me," James urged her. "If you don't, we'll have to go to the hospital."

"You know she has a heart condition, right Uncle JJ? Are you sure we shouldn't just call an ambulance?"

Cashell's eyes opened wide and, up this close and this personal, James was transported back to that night they'd danced and chatted well into the wee hours of the morning. "No, no ambulance," she exclaimed and sat up quickly. It was clear that she was dizzy, for she fell back dramatically and James caught her. She clutched her head. "No ambulance," she pleaded again.

"Okay, no ambulance, but you have to keep talking to us. You can't go back to sleep," James said sternly. He settled her back into the covers.

"My prayer was answered," she said groggily.

"What was your prayer?" James asked as he pulled the cover up, praying a prayer of his own that she would be all right. The kids were likely getting tired and dinner still needed to be made for them lest they wake up hungry in the middle of the night. The room was completely dark, save for the single lamp he'd turned on, and the soft light from the fire. He hadn't decorated or even furnished this room yet. There was a new leather sectional, but other than that the place was bare of any proper furniture.

James wondered idly what Cashell would want to do with the place, décor-wise… then he gave himself a little shake, wondering why on earth he was thinking about such things. As far as he was concerned, he reasoned with himself, she was too careless for her own good. She'd abandoned her car, and he'd found no purse, no cell phone and no wallet in all her outer layers. She had her bracelet on, yes; but what good would that do without a doctor who had the proper knowledge to interpret it? James's annoyance was increasing from bafflement to frustration and finally anger that Cashell would be so absentminded. There was no guarantee that he, or anyone else for that matter, would have found her. Why couldn't she have made a simple call to alert him that she was coming?

After the week you've had, you'd likely have refused her visit, chided his conscience. He probably would have refused to entertain her, he mused, but surely he would have taken her in and at least now she'd be safe and sound and warm. After more thought, though, James admittedly uneasily that a phone call from Cashell to ask if she could come over would likely have been met with a flat 'no'. Something also told him that nothing would have deterred her. It was highly likely that she'd be in this predicament no matter what conversations they might have had. Determination emanated from her like the delicious aromas of freshly-baked bread from an oven. Just in case she had called, James scrolled through his phone to look for messages, but he didn't see any unknown numbers nor any new voicemails.

As his thoughts wandered, he looked down at Cashell's face. She was a beauty... He found himself studying her features, until she interrupted his reverie with a frustrated sigh.

"I'm sorry, James. Honestly, I didn't know you were one of the players the Rebels management team assigned to us until I read all the background paperwork. I didn't get around to looking over it all 'til a couple days after we'd met that night."

James was taken aback. He set aside his phone.

"I didn't mean to end up in your front yard," Cashell continued. "My car broke down and I got out to look under the hood, then the door closed behind me and I realized I'd locked all my stuff in there. So I just started walking. What are the chances that I ended up here?" She looked embarrassed. "Just a silly accident, really. I felt so incompetent about it all. I'm... sorry."

In an instant, James's heart melted and he smiled. "You're not incompetent. You're so beautiful and smart - and you've been on television."

Cashell smiled dreamily. She mumbled something unintelligible, and moments later he felt her body relax as a grunting snore was heard over the crackling of the dying fire.

10

Heartfelt Stories

ONCE SHE COULD STAY UPRIGHT by herself and pay attention, Cashell managed to FaceTime her doctor from James's phone. She told the kindly older cardiologist about her symptoms and got a verbal 'pass' for a day or so, at least until the snow could be shoveled, her car could be fixed and she was able to leave. Although she felt like crud, she was thankful that the feeling was more on the groggy, cold, grumpy end of the spectrum than the heart-condition-related, seek-medical-attention-now side of things. Despite James's anxious vigilance and the cross-examination from her doctor, she felt confident that she was okay and her doctor agreed. Plus, right then, her elated brain urged her to resist the fog of sleepiness and pull it together just so she would not miss a minute of being inside James Parker's home.

Honestly, when the fog finally cleared and she looked around, she could not believe her luck. Not only was she going to see James Parker in action in his own kitchen - judging by the heavenly smells wafting past her nose, this was happening now – but maybe she would even get to taste whether or not he could cook. James's little nephew and the other girl, Hannah, were going to be the icing on her cake. Cashell had warmed to the kids instantly the moment she'd sat up, with Kira's caring ministrations accompanied by Hannah's quiet observance and little Jacoby approaching her as a prospective new friend to play with. She had slapped her hand down playfully in front of him and he'd laughed, tapping her hand. A simpler silly game could not be found anywhere. She loved children and these three would be no different, except that they were related to the man in front of her who had intrigued her and dominated her thoughts for the past week, even when he wasn't present. That made these kids extra special.

In the kitchen, Cashell watched James cook with the girls. The three of them moved around each other in the large, bright room as easily as if they'd been doing it forever – not to mention that there was more than enough room for them to do so. Her eyes lingered mostly on James's back. His broad shoulders and long muscular arms were constantly reaching down items that were too high for the girls to get at, handed them the things to set the table with and generally made sure they were safe. Now, he was browning meat that she'd watched him season. Her mouth watered as the raw flesh hit the hot pan and started to sizzle.

The girls were no slouches in the kitchen, either. Each of them handled a small paring knife without incident, all while keeping a watchful eye on Jacoby and ensuring his little snack piles of cheese and veggies were kept fully stocked. Every so often during their silly hand slap game, he paused to shove bits of this and that into his mouth.

"Ready!"

"Ready!"

"Ready!"

James initiated the call and the girls checked their work station before answering, each yell more jovial than the last.

"We watch a lot of Chopped," Hannah explained with glee.

"Oh, I love that show!" Cashell exclaimed.

"Yeah," Hannah continued. "Sometimes Cole and I make something out of a bunch of weird ingredients. It's so fun."

"I bet," Cashell said fondly. She salivated over the food that was being placed in front of her. Pretty glass bowls were filled with to the brim, looking for all the world like a meal in some five-star Asian-fusion restaurant, holding every conceivable kind of sandwich topping. This food was going to be out of this world.

James brought the grilled buns over from the toaster oven and set them near the bowl of browned meat. "Do you want me to make yours?" he asked.

Cashell looked up shyly. "Um, okay." James carried an empty plate to the opposite end of the long island. "Everything?" he queried, raising one eyebrow.

"Uh, everything?" She did a quick review of the spread before giving her assent: "Yeah, OK – everything except the onions."

Cashell watched him loading the meat onto the bread, still piping hot, then piling the mound high with shredded American cheese. On the other bun he put a slathering of avocado before adding the lettuce and tomato, skipping the onions as requested and carefully smushing the two sides together, finally adding chips and a pickle on the side. He raised his head to address Kira.

"That's more like avocado paste than slices, Kay Kay."

"Uh, so what? Anyway, the avocados were really ripe," Kira returned defensively.

Cashell looked from one girl to the other: Kira, who'd cut up the avocados, and Hannah, who was wrinkling her nose delicately at the less-than-perfect slicing job.

"Excuse me – what she meant to say was that it's total perfection," James said and winked at Kira, who stuck her tongue out at Hannah. "The tomatoes are also perfect, ladies - I like this salsa version, Hannah."

Cashell stifled a laugh. She could see how Hannah lit up when James found a way to compliment both girls without detracting one's strengths from the other. He was masterful: these girls were so lucky.

Everyone else fixed their own plate - except Jacoby, whose food was put together by Hannah. The little boy immediately fell to eating, forgetting about their little hand-slap game for the moment and becoming totally engrossed in his food. James said the grace, ignoring Jacoby's premature chomping. Cashell experienced contentment like she'd never felt before.

After the grace was said, everyone dug in and the chatter continued. Cashell could barely eat her food, and that wasn't because it lacked anything – in fact, it was delicious. The hamburger meat was flavorful and all the extras, from the lettuce to the avocado, were so good. But she did not want to miss a moment of their banter, either.

Hannah was tall and lanky and she wielded a knife almost as well as Cole. Her big brother must have taught her himself: either that or she'd simply been born a chef. Kira was a little more on the prissy side. The future doctor, like her father, was cool and calm but a tad melodramatic. She set the table, as she had the one time Cashell had been to dinner at Allontis's house. Thanks to her past encounters with Dexter, Cashell actually knew more about Kira than any of them.

"You doing okay?"

Startled out of her quiet observance of everyone else, Cashell wiped her mouth and looked up to meet James's eyes. He was eating standing up, and her throat felt dry watching him, but she managed to answer.

"Uh, yeah, so long as I don't look down. These chairs are kind of high," she quipped. He'd helped her climb up into the chair before dinner, but now that she was up there she clearly wasn't leaving without assistance.

"We can sit in the dining room," he offered, between hearty bites.

"No I'm fine." She wouldn't dare move: the girls were enjoying their food, and Jacoby was almost done.

Cashell kept pretending to be quietly aloof, when in fact she was busy observing the way James interacted with his awesome family. To her surprise, the pitches and magazine spreads she'd been struggling with for work had virtually been writing themselves since the other night. James couldn't have been an easier subject - and it was that very easiness that gave her pause. What if there were some skeletons lurking in his closet, as Bill had insinuated the other day? Was James Parker a genuine family man, a home chef and an attentive good looking

Uncle Bachelor; or was she missing something else completely?

"Kira, honey, you must be very excited about your father and Leedra's upcoming wedding, huh?"

Kira stopped eating and put her sandwich down, carefully wiping her mouth before looking up at Cashell.

"Actually, paint drying would be a faster process," she sighed airily. Hannah chuckled, but James turned and leaned against the counter to observe.

"Kay Kay…" James began in a warning tone.

"What? It's true. Everything takes forever. Lee is taking an age to decide on anything, and I know Daddy is getting frustrated. You'll probably get married faster than they will."

Cashell choked on a pickle spear.

"Excuse me, uh - " James fumbled, clearly embarrassed.

"Honey," Cashell interjected, clearing her throat and valiantly steering the conversation back on track. "I'm sure your father and Leedra will be married by Christmas. Their love is so evident."

Kira shrugged. "I just hate how lonely I feel when she leaves all the time. It's like I have a part-time mom. Can we just get on with it already?"

"You didn't tell me you felt that way," James said. "It's important not to pressure Leedra, though, Kay Kay. She's been through a lot."

"I have, too." Cashell felt a pang when she saw the tears standing in Kira's eyes. Instantly, James was at her side. He pulled out her chair and lifted her into his arms.

"Listen to me," he said softly. "You're gonna be fine. You can tell Leedra how you feel, but all I'm saying is that you need to do it in a loving way. Not in a way that makes her feel pressured, like 'hurry and do this or that.' You know? You are special and important too, honey, but you've got to remember that she's been through some hard stuff. It's important not to rush this sort of thing. Remember, what grown folks do is on their own time."

Cashell continued to eat, but her ears strained to hear what

James said to his niece as he led her through to the other room and sat her down. She couldn't see them, but she could just about make out their hushed whispers in the background.

"Kira's rather dramatic," Hannah said and gave Cashell her signature eye-roll.

"People handle things in different ways. You've been through a lot as well," Cashell replied gently.

"Yeah. You grow up fast when your mom's jacked up."

Cashell wasn't sure what to say. She smiled. For all their resilience, they were still just kids. This chance to talk with their uncle away from their parents likely brought things out that wouldn't be said at home.

"Wanna get down now, Hantah!"

Cashell looked over. She'd forgotten about Jacoby, who was, as he said, now done with his food and wanted to move on to other things.

Hannah sprang immediately to action. "Okay, Jac, wipe your face - are you finished?"

"Yesh."

Cashell watched how attentive Hannah was to Jacoby. The girl removed his plate, wiped up the food that didn't make it into his mouth with a damp cloth and carried it on his dirty plate to the sink.

"Can I help you, sweetie?"

"Oh, I got it, thank you. Wait for James - I don't want you to fall."

Miss Independent. Cashell nodded, suddenly feeling more childish than Hannah herself as she watched the girl pick up the chubby younger child like he weighed nothing. As soon as she set him on his feet, he toddled off in search of Kira and James.

"I started a movie for them."

Startled at James's voice behind her, Cashell whipped her head around so fast she felt her chair sway on its legs. He chuckled.

"Once they're all settled, I'll go get your car, see if I can figure out what's wrong with it," he continued, heading for the door. "I also dropped my mail out front when I tripped over you, so guess I'll get that while I'm out there too," he added.

She scooted her seat cautiously away from the kitchen island and stuck out a leg to slide down, hoping her dangling feet could reach the floor before her butt landed there first. She felt as if her head was taking her in a different direction, though: like wherever gravity pulled, that's where she was going. She grasped for the counter's edge, only to grab onto thin air as she fell backwards.

"Hey, hey!"

James caught her instantly and propped her back up.

She smiled up at him, ignoring the concerned look he gave her. "I love those girls and Jacoby. Those eyes of his are gonna break hearts. Did the new baby get Allontis's eyes too?" she asked, changing the subject.

"From what we can tell, it looks like it. I have pictures of her on my phone - I'll show you. She's only three months old: not even."

Cashell nodded, feeling James's eyes remain on her.

"James, about my car... I was thinking, should I just stay here?" she offered hesitantly. "I can sleep on the couch - looks like the girls are sleeping in the living room anyway. I can stay there 'til morning. Please don't go out to get the car right now. It's really dark. I'd feel more comfortable if you weren't out there in the pitch black. I can't help you with much, but please. The least I can do is wait."

"Well, as long as there's nothing you need in there."

She was surprised at James's lack of protest. Of course she wouldn't send him out there in the cold while she sat in here fretting he'd be hurt; but she suspected that the real reason for him wanting to stay inside was that he wouldn't leave the three kids. His love for them was paramount, and always would be. Nice try, that mean little voice mocked her. You're not so special. Kids and old folks rule, not almost-middle-aged single ladies.

"Um," she said, trying to get out of her own head. "I can call my brother. He'll tell my parents where I am, and I think his is probably the only number I know by heart - he's had the same number forever, you see. I'll do that now, if I can use your phone?"

James nodded. His arms were still around her from the swift catch. She leaned into him, more because she liked it than because it was necessary. He helped her to the living room and she took a seat on the couch. When she was settled, he handed her his cell phone.

"I don't know that I'll install a landline," James said, half to himself. "I likely will, but I haven't gotten around to it yet. Oh – the passcode is 4-0-9-1-2."

Cashell looked down at his phone. The black screen showed her nothing yet, but the code he'd just rattled off meant that she could see anything and everything on his phone once she punched in the numbers. His whole life, in this day and age. She hesitated. When she'd used his phone to call her doctor, James had been more cautious, holding it for her and tapping in the code and phone number himself: so much so that she'd guessed perhaps there was something on there that he didn't want her to see. Maybe she'd read more into that than she should have, for it clearly wasn't the case now.

As if reading her mind, James spoke up. "I don't have anything to hide, Cashell, contrary to what you've heard so far at work."

Cashell bit her lip. She'd hated that James had been lumped in with the other guys in the current controversy. So far, she had kept the information to herself that of the four players she was currently interviewing, Braxton Denton was clearly hiding something. She held out hope that it was something straightforward: that he just had a chip on his shoulder about his integrity being questioned despite his years on the team. She thought it was wrong of the management to treat him that way, too.

Cashell entered the phone's passcode, noticing that his

homescreen wallpaper was an old photo of the three people she'd just eaten dinner with. The individuals in question were currently sprawled out before her on the mounds of blankets covering the floor, half asleep. Cashell blinked at the digital image. She'd expected a photo of some random girl from his past, perhaps; or maybe a team logo, or a hot model draped over the hood of a dream sports car. She was not prepared for this family portrait of Parker kids to be staring back at her.

"Thank you." She quickly pushed the green icon to bring up the phone keypad and tapped in her brother's number. When she placed the phone to her ear, James tactfully wandered further away to the front of the room to pop in a DVD for the kids. The opening credits appeared on the big screen television, but the children barely paid any attention to it. Each of them had their covers pulled up to their chins and were slowly drifting off to sleep. Cashell spoke in a low voice to her brother when he answered, telling him she'd be spending the night with a friend during the blizzard and that she'd call him in the morning. She didn't mention her car, or the particular friend that she was with. She listened to James working in the kitchen, as dishes clanked and the water ran in the sink. He was cleaning up the space, likely putting the scrumptious leftovers away. She should have gone and offered to help him, but the day had been full of so much already: she couldn't quite believe the latter part of it had really happened. If she was seeing the true version of James Parker then he was such a dream.

After she ended the call with her brother, she felt herself drifting off too. The room was dark, with the cartoon's soft sounds of kids giggling and funny little animals burbling away in the background.

Somewhere in between sleep and awake, the man of her dreams reappeared before her. She wanted to stay awake to talk to him, now that they were semi alone, but she was forced to lay down when he deftly pulled her feet up onto the couch, removed her shoes with gentle hands and flipped a light comforter over her, which wafted a little breeze across her face as it fluttered down to cover her body.

"You're one of the kindest people I've ever met," she murmured drowsily.

"Really? Cash, you gotta get out more," James whispered, smiling.

She remembered only that she chuckled a bit at the fact that he'd given her the same nickname her brother had coined for her when she was just five years old. With that, she drifted off into a dream-filled, peaceful sleep.

11
Plays Well with Others?

———

"CATCH HELL? YOU LIKE THAT? Catch Hell. That's Ms. Bruer's new codename, because it's exactly what is going to happen to us if we don't do what she says."

"Then why don't you make the effort, Braxton? This is for our careers, you know?" James rolled his eyes.

"What career? I'm old. Haven't you heard?"

Old in age perhaps, but completely immature: a true oxymoron, James thought to himself. He shrugged. "Nope," he said aloud. "Your contract is renewed, you looked good at the end of the season. Your surgery was successful. What's the problem?"

James really didn't want to have this conversation yet again. His only saving grace was that they were in a morning meeting with a reporter this time around, and a photographer was setting up the photoshoot area behind them as they spoke. There wasn't any liquor involved, and no bars or bartenders in sight. God willing, things should go well for once. The photographer was testing the lighting. He'd get through this and be on his way for the day, thought James with relief.

"Whatever you say is what you shall become," he continued. "Try speaking positively, Brax - that might help."

"How do you know that?" his teammate snapped.

"I don't know it. I'm just saying, try it and see."

James crossed his arms. Their conversation was so repetitive that he quickly grew tired of listening to Brax. What was this, the buddy system? Why on earth did he always find himself next to this guy? He adjusted his clothes: not a suit exactly, but nice jeans, a button-down shirt and a vest. He'd read the memos that Cashell had sent around and spent quite some time the night before searching out the right outfit. Not that he'd been trying to impress her or anything, but he wanted to make things painless for her; and doing exactly what she asked seemed the easiest way to go about that.

"All right, gentlemen," the press guy began. "Ms. Bruer told us to get some shots over here: some of you guys holding the anniversary football. Then after the serious set, we'll do the team set. We've got a couple of girls from the squad here for those. Then we'll sit down to chat and ask you guys some questions. Sound good so far?"

James nodded and Braxton shrugged.

Everyone's eyes, James included, were riveted to the door as Cashell walked in, all business, accompanied by her intern. James tried to pay attention to the photographer, but it felt inarguably odd to be smiling a big fake smile at an older gentleman behind a camera, all while receiving chirpy instructions from a young woman who looked like she belonged in his old high school's Future Business Leaders of America Club.

Cashell, by contrast, stood watching them: smiling, cool as a cucumber yet looking nothing like the frozen Popsicle he'd encountered on his front lawn. He tried to keep his eyes on the camera, but they kept wandering back over to Cashell. Just like after the first time they'd met, it seemed she'd only come back stronger in the wake of catastrophe. She looked lucid, together... well. Once again, he questioned his feeling of relief. He'd arrived that morning wanting to say hello, but she'd been in a meeting so he hadn't bothered her.

He was glad she was there now.

"All right, now, you two stand together, please, shoulder to shoulder, shoulders in, bodies angled away from one another. Mr. Parker, toss up the ball. Put the other ball under your arm – that's it. Now, Mr. Denton, arms crossed, smiling, adjust your shades just a bit, that's it... you are the double threat here, guys. One can start it and the other can finish it."

"What does that mean?" Braxton's voice growled.

James looked over, not sure how to respond to this sudden and unprompted aggression. The reporter, sheepish now and unsure of what to say, was silent for a moment. The photographer lowered his camera, waiting for more instructions and the ensuing poses.

"Nothing!" the reporter responded eventually. "I'm just trying to get you to relax your features, that's all - trying to get you to look like you're having fun. I was thinking a sort of 'healthy rivalry but not really' thing, you know? It's good for business."

"Brax, calm down," James told him. "It's a photo shoot, not a competition."

"It's always a competition, Parker; but it looks like I'm the only one who's aware of anything."

"Awareness in your own head of your own made-up stories," James shot back.

"You shut up!"

Hearing the ruckus, Cashell looked up from her quiet conversation with her intern and came over to where they stood. She eyed the pair of them reproachfully.

"You guys are on the same team, you know?"

"Is that a question?"

"No, Braxton, it's a reminder." Cashell's eyes looked steadily at him, holding his gaze, unintimidated.

James spoke up. "Brax, could you just chill out for once? We work for the same team, we have a common goal. What's the problem?"

Cashell raised her voice to address the crew. "Hey Jess, why don't we take five, all right?"

James hung back as Cashell walked out onto the carpeted area, where the lights were bright and blinding for the photo shoot. He removed his shades so she could see his whole face, and their eyes met immediately as he took a seat. Braxton kept his shades on and slumped sulkily in a nearby office chair.

Cashell surveyed the situation before her. Well, her Men

In Black theme was going just super-duper so far... Approximately a hundred limited-edition silver footballs had been ordered specifically for the anniversary of the team's founding. Her movie theme went so well with the team's colors. The perfectly inspired theme idea had come to her in the middle of the night, color scheme and all. It fit in just ideally with the team's uniforms of silver and black.

"What's the problem, Mr. Denton?"

She looked at both of them but focused on the man who seemed to buck her at every turn.

"I'm not feeling this whole image-management- improvement-whatever thing," Braxton grumbled.

"Okay, well, we can do your shoot separately if you insist; but I'm on a budget, so I'd have to go and tell the budget office that we need to keep the folks here for double the time because you're being contrary." Cashell worked to conceal her disdain.

"Whatever."

Cashell exhaled through her nose. "Is there something more you'd like to share, Mr. Denton - or do you have something to hide?"

"I told you, I ain't got nothing to hide," Braxton snapped fiercely. "Now you can get out of my face."

Cashell's heart rate increased: not because the burly QB was now in her face, but because James had leapt out of his seat so lightning-fast that she was worried he would react more aggressively than whatever Brax had planned.

"Back up, Brax." James's tone carried a threat.

"What you gonna do? Huh?"

"Guys, please. What's happening?" asked Cashell, alarmed.

"I don't like the line of questioning your reporter people have," Braxton hissed, turning to her.

"Then you have the right to respond 'no comment'." Cashell tried to maintain smoothness in her voice.

"Well, that's what I'm doing now. No comment. No comment, no comment." He was right up in her face now.

"Back up, Brax. I'm not gonna tell you again." James moved

in closer, his large frame nearly edging Cashell out of the way.

She'd never considered that the situation might come to blows, but the way Brax was acting... Cashell was trying desperately to think of a way to diffuse the situation.

"I see you found yourself an ally," Braxton sniffed. "Way to go, Ms. Boo-her."

"Are you drunk?" James asked suddenly. Without waiting for an answer, he snatched the shades from the other man's face so fast that they fell to the floor before Brax could push him away. Angered, Brax shoved James much harder than was necessary.

"You shut up." Braxton rubbed his eyes viciously, but not before everyone saw the bloodshot whites and the red rims encircling them. Though James did not engage him further, Braxton stormed from the room, pushing people as he went. Cashell's luckless intern Brandon was in the way and Brax sent him flying. Wrongfooted, the slight young man stumbled into the lighting pole, which tumbled to the ground, catching the drop canvas. To the horror of all around, the thick fabric began to smolder, and moments later, flames curled up to lick the edges of the sheet. Fire!

Cashell, shocked and disbelieving that all this had been set in motion by one person's carelessness, saw everyone scramble ahead of her out the door as if in slow motion. She walked calmly, in a sort of daze, until someone grabbed her from behind. She let out a small shriek of terror. It was James, she soon realized, who hastily picked her up and almost ran with her until they were well away from the room, where he set her down away from everyone almost halfway along the hall. Despite his heroism in ensuring she was safe, all eyes were on her, including Braxton's. Then, after a long moment, he stormed off without a backward glance and disappeared around a corner, seeming not to care whether or not the place ultimately burned to the ground. He was gone.

James was back down the hall in a matter of moments, rushing past her to re-enter the burning room. Following his path with her eyes, she noticed the horizontal silver cabinet box on the hall wall, its door still swinging as a result of James's quick thinking. He had the fire extinguisher grasped in his hands and was already back in the room.

Waiting at a safe distance, Cashell spoke to the photographer and reporter, apologetically dismissing them for the day. She also sucked it up and asked them to send her an invoice for the damage to their equipment, thankful that the stunned gray-haired photographer had not one but two of his several costly cameras safely intact on their straps around his neck.

As the media guys trooped out, she reentered the smoking room despite the reprimands James would no doubt give her about doing so. The fire had been doused, and James wielded the extinguisher's hose expertly as a few more loud blowing sounds squirted from the apparatus. A white soapy-looking foam covered all that was left of the room.

12
Friendships

CASHELL WAS EXHAUSTED AND IT wasn't even noon. She re-entered her office with her intern hot on her heels.

Was she really expected to help keep the peace between two adult children – ones who played with fire, at that?

She glanced up at Brandon, wishing for the hundredth time that he were the type of intern who liked to disappear more frequently than he did. Right now she needed a moment. She wanted to talk to James. With sadness and anger, she'd noticed soon after the blaze had been quelled that he'd left, too.

"Brandon, I need you call maintenance and tell them what happened. Can you give me about an hour alone, please?"

"Yeah, uh, sure. Did you want me to get James and Braxton in here?"

Are you nuts? Instead of saying what first came to her mind, Cashell just shook her head. That'd be all she needed: to get her intern injured by Brax "The Bruiser" Denton. She took a deep breath, trying to marshal her thoughts. James must have saved her because he felt some kind of loyalty to her. Any positive connection of that sort would surely go out of the window if she sent her nineteen-year-old intern to summon him to her office to meet with a $24-million-dollar man-baby , as if she were some sort of principal.

"Thanks, Brandon. Once I let management know what transpired, I'm going to work from home for the rest of today. I want you to type up an incident report draft and send it to me ASAP. I'll email you a sample to follow - there may also be an official form on our intranet. Oh, and please call maintenance to come clean up."

A knock sounded on the door and Cashell sat straighter in her chair. Reflexively, she stood up, preparing herself to face whomever was on the other side, be it Braxton himself, management, or James.

Brandon got up and opened the door. Relief surged through her at seeing James standing in the doorway, and she released the breath she held. She stepped out from the behind the desk. Although her immediate instinct was to run up and give him a hug, she stopped short of moving toward him.

Thankfully, Brandon made no further comments and excused himself, scurrying silently off to do as she'd asked him.

"Come in, James."

She waited until the door was closed before taking one look at him and wrapping her arms around his neck, without invitation or permission.

"Are you all right?" His tone was cool.

Cashell moved back quickly. She'd question her boldness later. She nodded adamantly. "Of course I'm all right. Are you all right?"

"Well, I think Braxton should be suspended. I mean, we could have had a major issue back there - anyone could've gotten hurt. He's ridiculous - out of control."

"You wouldn't hear any arguments from me," Cashell sighed. She went back to her desk and sat down heavily. Despite having been with James just an hour earlier, only now did she notice what he was wearing. She liked what he'd chosen: it was just the sort of thing she'd had in mind... for the photo-shoot that never was, she reflected glumly. His jeans, button-down shirt, black vest and clean Converse high-tops gave him a rugged appeal. He had just a little facial hair, so the entire look wasn't completely playful but featured elegance combined with just enough 'play' to create a subtle but definite sex appeal. "You look really... well, I see my memo and instructions were clear enough," she grinned.

James moved forward and took a seat opposite her desk. He shrugged, giving nothing away. "You were clear. I mean, that's what the internet is for."

Cashell was a little taken aback by his coolness. "True, but some people don't care about - or aren't interested in - following instructions."

"Their loss. I like to satisfy certain people, only because their requests aren't difficult and I'm not the obtuse one in this situation. It makes my life easier."

Cashell smiled. Her word. Obtuse. She wondered if Braxton even knew what the word meant.

"I doubt Braxton even knows what that means."

"You know, I was just thinking that." She felt herself relax when they shared a laugh.

"I'm going out of town for a day or so," James said.

"Oh really? Just a day? Are you gonna spend time with Jacoby and the girls?

James shook his head. "I'm going to find my mother."

"Oh, your biological mom is... still alive?"

"She's in a nursing facility in North Carolina, according to the investigator."

"Oh, uh. Okay." Cashell hated the fact that she sounded liked like some sort of stunned parakeet. She didn't know what to say. "Um, have you told Dexter and Cole?"

"No. I don't want them to know yet."

"Well, why, James?" She was more than surprised he had chosen her to share this with.

"I just don't know who these people are yet or what they're like. I want to start with a bit of safe distance."

She paused. "These people?"

"I have a brother, too – well, a stepbrother. He lives down there too, the investigator said."

Cashell nodded her understanding. A part of her was glad that he'd felt enough... well, whatever he felt, to confide in her; yet another part wondered why he didn't also plan to tell the people he loved most. She suddenly wanted someone to be there with him, if not just to talk with him whenever he needed it. Her heart beat fast.

"Uh, James? Can you call me afterwards, please?

"Why?" he asked guardedly.

She shrugged. Good question. "I just want to know how it all goes, as a friend, James - that's all, I promise."

"I thought you might want to bring cameras or something. I'm kind of relieved that you don't."

"I wouldn't ever do that unless you wanted me to," she assured him. "My job is all about the image thing, James. It doesn't require me to insert myself into whatever you have going on personally. Perhaps after you meet your mom and give me a green light, I could talk to her, ask her about you... but not at this stage. Not when you're just getting to know her. That should be private. Sure, it would make a great human interest story - but whatever you want, okay?"

Cashell didn't want to tell him what else she was picking up about the report on his family: that if this stepbrother was alive and well but James's mom was in a nursing home, that probably indicated something unfortunate about the situation. Yes, it was the way people did business nowadays. Most nursing facilities were full of people whose children had no desire to make it work and keep their loved ones at home. Unfortunately, it might also say something about the home situation: perhaps that his mother needed more care than could be provided at home, whatever the exact nature of her needs. Illness, disability, dementia: all of it entered Cashell's mind. Or maybe the brother simply lacked the financial means to provide additional support. She hesitated to read all of that into just the little information she had, but she was starting to feel as if James could be in for a rude surprise. The thought just sat in her brain bugging her, for whatever reasons. She was also sad that it looked like James might be planning to go this alone. He shouldn't, and she wished he wouldn't.

As far as trailing along with him just to scrounge up details to sensationalize his private life, for a story that should have been his to tell? That just wasn't her. Cashell hoped that after all her years in this business, she didn't ever become that person.

James looked over at her as if he, too, had been lost in his thoughts. She moved over and took his hand.

"You've been a friend to me – pretty much a hero, in fact, rescuing me from burning buildings and dousing fires in a single spray as you wield your mighty fire extinguisher." That got a laugh and she was glad. "Now I want to be there for you. Please, tell Allontis or Cole that you're going on this trip down south – or… let me go with you?"

James raised his eyebrows but shook his head. Cashell nodded, knowing he wouldn't. She was surprised herself by the offer she had just made. It had just seemed like the right thing to say: the words had just come out, unbidden.

James stood. "It's important that I find out what it is I've got here before bringing any details of it back to my family. I'll call you."

She nodded. The fact that he'd hadn't refused outright was more than she had dared hope for, considering they weren't officially anything to each other.

"I just wanted to make sure you… didn't have anything on the agenda. The memo you sent had stuff scheduled for today, but nothing more till late next week – that right?"

"Yes, I, uh, wanted to make sure you have a summer," Cashell explained. "A lot of the guys go to the islands or the west coast: to their vacation homes and such."

"I don't do any of that," James said shortly.

"Were you invited?" she asked.

"Yes, I've been invited to numerous things. Thing is, I wanted to stay close to home until my brothers' kids are out of school. I want to have a family weekend at my house. Just as soon as I finish getting the place furnished and stuff, everyone's gonna be over. You can come if you'd like. But, just family, no one else: I don't want the guys popping over, so don't mention it please."

"Of course." Just family... but an invitation to her solo seemed to contradict that. She wasn't family. She made a mental note to examine what he'd just said later.

"What day will you go down to North Carolina?"

"Tuesday, probably."

She nodded. He moved to the door and she followed. She wouldn't see him for several days. Unexpectedly, he bent down and kissed her cheek. His warm breath and the softness of his mustache tickled.

"Think you can keep yourself out of trouble? Okay, I'll see you. I'll text you."

"Okay." She nodded, slightly stunned, wishing there was some way to prolong this goodbye. She could feel how heavy his heart was at the thought of meeting his mother for the first time. She hadn't known that was something he was dealing with at all. Perhaps that was one of the things that made him so much more mature than all of his peers.

Before today's revelation, she hadn't given much thought to what the adoption process must have been like for James. In addition, thinking about the fact that his mother had given him away angered and saddened her at the same time. Who could give him away? Come to think of it: who could cheat on Dexter? Why did Hannah's mother turn her back? All of these questions came to hit her at once. The whole Parker family was so complex, with so many intricacies. James was a wonderful person and, for whatever reason, his mother had missed out on all that he'd grown up to be. She could only imagine what that was like. And his brother? Something told her that whoever he was, the two of them would be different on so many levels. The fact that James wasn't telling Cole or Allontis or even Dexter meant that he, too, was uncertain about what he was getting into. Perhaps, she mused, it didn't feel positive to him. She wondered what exactly had been contained in that letter from the private investigator.

James left, closing the door behind him, and Cashell stared at it for a second before snapping into action. She moved back to the desk, packing up her papers and her laptop ready to put an end to this tumultuous day. She couldn't wait to get back to the bed in her small condo and commence burying her head under the covers until another, less overwhelming day presented itself.

13

The Scoop

A FEW DAYS LATER, CASHELL WAS physically back at work but her mind still refused to focus. It had been less than a week since the incident with Braxton and James. Now she could not get James off her mind. As far as she was concerned, though, Braxton could go take a flying leap. This week had progressed much too fast and the only thing she'd wanted to do that morning when her alarm clock went off was to pull the covers back over her head, just so she could reminisce about the unexpected but totally-worth-it near-death experience that had led to her weekend with James Parker and family.

Impressively, James had been able to fix whatever was wrong with her car to the extent that it was drivable. Something about the distributor cap, he'd told her, as if she knew what or where that was. Although she was loathe to leave the delectable warm breakfast, she'd said her goodbyes to James and his family that morning and went straight to the mechanic to have the car looked at. James had had to break her window to unlock the door, but the mechanic told her that was the only expense she had. James had driven it back to the house and let it run for a while to make sure.

His lips against her cheek... that softest, feather-light touch conjured all kinds of visions that lingered in living color every time she closed her eyes. She couldn't stop touching her cheek. Her weekend was over much too soon.

"Do you have a zit?" her intern Brandon piped up.

"What?"

"A zit. Is one coming in? I hate it when I get those. So

annoying."

"No - no, I don't have one. I don't think."

Brandon shrugged. "Oh. Well, you've been touching the side of your face all day," he said matter-of-factly. "Let me know if you want some of my Preventative. You can wash your face with some and it keeps zits and acne outbreaks from happening. I use it all the time."

"I'll remember that. Thanks." Cashell took a deep breath as the post she'd been working on blurred in front of her eyes.

As usual, Brandon's face was turned down as he spoke, his eyes perpetually glued to his phone. When they'd first started working together, Brandon had seemed very enthusiastic: perhaps even a bit overzealous. While he was pretty good as a researcher and all-around gopher, he had a troubling tendency to go rogue and start working on things she hadn't asked him to.

"So I didn't tell you, but I think that I've got the QB situation figured out," Brandon said casually.

"What figured out? What QB situation?" Cashell was immediately attentive now. She saved and closed the document she was working on. She would come back to it with fresh eyes in the afternoon, she decided: when she could focus. Sadly, she didn't think that was going to happen at all today, and probably not as long as James Parker occupied her thoughts every single moment.

"Brandon, are you trying to get a job with TMZ or what?" she asked sardonically.

"No, I'm just relaying information to you," Brandon replied coolly. "I haven't broadcast it or sold it to the highest bidder or anything like that - that would be the TMZ way, don't you think? And I didn't confirm or deny the rumors. All I said was that I'd gotten some news."

"All right then, out with it." Cashell looked at him piercingly.

"Well first, I got the scoop on Parker versus Denton, right," Brandon continued eagerly. "See, Denton is washed, up: old."

"He's thirty-eight! And he has two Super Bowl rings." Tactless kid, Cashell thought.

"Exactly. He needs to hang it up. At this point it's like a sixty-year-old woman wearing a mini skirt. Gross, right?" Brandon exclaimed. Cashell dutifully rolled her eyes at the visual.

"Let some young blood go for it, that's what I say. They're placating him out of a sense of loyalty."

"I don't know what you're smoking, but the NFL is all about business," Cashell informed him tartly. "They couldn't care less about loyalty."

"Not if you're chummy with the owner."

"What?"

"Yeah, as long as you're chummy with the owner you score whatever kind of deals you want, right? Like, oh I don't know, a token contract for a player trying to score past his prime? I mean, did they speak to you about his temper tantrum the other day?"

Cashell shook her head slowly. She was more than thankful that she'd missed the event itself, but it was odd that no one had mentioned it - and likely nobody had said anything to Denton either, when they should have.

"Fine, okay, that's one theory on Denton. So where does that leave Parker?" She tried to keep the new interest out of her voice, looking down and busying herself with riffling through the stacks of paper that littered her desk, even as she listened extra carefully for the response.

"Parker's green but he's talented, and they - the commentators, that is – they think he's gonna be a star. He's just gotta get past those issues he has. Word is he's looking for his birth mother or something: that could be a mess. Oh, and something big happened to him back in college, but it's super hard to get any information at all. I'm still doing some digging trying to figure out what it was."

Cashell nodded. So much for everything being on the up and up. She got a sick feeling in her gut. People with power were playing games as if the players were simply pieces on a chessboard. She hated it. This definitely wasn't what she signed on for.

"Braxton is hiding something too," Brandon continued, "but apparently no one is talking. You'd think that after being here for six years, which is an eternity in the league, someone would've found it by now."

"Well, uh, what are you working on now?" Cashell asked, not entirely sure she wanted to know.

"I'm trying to pull up some of Parker's old records – oh, and I got a possible location on his mother."

"Why?"

"I... thought you would want to see whatever it is he's gotten into," Brandon offered hopefully.

"You are here to find things that everyone else has access to," Cashell reminded him, feeling slightly panicked. "No hacking or underhanded information-gathering, Brandon. Besides, if someone finds out you have this information, how are you going to explain how and where you got it?"

Brandon stared at her and shrugged. "They all say they have 'a source' or something vague like that. Why can't I?"

Cashell took a deep, audible breath. She was certifiably worried now about what her employers were trying to do, and she didn't like it one bit. "Um, these so-called 'sources' can provide everything - but why would they give it to you? Brandon Smith, I want to tell you something right now: perhaps I didn't make it clear when I hired you. If you cross me with any information, I will fire you so fast it'll make your head spin. You want to start looking for that job at that rag, *Too Much Zeal*? Then you take your butt on out and find Mr. Garvey right now."

"Um it was bought by Time Warner when they-" Brandon started.

"Whatever," she said quickly. She was not comforted by the fact he was correcting her about the current owners of the tabloid talk show and publication arm. Perhaps this millennial had already researched his next employment options just in case. "My point is that I don't play around. I don't run unverified junk that hurts people and their families. I run a legitimate PR firm, not a tabloid. You understand?"

He nodded, but remained cocky. "You realize you work for the league now, though?"

"If they don't like it, I can leave at any time," she shot back. "I know exactly who I work for."

After this exchange, Cashell wasn't convinced that Brandon had heeded her warning. She hated the idea of firing him already: it would just anger him, making him that much more useful at some other company where he could provide out-of-context information and spin stories that tore people apart. She also realized that taking this contract in the first place was likely a mistake. Up until now, she'd only worked for individuals, plus some pro bono work for nonprofits that wanted to build their brand and increase their reach and fundraising targets. This was the first time she'd worked for a private organization with owners who contracted players - and employees - to do whatever they said: good and certainly bad. There was a degree of conflict in all of this. She wanted to work for the players, but she wasn't working for them. She was working for the team, the league and, ultimately, the owners. Players would come and go, be moved around, be cut, leave or get new contracts, but her loyalty would always have to remain with the management. She hadn't known about the intricate nature of these things when she'd first won the contract. With a cold shock, she realized that she'd even be expected to spin whatever potentially harmful decisions they made, finding a positive way to convey the messages to the press and public no matter how bad those messages were. No matter who got hurt, it was their 'brand' that had to remain intact. She had to do what they said.

Now that she knew what Brandon was after, the only thing she could do was get to the information about James's family before he did. That meant she'd have to work doubly hard on nights and weekends to get ahead of him.

Decidedly, she also needed to get over her growing feelings for James Parker – the family man, the rescuer, the fixer – and do so very quickly. A friendship with him, as alluring as it was getting to be, was wrong, too complicated; and it would lead her heart down the path of no return. Even though her mind told her what she needed to do, her heart whispered that James would eventually need protecting and, for that, she was the best person for the job.

14

Little Visits

JAMES WAS SURPRISED HOW EMPTY the house felt after the kids left. He still wasn't sure what to make of Cashell and her unexpected visit, or of his unforeseen need to tell her why he was going down south. That revelation came out of nowhere, he reflected: it had just sort of… tumbled out. He really hadn't wanted anyone to know.

He was still at home, taking stock of all the things he needed to get done to the house to render it worthy of inviting his brothers and their respective broods over for a couple days' stay. The bag he'd packed for North Carolina sat by the door: a small overnight bag, as he didn't plan to be gone long. And, right now, he was hungry.

James took down a clean bowl and poured cereal into it as he surveyed his kitchen. He looked in the fridge, annoyed that the pitiful amount of milk left in the carton wouldn't drown an ant. He laughed out loud to himself at Cashell's same sentiment on her birthday: she had used that exact phrase to describe their little champagne toast. He closed the door and noticed the list that had been taped to his fridge. In kid's handwriting, the letters on the first line spelled out the word MILK. The following lines listed waffles, syrup and a host of other things he didn't normally buy. He smiled: although he didn't eat any of that stuff, he liked the list just because the kids had made it. Plus, if he bought what they had listed, maybe it would somehow mean they'd be coming back. That gave him some comfort.

Why are you such a loner?

James tore off the list, folded it and shoved it into his pocket. He pushed the cereal bowl aside and was about to restart his search for something low-effort to satisfy his growling belly when the doorbell rang.

Allontis Baxter Parker, his sister-in-law, stood on the doorstep. On one shoulder she balanced a small blanketed bundle and, on the other, a diaper bag. Before James could welcome her, she breezed past him. James looked outside to see if Cole was with her, since they were rarely apart.

"I'm by myself – well, me and this one," she said over her shoulder, as if reading his thoughts, indicating the bundle.

"Okay. Um, how are you?" he said, shutting the door behind her in some bewilderment. He moved to follow her, taking the diaper bag from her shoulder.

"I'm good, thanks – and I brought you my latest heartbreaker, Ms. Sophia Renee," Allontis beamed. "Uh, how are you?"

"Good." There was a short pause. "Er," James continued, "this is unexpected. Why didn't you tell me you were coming?" It seemed to be a pattern of late with the women in his life. Who said Cashell was 'in your life'?

James dismissed the thoughts and joined Allontis in the living room. She had sat down and was unwrapping her newest bundle. For her to appear without calling ahead wasn't a huge deal, but it did seem odd that neither she nor Cole had told him to be on the lookout for her.

"I'll call Cole in a little bit. Don't worry so much." Again, Allontis was reading his mind.

James took a seat across from her, and shrugged nonchalantly. "Who says I'm worried?"

"It's the Parker worry vein right here," she said pointing to her forehead.

James made a face. The remark was all the more laughable considering none of the adoptive brothers were blood relations. While the five of them had grown up together, their blood was all different: a point he'd always tried to dismiss but had been bothering him more and more of late. It really shouldn't have, after all these years.

James knew he was touchier than usual about family issues today, because he'd just been contemplating the best day to start the trip down south. He'd also finally found time that week to review the agency's more detailed report about his biological family.

When James looked up, Allontis was in front of him, her arms outstretched.

"Can you hold her? I have to pee."

She kissed his cheek and put her baby in his lap without waiting for an answer. "I haven't seen you since she was born, by the way, and even then you only stayed one night - like you had to get away or something."

"Sorry," he said guiltily. He carefully adjusted the infant, who was either just coming out of or just dropping off into her slumber. He wasn't sure: he didn't know much about babies.

"What made you come?"

She lifted her eyes heavenward and slapped her hands dramatically against her thighs, as if he'd asked her that already – or, for that matter, for the umpteenth time.

"I just needed to go for a drive, that's all," she snapped irritably. "Where's the bathroom?"

James jabbed a finger over her shoulder to point through the kitchen, hoping the kids hadn't left the washroom in a mess. He really hadn't checked around much since they'd left. A part of him had sort of hoped to find more little remnants of them, like the grocery list on his fridge or the little fingerprints covering just about every surface. Those telltale signs of a young family made him happy, reminding him of the recent influx of little visitors to his new house. At the same time, though, he was sad to remember that at the end of the day, this place was just a lonely bachelor pad.

When the baby's mother returned, James handed the baby back, and the little thing wailed loudly as Allontis started to fumble with her shirt. Suddenly embarrassed, James pretended to be busy with other things. In seconds, the baby ceased her fussing, now otherwise occupied with the tasty offering under the nursing cover.

"I'm a busy Momma now - can you believe it?" Allontis said in quiet awe.

"Truthfully? Heck no, I can't," he replied, with a fond smile.

"But I'm still Lonnie - although that's debatable, I guess."

James did a double take, "Now you sound like Cole." When Allontis looked quizzical, he clarified: "Cole... when he brought the kids over, he said the exact same thing: that he was still Cole." James paused. "I know you're still my family, but you've gotta admit it's just... different now. You've got a family of your own. No time these days for the last little kid Momma G brought home from the foster-care store," he finished, with just a hint of forlorn bitterness.

"That's not true," Allontis soothed. "You'll always be my first baby." She smiled. "Hey, when Momma G brought you home, I thought you were my baby, remember? I helped her take care of you."

James shrugged. The truth was that as a boy he'd been in love with his girl next-door sister type of friend Allontis Baxter then - but even then, she'd belonged to Cole and everyone knew it. Reluctantly, as everything had changed, James had had to grow up along with everyone else.

Wandering through to the kitchen, James wiped down the counter with gusto, still trying to pretend he was doing something else besides wondering about Allontis. Once again, his thoughts returned to his childhood, and what it was like for her making the transition into motherhood, which she did so seamlessly and without much apparent effort.

Jolted from his reverie, James pulled his phone from his pocket when it buzzed. He looked at the caller ID and then confusedly up at Allontis, still seated in the other room. "Hello - hey Cole," James began – then his mouth dropped open as his brother's stern voice asked him about Lonnie's whereabouts. He covered the mouthpiece and looked at her incredulously, pointing to the phone in alarm.

"Lonnie, Cole's on the phone," he hissed, trying to keep his voice low. "Sounds like he didn't know you were coming out here."

"He'll be fine," Allontis replied with uncharacteristic abruptness. "It's a really beautiful drive. Tell him I'll call him before I leave and that I had no trouble driving. Tell him that." She waved James away dismissively as she transferred his hungry niece to her other breast.

Disgruntled about her nonchalance yet not wanting to see anything as she was feeding even by accident, James turned his back on Allontis. With somewhat less confidence, he relayed her words to his brother on the line, but the significance of Cole's curt, clipped goodbye before hanging up was not lost on James. He turned to face her again, keeping his eyes low until he was sure Lonnie had covered her chest again with the blanket.

"For crying out loud, Lonnie - you had a really hard pregnancy, and now Cole's mad at me, and you drove all the way up here without telling him," he began reproachfully. "What's with these women coming over here without letting someone know?" James shook his head, dismayed. Of course, another woman of equally perplexing demeanor leapt to the forefront of his mind. Filling his cheeks with air, he eyed Allontis disapprovingly and sighed his frustration.

"James, listen to me. Cole is not mad at anyone, certainly not you. He's just protective."

James smirked, not believing a word of it. Whatever Allontis said about Cole's reaction, he was right to be worried. Her trek up there had likely taken her over an hour, plus she'd never actually been to this house before. When James had first moved, she'd been too pregnant to do anything, and she'd been on bed rest the last several weeks of her final term.

Allontis had been more like a second mom to him than a sister. Before she married Cole and started her own family, she'd been at his house, seeing to Momma G when David died and James and Momma G had been left alone together. Dexter lived in the area, but Allontis was constantly over at Momma G's house to help because she lived just a few blocks away. When she and Cole married, they'd kept Allontis's house as their base as their family grew. Then Dexter had lost his wife three years ago and asked to move into Momma G's house. James supposed that's where some of his own feelings of displacement really stemmed from.

From that point on, Dexter and Kira had been the house's occupants. Yes, there had been more than enough room for James to stay with them, but until he figured out what he was doing with his life and career after college, he had wanted his own space. Kira likely wished he was still there and a part of him did too - but at this point, he'd been away so long that he'd just decided to stay away.

James took another look at Allontis. Motherhood made her still more alluring: capable was the word. As a teenager, he remembered borrowing her brand-new car for junior prom, and she'd helped him with all of his school subjects.

"What are you thinking about?" she asked.

James shrugged. "How things used to be."

"You turned out great… you know that, right? You're a good person with a true and kind heart. We're all so proud of you."

James laughed. She talked like he'd won the Nobel Peace Prize.

"Don't you scoff at me! I'm serious. You turned out wonderful." Allontis looked searchingly at him. "James, whatever relatives or whoever you find as you search through your biological roots, just remember that you're good, kind and decent. No matter what. Okay?"

James shrugged again, surprised that once again she'd read him so well. Momma G and his adoptive brothers, however good and decent they had turned out to be, still weren't of any real relation: not grown on any genealogical tree he'd fallen from.

"They are not you, James. Look at me."

James looked over reluctantly at his sister-in-law.

"We all have some skeletons, James," Allontis went on. "We can have them, but that doesn't mean we are them - or have to become like them."

"You don't have any skeletons," James replied. "Your family was all good - on the up-and-up."

"But my decisions have been very wrong. I made some bad choices; I almost died because of a few of them. All of my family - you were all at risk because of me."

James was sorry he'd brought the tears to her eyes. He couldn't help the alarm that must have flickered across his face.

"Lonnie, I'm sorry. Is this what Cole was talking about? I'm sorry - jeez... please stop crying."

"Don't worry, I'm fine. Breastfeeding can be emotional. All these hormones floating around. Can you burp her?"

James reared back: he hadn't burped anyone since Kira. Oh, wait - he might have burped Jacoby right at the beginning, but the time surrounding the child's birth was a blur. He'd been a rookie back then, just starting his career in the NFL, and had rarely visited home at all. He stood by awkwardly, feeling like a rookie all over again, as Allontis adjusted her shirt, plunked the child unceremoniously in his arms and walked to the kitchen.

"Rub in a circle and pat gently, just like you did with Jacoby," she said over her shoulder.

James nodded. The child looked at him, curious, and all he could do was pray she waited just a few minutes to start crying. Over in the kitchen, Allontis proceeded to make herself a cup of coffee.

"Lonnie, I can do that for you," he began.

"So can I, okay?" she snapped.

At her raised voice, James was silent. Turning his attention to the child, he awkwardly put her on his shoulder, remembering the towel in case more came out than just air, and gingerly rubbed her back in a circular motion while rocking up and down.

Fixed to the spot with the baby, he watched Allontis scrutinize the fancy coffee machine and insert the pod cautiously into the chamber. She stood there a moment and although he wanted to help, he held off.

Before long, baby Sophia produced the air they'd been waiting for in a cute little belch. "That was great," he whispered to the tiny girl. He held her up to look at her and felt transfixed by those eyes. He smiled at her and her eyes twinkled, a beautiful light caramel color. "Heartbreaker," he whispered, kissing her soft little cheek. "You can't take my heart too, though. I don't have enough of it left to give away. Kira's my girl, then Hannah too, and they will kill me if I fall for you as well. You got a daddy - I'm just your uncle. I'm only here for fun and games and no discipline whatsoever, okay?" James smiled when the baby laughed, caught off guard by the emotion that came to him. "Are you mocking me?" he whispered. Figures. He grinned to himself.

"How's Cashell?" Allontis had located the sugar and creamer and carried her steaming cup back to the sofa. The word 'nonaya' came to James's mind in response to Allontis's question - as used in the phrase 'nonaya business' - but he bit that one back. Frowning a little that she did not immediately take her baby back, James sat on the other sofa, shifting Sophia conspicuously to his lap. He'd better figure out a response pretty darn quick or risk looking even more suspicious. After a moment's thought, he chose the aloof route.

"What? Oh, uh, I don't know. Fine, I guess," he said casually. "And by the way, I think Kira and Hannah are just your little spies."

Allontis raised her eyebrows. "If nothing is going on, what is there to spy on?"

Gotcha, she might as well have said.

"You like older women," Allontis declared triumphantly.

"What? No..."

What was this? He did not consider Cashell 'older,' anyway.

He didn't think about her age at all. She was young enough as far as he was concerned: desirable, confident, caring... The words to describe her presented themselves quickly in his mind. He shook them away, keeping all those adjectives to himself. Aloud, he continued: "What does that have to do with anything?"

"It was just an observation," Allontis countered, a teasing twinkle in her eye.

James was tightlipped. Whatever he said or didn't say, it would be to no avail: apparently, the jig was up. There was no telling what Kira and Hannah had blabbed to Allontis, Cole, Dexter and now Leedra too: yet another woman they could tell his secrets to. The entire time Cashell had been in his home, he'd felt especially protective - only because he knew of her heart condition, he told himself, that was all. He didn't remember showing her any special affection, but that wouldn't have stopped the girls from sharing every single detail about what was really only one night and half a day with Cashell in the house. The TLC, the fireside warming cuddles... James, meanwhile, tried to dismiss how right it had felt holding her in his arms: the sweet way she'd buried her face in the crook of his shoulder, and how looking into her eyes was like seeing her perfect soul.

Wax poetic much? his subconscious jibed. Perhaps that's the way Cole felt about Allontis. James couldn't say: he'd never been in love himself. He wasn't now – he couldn't be, surely? He cleared his dry throat a few times before speaking.

"I think you and that baby need to get back on the road," he told her. "Cole will likely send out an All Points bulletin if your GPS doesn't show that you're en route back to Alexandria pretty soon. Oh, but before you go I need to check the tire. He said something about a tire."

"Wait - what? Oh - oh my God, I drove on the tire. Oh man, he totally told me that, oh my God. I forgot. How could I forget? I'm so sorry, my baby." She looked tenderly at little Sophia, now asleep in James's arms. Fresh tears welled in her eyes. "M-maybe you should take the car to the dealer or a shop around here first," she stammered. "Perhaps I should stay here and let Cole come get us? Oh man. I can't do anything right."

James listened as she blew out a flustered breath, talking to herself as if there was no one there but her. With growing alarm, he thought back to the dramatic tension he'd heard in his brother's tone. He regarded Allontis with a new level of apprehension, hoping he wasn't missing something important.

Lonnie inhaled deeply, put her coffee aside and tucked her feet up under her on the soft seat. She placed her fingers delicately on her temples and massaged them in a circular motion. With the child still in his arms, James looked at her. The baby looked up at him sleepily and then back to her mom.

"I'm in complete control," Lonnie murmured. "I'm fine - I'm fine. It's kind of cool out... is the baby warm enough? I have a blanket in my bag, okay? I – I just need to rest."

"Lonnie, is there something you want to tell me?"

She looked up, embarrassed. "Um, I just been kind of stressed, that's all. I'm gonna be fine. I... just need a few minutes."

James nodded slowly, taking in the situation with mounting concern. He was gradually remembering all that the girls had said during their stay: Hannah asking him if he had any detergent, Kira's comments that they liked to help Allontis out around the house, that this pregnancy had been 'harder' than the last – not to mention the fact that the woman sitting before him had apparently left on a long drive this afternoon without telling her husband where she was going. You didn't have to be a doctor to tell that something was amiss with her mental state. Allontis lifted her head to gaze at her baby, but she still didn't make a move to take her.

James felt his heart sink and he steeled himself for some sort of bad news. It scared him not knowing what was going on in his own family, and it made it worse that they were clearly going through it without him. He cleared his through and moved closer to Lonnie.

"Lonnie, it's me. You used to be able to talk to me about anything... but that was before you got married, I guess," James whispered. "Is it you and Cole? Are you guys okay?"

"Cole's fine; it's me, as always. What I'm going through isn't a secret - not really. I just hoped it'd go away before there was any need to tell anyone anything."

"Tell what?" James couldn't help himself from asking outright, even though he knew she was getting to it. He couldn't wait.

"It's just that – well, this pregnancy was rougher on me than the last, psychologically. I've felt a little... batty." She laughed nervously at her old-fashioned choice of word, startling the baby. James held Sophia closer, comforting her in hopes that she wouldn't cry, even though he was feeling emotions up the wazoo himself. Allontis continued.

"I, uh, think bad things sometimes: like something bad is going to happen, like - like I might even hurt my own child." She bowed her head, shamefaced. "I'm on some meds, but they keep changing my dosage. It's not right... I'm not right. They say I have PPOCD - that's Postpartum OCD - with anxiety."

She was crying in earnest now. With his internal alarm going up a notch, James moved closer and placed his arm gently around her, realizing he had no idea what any of that meant. Whatever had just happened, he was suddenly very sad too.

15

How I Met My Mother

JAMES KNEW HE COULDN'T PUT off meeting his biological family forever. Early the next morning, a combination of worry about Allontis and that old feeling of helplessness pushed him into hitting the road at last, headed for Interstate 95 South. Hanging around at his new house just kept his mind circling around everything he couldn't fix, so now was the time to flee.

If he was going to have any sort of future, James reasoned, then knowing what his past looked like was an important step. He didn't want to look up one day and realize he was lost to a family he'd never even known.

When he arrived at the parking lot of the address the investigator had sent him several hours later, the first thing he noticed was that the yard needed a good mowing. If Momma G had ever lived here, he found himself thinking as he gazed around, she wouldn't have stayed for long. He used to cut her grass himself, once his adoptive father got too old to do so. James had picked up his foster father David's love of fixing things, and even if he couldn't fix much, mowing was an easy one. There was absolutely no excuse for letting overgrown shrubbery take over.

Getting out of his truck, James surveyed the lot as he walked slowly to the front entrance. He wondered about the scant number of cars: only about five in total. It wasn't lunchtime, but surely the place saw more visitors than this at any given time?

Before he entered, a thought of Cashell crossed his mind.

Wouldn't she want to see this? She'd probably consider it a prime photo op, he thought, somewhat wryly: he and his mother reunited, meeting for the first time after all these years. Surely scenes like this one didn't occur all the time.

He shoved those thoughts out of his mind and tried to reach for something else. The strange unkemptness of the yard: that's what he'd been thinking of before Cashell had infiltrated his thoughts once again. Now he noticed a tattered sign, clearly taped and mended several times over, cautioning those who were entering about "Resident Flight Risks". While he hadn't been to many nursing facilities, he would have thought that signs such as this one would only apply to folks who were mentally ill. But what did he know? Perhaps only a small section of this facility housed those kinds of people.

Entering through the front doors, James walked quietly down the hall. The smell greeted him instantly: a mix of breath-stealing ammonia and whatever today's lunch special was going to be: fried, green, disgusting.

Noticing a nurse sitting at the reception desk, he approached and leaned over to address her, keeping his hands at his sides to avoid touching the grubby and battered counter.

"I'm here to see uh, Stella Foxx," he began tentatively.

The nurse glanced up, peering at him through thick eyeglasses. "Oh hey. Uh, Bobby? Is that you?"

"No - uh, I -"

"It's been quite a while since you seen your Mom. I didn't even recognize you," the nurse continued.

"Look, I'm not Bobby," James clarified hastily. "I am his... I'm Ms. Foxx's other son. James."

He hoped that he hadn't somehow just messed up his chances of seeing the woman he'd driven the better part of the day to meet, just by having the wrong name. He had no papers giving him any rights; and while he had identification in his pocket, it naturally didn't prove he was any relation to the woman in question.

The nurse brightened and James graced her with a tighter,

nervous smile.

"Well, you're in luck! Ms. Foxx is having a good day so far. Could you sign in, please?"

She led him down the hall, past several other rooms. James did his best to take in small details about the facility and to keep focused, despite the walk feeling a little like a slow and tortuous march to some kind of chamber. His anxiety growing, he looked at the faces that passed by him, wondering if any of them knew his mother; whether any of them were her friends.

They neared the end of the hall. A window with bright sunshine streaking through stood out at the end of the dim hall, in stark contrast to the melancholy, disappointed, almost deathly feel of the space within the walls. Finally, the nurse stopped to turn into a room with a metal door so heavy that he had to reach out and help her push it open. More red flags, he thought.

"Ms. Banks, we hit the jackpot today!" chirped the nurse. "We got a good-looking man here for you today, Ma'am, yes-sir."

James resisted the urge to roll his eyes but smiled politely at the nurse instead. A woman was sitting on the edge of the bed, her fingers playing nervously with something that looked like a yellow string. She twirled it absently, around and around.

"Hello. I'm James."

He didn't know what else to say. Before he could ask the nurse for any details about the woman's condition, the nurse turned on her heel with a professionally caring smile and exited the room just as quickly as she'd entered.

With her gone, James focused on his mother, trying to keep his breath from hitching. The woman's face was twisted and when he looked closer, he saw she had no teeth: her mouth was sunken in and she worried her lips, shifting them back and forth tightly together as if she was trying to figure something out. Glassy eyes rose to meet his. They were large and almost luminous behind their blank stare. Her body was skinny; she looked frail, bone-thin. James looked around and noted that her room was, sadly, just as spare as her body. No pictures crowded her walls, as in the other residents' rooms that he'd glanced into briefly on the death-march to get here. This poky room, right at the end of the corridor, was so far removed from the other residents that the background noises of the facility were barely audible from here.

"Oh, Bobby, honey, where you been?" Mrs. Foxx began. "Why you not come to see me? You look just like your father. Oh well. Now, now, you on that stuff 'gain?" Her eyes dimmed and she looked at him with her head lowered, her milky eyes scrutinizing him closer through her sparse eyelashes. "I told you that stuff ain't no good."

"I'm not on any stuff, uh, Mom." His throat went dry. She didn't know who he was. She thought he was Bobby.

"Good den… but why your eye watering?"

"I just, uh… I missed you, mom. I was sad." He missed a lot.

"Don't be sad," his mother went on, suddenly cheery. "I been here but you ain't come t'see me. I told you I don't likes it here. They ain't very nice here, they real mean. Boy, you taking care of my house?" she shot out, abruptly suspicious. "You got those no-good girls… keep putting out all dem babies in my house? Eatin' my food, drivin' up my water bill. I'm not crazy as you make me out to be. I'm all right, I'm not crazy. Nope. No sir. I am not crazy…"

Silently, James crossed his arms, standing a little taller. His mother balked. "Why you looking' at me like I'm crazy?" she demanded.

James relaxed his arms and let them hang limp at his sides. He felt helpless. He really had no idea what to do or say - but the next thing he knew, his mother had started to scream. Before he could move out of the way, she'd lunged and managed a good smack against his face. He didn't push her away. He was too stunned and too sad to do anything but stare.

Within seconds, the nurse rushed back in. "Ms. Foxx - Ms. Foxx! Now, we talked about this - you need to calm down.

Oh, man, Ms. Foxx, you were doing so well that we eased your medication dosage, but it doesn't look like that was a good idea, now was it?"

"Wait, wait - don't – uh..." James had no idea why or how he was intervening, but it came out anyway.

"I'm sorry, sir, who are you?" A doctor had entered the room too, hot on the heels of the nurse. He carried a large tubular vial of something thick and white that looked for all the world like Elmer's glue.

"I'm her son."

"Bobby?" The doctor pushed his glasses further up on his face to peer at James.

"No, no - not Bobby; James," said James impatiently. "Her other son. James."

The doctor looked at him skeptically but without argument. "Well, uh, I'm afraid we'll need to speak with Bobby. He's the only son of hers I've met up until now, and they've never mentioned you before. Mrs. Foxx becomes upset often enough as it is, and she has few if any visitors... but I can't give you any more details about her care or treatment until I speak with Bobby," the doctor repeated matter-of-factly.

Without further comment, he turned his attention back to James's mother. James looked closer as the doctor held up the large syringe to inspect something before carefully, slowly pushing the tip of the needle into her arm. James gritted his teeth as he saw her wince in pain momentarily, but soon her eyes seemed to grow smaller and her body relaxed visibly in just a matter of moments.

The injection administered, the doctor turned and placed the syringe in a tray the nurse was holding as she exited. He adjusted his white coat, as if he'd just done nothing more than fix his hair in the mirror.

"Now, Mr. ...?"

"Parker."

"Mr. Parker. Your - uh, your mother has a serious mental illness, son. It's getting worse as she's getting on in years."

"She's just sixty-two," James said, almost to himself. "What's the name of her condition?"

"Look, Mr. Foxx - "

"Parker," James corrected quickly and saw the judgment flicker across the doctor's eyes before he spoke again.

"Mr. Parker, I assume you know Bobby. He is Ms. Foxx's guardian."

James nodded. He had a feeling he'd be meeting the fabled Bobby soon enough.

"As such, you will need to see Bobby to be added to the authorization to release information. Then I'll be glad to inform you about your... mother's diagnosis, as well as her prognosis. Until then... well, if you'll excuse me."

The nurse returned to haul his mother into a wheelchair and wheeled her away without a backward glance, leaving James standing alone in the empty room.

Certainly not the kind of reunion he'd been hoping for. Not by a long shot.

James stood there a little longer in the emptiness. He hadn't even been there a full hour and he was already exhausted. Tears, as his mother had noticed earlier, pricked the corners of his eyes once again.

He didn't care to meet Bobby now. This first encounter had likely been an indicator of how the rest of his day was going to transpire. However, if Bobby held all the cards, James couldn't leaving town without meeting him. That, it seemed, was the only way to get this whole messy business over with.

James exited the building and headed for his truck. He got in and placed the keys in the ignition but didn't start it up right away. He simply sat there. It was warm back down here in the Southern state, and the stale air in the car stifled him. He leaned his head against the leather headrest and did everything he could to keep from crying. He should meet his brother, that's what he thought: he was here, and he'd wanted to finish all this in one day. What else could possibly go wrong? That his brother rejected him, too? So what, he shrugged:

that couldn't possibly feel any worse than what he'd just experienced. The fact that his mother was ill didn't ease the sharp feelings of rejection the way it should. Despite everything, he still wanted to know her.

Clearing his throat, he felt on the passenger seat for his shades and started the truck. The tears were still in his eyes wanting out, but he ground his teeth to take his mind off the pain inside.

As he was about to put the car in reverse and back out of his parking space, he glanced to the left side and couldn't believe the face that caught his eye. His heart beat double time, thinking for a second that this vision was merely a figment of his imagination. Blinking in disbelief, his eyes adjusted from the face to the long and delicate fingers resting against his window.

16

Friends to the Rescue

REMOVING HER FINGERS FROM JAMES'S car window, Cashell smiled shyly and James opened the door, bumping her in the process. Feeling silly, she moved back to let him out. All six-feet-four of him climbed out of his truck to stand in front of her, staring down as if he couldn't believe his eyes.

"What are you doing here?" he uttered eventually.

She smiled only a little: she recognized James's closed-off defensive stance even as he leaned against his truck, his arms folded across each other, awaiting her answer. She was silent, debating what she should say first. It wasn't like she trekked six hours away from home every day – well, technically today was only an hour's trip, because she'd caught a flight right out of Dulles Airport. Just an hour ago, the pilot had announced that they were descending to sunny North Carolina… only, from where she stood at this moment, it wasn't that sunny at all.

Cashell had talked to Allontis, saddened to hear that James hadn't told anyone about his planned trip. When Cashell had put forward her idea of going along to look out for him, the family had jumped on it, begging her to be there for him. They didn't know that no begging was necessary to get Cashell involved as far as James was concerned. She didn't need any pushing. Now, standing here in front of him in such an unexpected situation, she was thankful she had his family as a back-up excuse - but all her practiced words left her brain.

"Cashell?" James prompted, looking perplexed.

"Uh," she stuttered in a rush, "y-your family isn't here. You didn't tell Dexter or Cole you planned to visit, you didn't tell the guys or your coach - "

"Please tell me you did not drive all the way down here by yourself, Cashell?" James interrupted her. His concern for her safety endeared him all the more to her.

"I didn't," she replied quietly. "I flew."

"Oh - well, peachy!" He looked away from her.

"How did it go?" she ventured timidly. "I - I thought you'd appreciate a friend being here."

"Good and terrible." James's face was cold. His stance alone was an indication that things didn't go smoothly. Well, she thought, if silence was what he wanted then they'd just stand there for however long it took, and see whose patience wore out first.

"A friend, huh? Is that what this is?" James looked skeptical. "Where's your notepad? I thought for sure you'd have a crew with cameras to film my family disaster for your biopic," he added sardonically.

She touched his arm and was somewhat encouraged that at least he didn't flinch away. Her hand moved to grip more of his arm.

"My mom has, uh, some mental illness. She's batsh..."

He stopped himself, then gave a harsh laugh, but she didn't join in.

"It's okay," Cashell said.

"It's not," he snapped.

She didn't flinch. "It is," she reinforced firmly, and didn't hesitate this time to get in his personal space: to lay her cheek against his chest, because it was the only place she could reach owing to her short stature. His arms didn't embrace her in return, but remained resting at his sides. He seemed at a loss as to where to put them. Finally, she felt him lower his head to rest it gently atop hers, inhaling a deep breath which she felt echo through his broad chest as if it were her own. The tension eased the more she held onto him. Eventually, his hesitant arms came around her back and held her tight.

When she turned her head to look up, his sunglasses were gone and she saw the rawness around his eyes. It startled her, made her painfully sad for him and made her want to cry, all in a rush of feelings. Her heart was heavy about the grief he was experiencing: that much she could understand. She stood on tiptoe, her face raised, but he leaned away from her as if contemplating everything. She'd already contemplated her actions enough. The only thing that mattered right then was that she was there for him. There wasn't a camera crew, another player or an annoying intern in sight.

One arm still cradled her back as he brought up one of his hands, which then proceeded to hold her chin tenderly as if she were a delicate flower.

"What are we doing, Cashell?" he asked softly.

"I don't know, but it feels really... right," she replied.

"Is that all that matters?"

"Well, no, but if..." She trailed off, preparing herself for a let-down; but he didn't disappoint her. He kissed her, tentatively at first, and in a rush of happy relief, she kissed him back. His arms were around her fully now, pulling her up, and finally he started to kiss her back with vigor, with a nibble that stole her breath away.

When they eventually broke apart, she stared into his eyes and fell harder in love with him, if that were at all possible.

Now that he was convinced she wasn't out to get him, it was back to their usual friendly banter.

"Where's your car? Thank you for being here - I appreciate it," he said quietly. "I don't want you to go yet, but I had planned to go see my brother – being as I'm here and all."

She was glad he still held her, even though the pain had now passed from his eyes. The heat of his kiss lingered on her lips.

"I'll come with you."

"What about your car?"

"You can follow me back to the rental car place." She held her breath as soon as she said it, unsure whether or not this was one of her better ideas; but for now, she was there and she wasn't inclined to leave. She wanted to be there for him. The fact that he hadn't immediately dismissed the idea of her coming along with him meant that he wasn't opposed it: that she hadn't been wrong for coming after all.

Back at the rental office, it took mere minutes for them to return the car. She got in the truck and he gave her a leg-up to help her scale the high step. She was glad he didn't comment on her inability to get into the truck gracefully, but the strong hand against her backside left a tingling feeling she strove to ignore. Lucky footballs. She smiled to herself.

James went around to the other side and pulled a paper from the thin folder on the seat.

"Can I see?" she asked.

He hesitated for just a moment, then handed her the folder. She read the letter the detective had sent as he pulled out of the parking lot onto the main road. The summary wasn't at all lengthy - under two pages – but it outlined the usual whereabouts of James's mother and brother. It went on to mention the brother's jail time and the mother's mental illness. It didn't specify what condition she had, but it did say that she'd been moved a number of times from one facility to another.

"James, I wanted to tell you that I – well, my intern had found out some things about this nursing facility," Cashell began carefully. "And I, uh, looked at the facility's record while you were inside."

He looked at her. "How long have you been waiting for me?" he asked.

"Not long, but I saw your truck and I just decided to do some more research while I waited. The place was so sad-looking."

A muscle twitched in his jaw, but he stared straight ahead at the road. "That's putting it mildly." He hesitated again. "What, uh, did you find out? The place is crap: I don't need to read any Yelp reviews to know that. The writing's on the wall."

"Yeah, that's kind of what I found," she replied. "They um, have been fined upwards of two hundred and fifty thousand dollars in the last five years. There are reported cases of dehydration, malnutrition of residents, injuries, overmedication… it's all in the public record."

Cashell stared fixedly out of the window as the truck jostled her just a bit. James's hands gripped the wheel tightly. It was evident that he was angry.

"Does you Mom look okay?" she asked.

He laughed bitterly before a note of incredulity that she even needed to ask leapt into his voice. "No."

"I just mean her clothing, James – her weight. You know."

James just shrugged.

The drive to Bobby's home wasn't bad. The trip from there to the facility where James's mom was located only took an hour, and that was with the midday traffic they'd run into. Otherwise, it seemed like a normal drive.

Cashell didn't say a thing: her thoughts likely mirrored James's own. "Listen, I'm gonna make some calls," she said. "I'll stay here, okay?" She reached for his hand and he squeezed hers.

"Lock the doors," he instructed briskly. "If stuff happens, just drive off."

"It's the middle of the day," she reminded him. "Anyway, I wouldn't leave you here James - be real. Come on: the place doesn't look that bad." She turned and followed his eyes to assess the front yard. It wasn't nice, but there were toys littering the yard, so that could indicate some degree of safety - maybe? She squeezed his hand again to reassure him and he gave her another kiss, rendering her momentarily speechless, before he hopped out of the truck and strode up the rickety steps to the front door.

Cashell prayed that this time James would get a more favorable outcome.

17
Strained Relations

ONCE OUTSIDE THE TINTED WINDOWS of his truck, James could take in the dilapidated house in full technicolor.

Still pathetic, he thought to himself.

The thought of Cashell's relentless optimism the entire ride over there made him smile. Though he hadn't expected himself to, he had admittedly felt better telling her about everything that had happened with his mother. Now he stood there at the front door alone, with Cashell waiting in the truck, and her idealism was fading fast in the face of the reality he was now witnessing first-hand.

Considering it was a six-hour drive back to Virginia, James decided it was best not to drag this particular meeting out any longer than necessary. When he knocked on the door, the sound of dogs barking fiercely could be heard from somewhere inside. The sound was distant, though, and as far as he could tell there wasn't anything rushing to the door, so he knocked again, hoping it was safe. Upon closer inspection, the yard was full of old toys and rusting car parts with long grass growing up around each item. An old broken blue-and-green plastic table with missing legs looked like it should have been taken to the dump long ago.

All at once the door swung open and a tall, thin man looked out. "What's up, goon?"

"Hello – uh, hey. I'm James."

"I hear tell you met our crazy mother. You look a little - what they say up there in northern Virginia? - green around the gillis?"

"Gills," James clarified.

"Uh oh, certified. I know you'd know what I was talkin' about." Bobby grinned as if he had this sort of conversation every day.

The man before him backed up and James, hoping that meant 'come in', entered but didn't step too far. He stood just inside the door, on the three-by-four-foot area of tile before the carpet began. There was a tattered doormat inside, and although he didn't think he was going any further in, James courteously took a moment to wipe his feet.

"Oh boy, you got manners. Look atcha, boy." Bobby raised his voice to address the other people James gradually noticed as his eyes adjusted to the indoor gloom. "Y'all need to pay attention, this man got manners."

James nodded to the other folks sitting in the stale living room. There was a big man seated on the couch, a younger woman sitting so close to the man that it looked like they were conjoined twins, and two little kids playing at a coffee table littered with beer and soda cans. James smiled at them but they didn't pay him much attention.

"I'm James," he said, by way of breaking the awkward silence. They merely waved in return.

"This my bro, y'all," announced his greeter. "He come down here all the way from Virginia."

"I, uh - I went to see Mom." James swallowed hard. It was still difficult to picture her as that, however hard he tried.

"I know - I told you, I heard dat. They called me from the place," Bobby informed him.

"How long has she been there?"

"How old are you? That's how long she been there," Bobby cackled.

"What? Uh..."

James couldn't find the words to pose the right questions.

"They wouldn't let me see her for too long," he began. "She, uh..."

"Don't tell me: she went batty, right? Thought she'd be all right for you, a visitor and all, and with you the favorite." Bobby studied his fingernails with apparent nonchalance.

James blinked. "How can I be the favorite?" he queried. "She gave me up."

"Not really. They took you away from her."

James listened, but he was finding it hard to have such a personal conversation in the presence of the two adult spectators. The pair looked like they hadn't moved off the couch since Happy Days went off the air. He looked away from them, but not before he met the eyes of the woman and noted her blatant stare. James tried to register what Bobby had just stated.

"What did you say?" James asked.

"What I said was, she didn't give you up," his brother replied. "Social Services took you away from her. That's why she went crazy, you know. Lost her man and her precious baby, all in the same week."

James was confused. He wasn't sure whether his brother was deliberately talking in circles just to irritate him. "Did she try to look for me?" he asked helplessly.

Bobby shrugged. "I tried, but, well you know how life can get in the way, man. When you came to school here and started playing ball – yeah, I thought that mighta been you."

"Why didn't you come ask me?" James asked.

"Why didn't you come ask us?" Bobby rolled his neck, suddenly indignant. He moved back to the couch and sat down on the arm. He eyed James, then snatched up a loose cigarette lying on the table, rolled it between his fingers and laid it on his upper lip, giving it a careful sniff before putting the beige butt between his lips. He took a deep drag and exhaled a thick, white cloud of smoke into the already-stifling air. It smelled. Bad.

"Why you come sniffin' around here now, anyway?" Bobby continued. "What you care? We been around here a while, an' I ain't see you spread none of that new money you got our way."

"I would have if I'd known," James countered defensively. "You had a birth certificate and all my papers in mom's information: you didn't look for me either."

"I ain't wasting my time looking for no crazy couple's offspring," Bobby snorted disdainfully.

A twitch leapt into James's jaw. Despite the strange feeling that he didn't know what he was defending - he hardly knew either of his parents - the need to defend them was still inherent and strong, whoever they were.

He took a moment to calm himself down and looked away, lest he find another reason to smash Bobby's face in. However little he knew about his past, at least he now knew that his brother didn't mince words. Bobby wasn't ever likely to be friendly, even toward his own brother, so James was very much aware of what Bobby thought. His brother seemed awfully crass, not to mention dishearteningly pessimistic about their mother's condition.

James wanted to leave. He hadn't gotten the information he sought, so what was the point in hanging around? He tried to keep from wrinkling his nose at the numerous bad smells mingling in the close air.

One of the children reached for a can of soda and put it to his lips. James thought immediately of Cole, who would have a heart attack if Jacoby ever so much as touched anything so loaded with sugar before he could even speak complete sentences. Even Hannah and Kira were only allowed to split a can of soda between them, and only on special occasions at that. By contrast, the child before him that could barely walk was guzzling the drink on the table as though it was a habit. His thick diaper sagged heavily between his legs, further impeding his wide-legged gait as he moved around the dirty table.

When the child approached him, James picked him up and the child smiled a toothless grin, trying to reach for James's ear.

"What's up, li'l man?" James grabbed his sticky hand and shook it.

"That's my son," interjected Bobby airily. "So, like I said, I can't see you coming up here to visit me just for some lemonade. What did Momma say?"

"Uh, I didn't get to talk to her," James said. "She – uh…"

Sensing Bobby eying his every move, James set the child back down. The tike trundled away around the corner, but not before stopping to turn up the can on the table once more. Visibly disappointed that it was empty, he threw it to the floor in disgust and left it there.

"Yeah, you guys didn't get too well acquainted, huh? 'Fore she went off all crazy? Oh well. I thought she could at least act right for some new company, but – well, you know. Guess you ain't nobody special after all. Not much going on 'round here." Bobby picked his teeth.

James shrugged. "I always wondered about my folks."

"For real?" Bobby laughed, "James - whatever your last name is - wondering about his folks? Not Mr. All-American, Heisman-Trophy-nominee, already-got-a-thousand-passing-yards? You's 'bout to knock out Donnie's record and you ain't even over thirty. Why you wonderin' about some po' broke-down pigeons 'round here? I can't belee dat."

James regarded him a little more closely. The man had done his research, obviously. That said, any old search engine could yield that much information online, now that James played professionally. It wasn't exactly a secret. He wondered why Bobby had bothered to retain all those stats if he wasn't planning to look James up, though? The hairs on the back of his neck stood up unaccountably.

"Say, did I hear you got into some trouble while you was here at that fancy college?" Bobby asked innocently. "They sent you packing, huh?"

James's mouth went dry. "No trouble. I didn't do any time."

"Oh, but I did - is that what you're saying?" Bobby's eyes narrowed.

"No - I don't know. I don't know anything about you," James lied. "I'm just here to find out more about my mom."

So he kept telling himself - but for what? What more did he need that he hadn't already seen earlier that day in her hospital room? "I'm not here to judge you. I just want to get to know my mother."

"Yeah, well, whatever," Bobby replied. "I been in jail a couple times, just me and my - excuse me, our crazy Momma holding it down. After she tore up the world, had to put her away: can't take care of her no more, you know?"

"Is that place nice? She said they are mean to her."

"They nice to her compared to how she treat them," Bobby snorted.

"That's not what I asked." James tried to keep his voice calm. "She's ill. They should be equipped to handle her."

"Well, like I said, you get back what you put out. She be screaming and hollering and carrying on and ain't nobody even touched her, so she need to get over it. That all is expensive. You don't get good treatment if you can't act right, now do you?"

"She's ill," James repeated more forcefully. "What kind of place is it? It needs a lot of work, could use remodeling, that's for sure. They don't keep the grounds up."

"Oh well, Mr. Money Bags, why don't you go on down there and tell them that? She can barely afford to live there on your dad's retirement check and her small-ass pension. Ain't got much to work with."

"What kind of work do you do?"

"What? What you saying?"

Clearly spoiling for a fight, Bobby scrambled back up and leaned menacingly into James's face. His cigarette fell to the carpet and instead of picking it up, Bobby's black sandal ground it further into the rug. "I'm a convict, punk. What type of work you think 'round here? Odd jobs. I work with my hands, fixing this and that."

When Bobby mentioned his time in jail, James wanted to sound curious, to offer something to assure his brother that he wasn't judging him, that it really was about their mother;

but the fact remained that he was merely feigning interest to see if he could get somewhere. Aware of all that the doctors wouldn't tell him concerning his mother's condition, he was hungry for any little thing Bobby might offer to supplement what he'd seen.

After setting foot in this house, James wanted nothing to do with this bunch at all. A part of him wished he'd never come. He'd visit his mother another time by himself, if he was allowed, and would just hope that their next encounter went differently. Maybe he could move her up north, he thought, where there had to be a better home available than where she was at now. He'd look into it as soon as he got back. This place felt, smelled and looked like bad news.

Cashell was waiting and he knew he needed to get going soon. The mere fact that she was there made this entire scene seem just a minor setback, and this ill-fated trek to meet everyone somehow more bearable.

He looked back at Bobby. "What did you go to jail for?" he asked, managing to sound interested.

"Ah you know, just a little time for cutting a fool."

James nodded mutely, trying to seem as though he could relate.

"You a fool?" Bobby asked quietly.

"What? No. I had, some good adoptive parents," James replied.

"Oh yeah? Dey rich?"

"They're dead," James replied shortly.

"They leave you some dough? Thought you had some bank of your own. But, I mean, you come sniffing around here now, to see what we got?"

James looked around pointedly, his eyebrow dipping in confusion. It didn't look like they had much of anything. Unless Bobby had something he didn't know about stashed away somewhere in this dump, James didn't see anything worth taking, even if somebody wanted to try.

"No, I don't want nothing – I mean, anything," he answered.

"I'm just trying to see who my folks are, like I said. My adoptive mother was old: I didn't want to hurt her feelings. If she ever found out I was looking for you... well, I didn't want her to feel bad."

"Oh you got a lot of nobility, ain't that what they say?" sneered Bobby. "You care about what people think and how they feel and stuff. You soft. My brother soft, y'all," he announced to their stationary audience. Though they'd been largely silent, staring at the television like zombies, the two couch dwellers responded with chuckles.

"I'm not soft; but I'm not callous and heartless either," James returned hotly. He didn't consider himself 'soft' just because he cared about people. It was true that he hadn't wanted to upset Momma G in her old age. He also believed that, even if she had known, she'd never have tried to dissuade him from looking into his past. The facts so far still seemed like a slap in the face as far as he was concerned: part of the reason he'd held off from mentioning it to Cole or Dexter. He just wanted to know what he was getting into first. He didn't want to invite any trouble to his door. Though the day had been filled with disappointment, he was now glad he'd waited. Time wouldn't have made things easier if he'd found all this out any earlier. It certainly wouldn't have canceled out his mother's mental illness.

It was clearly time to leave. "Look, Bobby... I'd like to visit Mom again," James tried one more time. "They said you have to call them and tell them that I can see her. Can you - will you do that?"

"Yeah, 'f you're still here, I'll see what I can do."

"Is this Mom's house?"

"Yup."

"She was asking me about it," James began cautiously.

"Yeah? I took real nice care of it for her," Bobby said shortly. "Don't it look good? Piece of crap was falling apart when she left."

James looked around: soiled carpet, walls riddled with holes from God-knew-what, and dingy yellowing furniture with stuffing spilling from the cushions wasn't his idea of 'taking care of things'.

"Could you just... put my name on the paperwork for Mom? I'll come back in a couple of weeks." James was disheartened. It was already time to go, and he wasn't hopeful about getting any cooperation out of his brother. He supposed that he could hire a lawyer and file the necessary paperwork, if it came down to that. He hoped it didn't. Despite her reaction to him, he wanted to know her until she died. "Like I said, I'll... I'd like to visit our mother again, okay?"

"Really?" Bobby said. "Seriously though, why you wasting your time, dude? You can see she crazy."

"I'd still like to get to know her. Did you know my father? - Is he still alive?"

Hair raised on the back of James neck again when Bobby's face turned grave. After a beat, Bobby bent over laughing, mocking him at having been taken in.

"Your adoptive parents must have given you either some serious love or a lot of bullcrap. Maybe this will help you get rid of this fantasy you done conjured in your head and move on. And how about, instead of coming around here judging me, get yourself some of that genetic testing make sure you ain't crazy too, because your - excuse me, our Momma is even crazier than you witnessed today."

Bobby moved toward James, but James stood his ground. Bobby's eyes narrowed maliciously.

"You tough, right? Well, that's too bad. See son, your daddy was a rapist and Momma shot him dead while she was pregnant wit' you. Now it's time for you to leave me be and get yourself on back to Virginia."

18
Nostalgia

CASHELL WAS SILENT ON THE long drive back to Virginia. The rigidity of James's jaw and his tense, jerky movements as he navigated the highway in the large SUV indicated that, once again, things had not gone well. She hated the thought that he'd had yet another let down. She was sorry.

James's thoughts were racing. Even though he had a healthy sum of money in the bank at this point in his career, it meant nothing to him. He'd trade it all in a heartbeat for a healthy Momma G, a healthy birth mother, maybe even a cordial relationship with his half-brother. His money wouldn't buy him any of those things. Momma G and David had taught him that. He hadn't wanted for anything growing up; his main goal had been to make Momma G and David proud by doing the right thing and being a person of integrity. Nowadays, as life moved on, his goals had expanded to finding out who his people were: where exactly he'd come from and what, if anything, he could do to support the people who'd first given him life.

Cashell wasn't sure when she should start talking, but eventually she knew she had to try something. She thought back to that night when they'd first met. Right then, that night of dancing and fun seemed like several lifetimes ago: so much was happening, so much changing for her since that time. That night, she'd plunged from elation at dancing up a storm with a mysterious stranger to mortal terror about her heart giving out – either that or being burned to a crisp, unable to exit the building without assistance. The man beside her in this car had managed to distract her from her fear of being left alone and had ensured they'd gotten to safety together.

She reached into her proverbial bag of interview questions and pulled out a few to get things going again. "James... when you were growing up, did Dexter and Cole play with you?"

"What?" James snapped.

Cashell didn't waver, even in the face of his irritability, but she fell silent again, looking out as he ate up the road ahead of them. Eventually, he replied.

"Yeah, sure they did," he said, more softly this time. He looked at her briefly, as if weighing whether or not to engage, to trust her. She smiled at him reassuringly. He stopped slumping against his window and sat up straighter as he spoke.

"Uh, I mostly played with Dexter and Adrian, I guess. Cole left for college after high school but he was still in the state, then he became a cop in DC, then he moved to New York and opened his first restaurant."

"I thought he sold that one, in New York?"

"Nah, he was going to, but he made a go of it," James replied with some pride. "He's kept both for a while now, splitting his time between NYC and Virginia, but I think he's contemplating selling it again, what with all this stuff Allontis is going through."

Cashell didn't know what he meant, but she assumed he was just talking about Allontis's second motherhood: with three children in the house now, she figured it was so self-evident she didn't have to ask. "I think Adrian's the only one I haven't met, right?"

"Not Deon either: he's in jail," James reminded her. "Adrian is a good dude. He's not as close as the three of us. Honestly, don't know how I could have left any of those guys to come see about this junk down here."

"There's nothing wrong with knowing. It's okay." She touched the hand that rested on the seat next to his thigh. His fingers gripped the leather, pinching it so hard that it was a wonder he didn't rip a hole in it. He grasped her hand and she had to shift closer to accommodate him. She loosened her seatbelt - their thighs were now less than an inch apart. He held her hand tenderly as they drove.

"What kinds of things did Momma G like to do?" Cashell asked. It was good to get him talking.

"She loved to cook, like Cole. Actually, she also loved to go thrifting," James said thoughtfully. "When she helped me move into my college dorm, she bought half the stuff for my room from the thrift store," he added with a chuckle. "It didn't bother me. A lot of it was really nice."

"I think I've been to Carolina Thrift maybe once. Do you think we could go now on the way home? And we can get some sweet potato tots, too," Cashell suggested.

"What?" James asked, nonplussed.

Cashell smiled, letting go of his hand to touch his arm in mock horror. "You lived in this area for four years and didn't experience the sheer joy of sweet potato tots? You're not for real. Let's see," she continued, counting on her fingers. "We got our waffle fries, curly fries, tater tots and sweet potato fries - but if you haven't had sweet potato tots, well, that's just not right."

"Sounds greasy," he rejoined with a smile.

"And sometimes you just want something greasy and artery-clogging, you know?" Cashell laughed for the first time that day, silently congratulating herself when James graced her with the best, broadest, pearliest-white smile since she'd arrived. Boo-yah. Every one of his smiles were awesome, but this one had been particularly hard-won. As always, it did things to her insides.

She breathed a long sigh. All that time she'd spent fretting about the bold move of coming down there, and now she was actually here doing it, it seemed fine. Nevertheless, the fact remained that the two of them weren't technically a couple. She didn't want that either, not yet. It had to start out as a friendship, she reflected. She wanted desperately to show him he could count on her: that she could be his friend and he could trust her. Her subconscious laughed at the deceptive word 'friend'. She leaned on his shoulder, thinking about her last-minute flight, her tenacity and her foolish heart. Had it once again led her into big trouble?

Half an hour later, James pulled into the lot of the Carolina Thrift Store and gazed around. "I remember this place. It was always impossible to get a parking space, and the parking is still terrible today." Though it was getting late, the combination of his full belly from so many sweet potato tots, the nostalgia of the road trip and the questions Cashell continued to prod him with really were helping to take his mind off things. They also brought up other things, though - like Momma G, whom he was thinking of now as he found a rare empty space and maneuvered his big vehicle into it.

"Momma G liked coming here, even when it got hard for her to drive," he said to Cashell before getting out. All those years ago, he'd taken Momma G there because it was the only thing that brought a smile to her face. The thrill of the hunt, she would say, even though it was more likely that she shopped there out of budgetary necessity than for the frivolous thrill of the rare find. They walked side by side through the main entrance.

Momma G's only real luxury that he could remember was hunting for treasures at the local thrift or antique stores. Outside of that, she really didn't seem to want much. She was a woman with a truly simple life.

James smiled at the thought. He didn't usually shop much at all, but something about pottering around this store had gotten him thinking - not to mention the fact that Cashell's company had only enhanced the day.

He watched Cashell lead the way, her excitement palpable and infectious. He wasn't looking for anything much himself, just happy to be doing anything that kept him from being alone with his thoughts. He trailed along after her, pulling out his phone to start a list of the items he needed for the special weekend. As they passed the Housewares section, it occurred to him that he should take a look for some more furniture for Hannah and Kira's room while they were here. Cashell stopped to stare into the jewelry case, and James stood by her side to look with her.

"Even though I love old things, there is something about the thrift store that's partly sad, you know?" Cashell murmured. "It's the thrill of the hunt, sure, but half the belongings here are..."

"Dead people's?" James supplied, raising an eyebrow.

"Not necessarily," she shrugged. "Just someone's life, regardless of their current station. Little stories, tidbits, snippets of life lived, memories... If these trinkets could talk, wouldn't that be interesting? If that dresser could talk about holding the brand-new baby clothes for the arrival of a couple's first child. Or that ring there: small, probably all that young man could afford."

James smiled at her stories. He liked thinking in that way. "Well, by purchasing something, you give it new life: you tell a new story, give a second chance. It's recycling at its best."

"That's the most optimistic thing you've said all day! I'm so happy."

"Well, my life is complete," James replied sarcastically. Although it was supposed to be a joke, Cashell looked crestfallen.

"Come here. I'm kidding." He pulled her to him and, caught off guard, she fell into his chest. He embraced her tight.

"Thank you," he whispered into her hair, trying to convey so much more than a simple word of thanks. No pen and paper, no voice recorders now... sure, maybe she was gathering some information for her press-fodder stories, but this way at least it wasn't so blatantly, intrusively obvious.

She stood up straight again, leaning away from him, and nodded. Now that they were no longer holding her, his hands dove into his pockets, and he scuffed a toe awkwardly against the worn carpet.

"I uh, got a lot of work to do to get the house together for

Family Weekend," he said.

"What's that?"

"My harebrained idea," James said, and she chuckled.

"It sounds like fun," she replied.

"Do you want to come?"

"What?"

"You can come if you'd like," James said seriously. Cashell smiled, almost in disbelief, but stayed silent, not committing. That bothered him, but at least she must have been considering it: she worried her lip nervously.

"I, uh, like old shirts and oversized jerseys. We can go as soon as I look in the Men's section," she said hurriedly. James nodded, pulling out his phone to pass the time. Despite how the day had started, he really wasn't in any hurry for it to end. The drive home would obviously end with dropping her off and saying goodbye, he thought glumly. Home was still a bit of hike from here, but for the time being he had a companion: the most wonderful person he could think of. For now, at least, all was right with his world.

Sheesh. The store and its memories of Momma G were wreaking serious havoc on his brain.

Suddenly, Cashell squealed and snatched a shirt from the rack. He put his phone back in his pocket as she clutched the garment close to her chest, her eyes closed so tight that he touched her hand gingerly to make sure she was okay. Whatever she was holding looked like nothing more than a tattered old school football sweatshirt on a cheap wire hanger. She opened her eyes and held it up reverently. Their eyes met. Grinning as if she'd struck gold, she turned the shirt around with a dramatic gesture to show him the back. He was about to roll his eyes but then he understood, finally, why she'd been so excited. The telltale red-and-white jersey swung in front of him and his mouth formed a perfect O as he realized it had his own name embroidered onto the back.

He caught his breath and collected himself. "You're squealing over junk?" he said. "That's junk you're holding."

"It's yours! Please tell me you did not give this away?" she exclaimed incredulously. "Oh James, I'm so mad at you! Why wouldn't you keep it? You should have kept it. This is... you sweated in this." She held the shirt up again as her eyes roved over it, admiring it. "Don't you know that's epic?"

"Um, that's gross, for realsies." He wrinkled his nose and she laughed. He felt relaxed for the first time all day. "I'm sure I have others somewhere that are clean," he assured her. Although it was true that he must surely have at least one, it occurred to him that he wasn't at all sure where in the world it might be stashed.

He was just a teen the last time he'd worn that shirt. He must have dumped it into the local donation center's drop box. He remembered the excitement he'd felt, to finally be moving out of North Carolina and back to his northern home. While he'd played professionally in Carolina, he'd been more than happy to get rid of anything and everything that reminded him of his time here. He'd been making a clean start, so he'd stored, given away or trashed most items that reminded him of that time in his life.

Despite the attempt at a fresh start, half his current house was still crammed with boxes. In signature fashion, he'd pulled out the basic stuff he needed when he moved in, and the rest remained packed away. So much like his beginnings in life, his belongings remained hidden; and, from what he could tell so far, it was best that they stayed buried.

"I want it - I'm gonna buy this one," Cashell declared ceremoniously. "This was meant to be."

James smiled. Something seemed true in her statement, even as something in him resisted how natural and comfortable it felt to be with her. She turned and bumped into him, stopping short as if considering something new.

"Were you happy here?" Cashell's eyes searched deep into his, as if reading him. "If you weren't happy, then I won't get it. I'm sorry." She made as if to set the shirt down.

He shrugged. After all, it was just a shirt. Despite them not being romantically involved, the thought of her wanting to wear his team jersey did make him feel a little warm and fuzzy on the inside. He steeled himself against the emotion, even as her elation seemed genuine.

"It's fine, get it," he told her. "You should be fine wearing it in VA, but don't wear it in Florida. We still have all kinds of beef with a few Floridians: Hater Gators." Grinning, he avoided her question about whether or not he'd been happy.

"That's not what I asked you," Cashell said firmly, standing her ground.

James watched as she put the shirt back on the rack, but he pulled it out again and held it for her.

"It's a shirt, not a cloak." He moved in the direction of the register. "It was hard here," he said over his shoulder. "You grow up at college, you know: lots of stuff happens. Lots more stuff happens when you're about to be drafted. Then, while I was here, Momma G was diagnosed with the big C. I spent a lot of time going back and forth to see about her. Pretty stressful. She never got to a game." James was speaking more than he'd meant to. "She watched it on television," he continued. "I told Allontis where I'd be, and she and Momma G would call and pray with me over the phone before the game started. I felt her everywhere. She's still here." He thumped his chest roughly.

Cashell watched him without speaking. It seemed that her eyes could see straight through his tough-guy façade to the pain it hid. He tried desperately to move on, to talk about something else, but he couldn't seem to stop now. "There were other things here, all bad. Long story short, I did well in school, I did well on the field. I just wanted to forget about it, really. That's…"

A voice interrupted from behind Cashell.

"Jamie! What is your fine self doing here?"

19
Time Warps

CASHELL TURNED TO LOOK AT the woman that had called James. Jamie. The woman moved close, her arms outstretched, her face with too much makeup and her body with too-tight clothes.

James sidestepped her, all but knocking Cashell out of the way to avoid the woman's embrace. He hustled over to the cashier and pulled out his wallet before Cashell could get to her credit card.

"What the heck, Jamie? You can't even talk to me?" the woman exclaimed indignantly.

"You don't talk much, Michelle. That's the problem."

"Oh, you still upset about that? 'S'matter, you can't forgive a girl?"

"I can, but I don't have to make small talk with her."

James snatched the bag from the older cashier's slow fingers, took Cashell's hand and almost dragged her toward the door.

"What, you can't introduce your little princess B to me?"

"Stop it, Michelle. This is Cashell, a friend of mine. Glad to see you're doing good. We gotta go."

"You talked to Kirk?"

"Yes, I've talked to him." It was clear James wanted to leave, and fast. "Get in the truck, please," he told Cashell in a low, urgent voice as they exited the store. He opened the door for her, gave her the necessary leg-up and let the door slam.

"Oh, you got one of those obedient wenches, huh?" The woman had followed them out to the car.

"She's not anything to you," James snapped. "Hey, what are

you doing with yourself these days, Michelle? You got a job, you take care of your kids now, or you still working the football circuit?"

"Oh, see, there you go... why don't you shut up? You always judging."

"I was trying to leave, Michelle. You followed me out here." He was angry - but he was a different person now, he reminded himself. He would remain unprovoked.

"Oh yeah, how about you? You been to see Macy and her Momma? You got all the money in heaven. You could help them now."

"You don't know what I got, and you don't know whether or not I help them." He was instantly mad he'd said it: responded to the bait. He didn't want to acknowledge her either way, and he didn't want to tell her anything even in passing that might fuel her gossiping and lying around town – which would cover just about everything that came out of her mouth. Yet now here they were in a parking lot, arguing, just like the last time things went south.

"Kirk made his choice. I didn't have nothing to do with that," James continued coldly. He opened the driver's door and got in.

"Oh yeah? Well now, in all this you the only one doing real well. Ain't something wrong with that picture?" she yelled, loud enough for them both to hear. "You the only one real successful right about now." She was around at Cashell's side of the truck now, her face all but leaning on the glass.

"Stop blaming me for how your life worked out, or didn't," James said, under his breath.

Cashell kept quiet. She guessed he was thinking back to the similar aspersions cast by his brother earlier in the day. This made three meetings in twenty-four hours that had ended in disaster. Poor guy.

It was clear that James strongly disliked the woman outside the truck, but despite his efforts to leave she kept yelling and eventually banged her hands on the window. Cashell wanted to say something, but James was keeping his cool and that's all she could ask for.

"Let's go. Got your seat belt on?" James said as he clicked his own. Cashell fumbled with hers for a moment before his deft fingers grabbed it and secured it for her. He checked all his mirrors and threw the truck into reverse. Cashell prayed that this woman was above doing something drastic - like throwing herself under James's wheels, say, in some deranged attempt to get herself injured, then yelling to some poor bystander to call the police, thus detaining them longer. Despite not wanting to believe anyone could do that, she'd been in public relations for long enough to know. She'd worked with many a wealthy man, not least on some heated divorce proceedings, and as such she'd already seen a lot of wild schemes.

To both their amazement, the woman kept banging on the window even as the truck began to move. James backed out of the parking space slowly, his eyes watching her the entire time, before gunning the truck out of the parking lot as soon as he was able. Cashell turned to see the woman scrambling behind them, and she took a deep breath as he drove them away at last.

"When people are unhappy with themselves, James, they look for a scapegoat," she began.

"Everyone is stuck in a freakin' time warp, here," he shot back. "It gets on my doggone nerves."

"Was she your... girlfriend?" Cashell ventured.

"Hell no," he said curtly. "She was Kirk's, and when she saw he wasn't gonna make no money in the NFL, she turned her eyes on me - only she was already pregnant with his baby by that time. Just a mess, okay? I'm gonna tell you right now, if you want a baby outta me so you can get yourself a television show and move to Los Angeles, live next to the Kardashians and Ray J with your child support Go-Fund-Me, we would be best to end this right now."

"I would never do that," Cashell whispered.

"Good," he said. "I already know that. I'm sorry."

She nodded, accepting his apology. She knew he was just angry and emotional after the crazy day he'd had.

"I'm sorry, Cashell," he said again.

"It's okay."

"It's not okay," he insisted. I was having a really good time before this went down. Today is just jacked up. You made it better, then I made it worse again. I'm sorry."

To both his and her surprise, she shifted over and touched his back as he drove. His entire frame was tense, hunched over the wheel. He grabbed her hand and pulled it to his lips and kissed her knuckles before keeping her hand locked in a death grip like a drowning man, her fingers sandwiched between his as he continued to drive.

"Cashell, my personal life is a friggin' mess. You know: you grow up and you mature, while everyone else does nothing but stay stuck right where they are. People just stick around to call you out on the things you didn't do for them… well, what did you do for yourself, huh?"

He was talking to himself, pretty much, and she just sat and listened. He was so right, she thought. He'd grown up and become someone to be proud of. He was about to be an awesome football player, while whatever it was that the people they'd met today were on the brink of doing, she wasn't sure. Just about to stay in exactly the same place doing the same things, perhaps.

If James came back in ten years, she reflected, they'd likely still be there: still stuck in the past, still reminding him of whatever they felt was wrong with him, never considering their own choices or the logs in their own eyes, as her dad used to say. That was a verse from the Book of Matthew: chapter seven, if she recalled correctly.

Cashell was sad. She could see all that he said being borne out in what they had seen that day, and she knew that he likely wasn't referring only to the woman at the store with his comments: also to his brother and perhaps some of his wayward teammates. She wondered about the girl that the woman

Michelle had mentioned, Macy, and her mother. She didn't know those people, but they had obviously been something to James at some point.

James eased back in his seat and draped his arm around her.

"I hear your brain wheels turning. What's this, you don't have any more questions in your interview bag?"

She moved her head back and forth. "I was having... not-very-nice thoughts."

"What are they?"

She felt James's eyes on her for a second, before he looked back at the road again.

"What's not nice about them?" he asked again.

"Just, uh – well, that stuff I was saying about if the items in the store could talk?" He nodded and Cashell continued. "I was thinking that if your girl Michelle's clothes could talk, they might say: 'Could someone please return us for store credit?'"

She gave an apologetic little giggle, but when she and James caught one another's eye, they both burst out into full-blown laughter

20
Soup Changes Things

THE FAST PACE OF THE weekend had caught up with her. Cashell made it to work on time for the better part of the week, but she was dragging. Exhausted, she entered her office and sat down heavily at her desk, leaning back in the large leather chair and swiveling away from the door.

She stared at the ceiling, recounting the last series of interviews, thinking about articles to be written for people who were too lazy to do their own jobs, not to mention an intern who had lately managed to spend more time talking to a coach's teenage daughter than doing any of the research she'd requested of him. Then there was her one very problematic client, Brax Denton, plus a certain other player who stayed on her mind constantly for all the wrong reasons.

As far as problem number one went, she dismissed Denton out of hand. Dealing with him in person swallowed up enough of her time: she refused to let him invade her mentally as well, to let him consume the few moments she had alone before spending the rest of her day creating a social media strategy for the team's upcoming trip. The squad would start their practices and training at the state-of-the-art facility in Richmond, Virginia.

The rest of her time had been devoted to research: which, in translation, basically meant getting on the phone and hobnobbing her way into different editorial circles in order to build up the media image of the team's recent additions. Trying to win coverage of this particular team's 'problem children' was proving more of a challenge than she had expected. As always, her goal was not to dictate what the press published but to render her clients so charming that they won it over by themselves. Many of this team's players needed polish – that was putting it mildly. As things stood now, it was like they'd been raised by Tarzan's cousins: none of them seemed to have any manners. She should have started with a series of public speaking classes, coursework on discipline and most likely an intensive run of etiquette sessions.

That's what we need - a class! She snapped her fingers and swiveled her chair back to her desk, reaching for a notepad with renewed energy. She couldn't let this little PR hiccup get the best of her: she just had to arm her surlier clients with the right words and coaching to handle difficult situations.

Even though she was supposed to be getting rid of the negative energy, a part of her wanted to tell her boss and the team owners that as far as she was concerned, Brax Denton wasn't worth the trouble. He didn't care about his teammates and, truth be told, he wasn't such a great player as they all seemed to make out. Her intern had been right: she hated to use the phrase 'washed up', but Denton was just that. He was too arrogant to admit he needed to retire, and he had the biased support of the team owner. In any case, the fire he'd allegedly started that night at the hotel was such a liability that the team may eventually regret keeping him on, when the associated costs were sky-high even by the League's usual lax standards.

Opening her eyes to gaze at the ceiling, Cashell listened meditatively to the silence... and heard the tinny yet distinct sound of distant music. She raised her head and was astonished to see a very long, completely male and utterly sleeping body stretched out on her office couch. One of her smaller throw pillows was over his face and his hands were in the pocket of a gray hoodie, the hood pulled down low. The hiss of music she could hear came from his ear buds.

It was the length of him, scrunched awkwardly onto the compact couch, that instantly gave away his identity. The fact that James was there in her office initially alarmed her: something must be wrong. She hoped it wasn't news of his mother, or of more strife with Bobby. She was surprised that he'd sought refuge here. Her office was her one little private oasis of calm in the entire building: any meetings or discussions always happened in the larger conference rooms that lined the adjacent hall.

"James?" Cashell perched on the long narrow coffee table beside the sofa and touched his chest. The warmer weather meant looser fitting clothes, and her fingers met with solid warmth through the thin material of his shirt. Ready to wake him up, find out what he needed and send him on his way, she tentatively patted his chest. His right hand came out of his pocket and took hers before she could withdraw it. He squeezed her hand gently. His other hand emerged from his pocket and reached up to remove the pillow from his eyes and pull the hoodie off his head.

Startled and groggy, he sat up and looked around, rubbing the sleep from his face. In doing so he was forced to let her hand go, which should have made her feel better as it was slightly less intimate. When he sat up, his knees jutted out from the low seat so far that they were now touching hers. She scooted back on the table, in hopes of putting some distance between them. What had always seemed like a spacious office now seemed to shrink in an instant.

"How are you?" he said.

"Good. Uh, what are you doing here?" She stared at him. Maybe they'd talked so much on the drive from North Carolina that she'd run out of words: now the cat had her tongue. That, and she felt something deeper seeing him again now. A shared connection.

"Thought I'd take you out for lunch," James replied.

Cashell was annoyed and elated all at the same time. Of all the days, he would ask her on a day when her schedule was packed.

"I uh, have to stay here. I want to go, but…um, are you super hungry?".

"Yes." James replied.

"Then I can make you something - let me, uh, put something together."

Thrilled that he would stay, Cashell went to move from her perch on the narrow table.

"I liked the first article you wrote. It doesn't seem like it's about me, though," James commented as he watched her.

Cashell smiled to herself. She'd try to hide the fact that his having actually read and liked her writing meant the world to her. She figured he wouldn't find her descriptions of him accurate, simply because he doubted his own talents and strongpoints. Whatever he thought, she'd written the truth. It wasn't even a lengthy article: she planned to ration out what details she had about each of the players a little at a time, just to draw nibbles from other media outlets as she navigated the team through this process. "It's all true, James."

"It's embellished," he said, rolling his eyes.

"Never."

"I thought you'd talk about what happened," he said quietly.

She shook her head. "I wouldn't share that: not now." It was too soon, too raw; and anyway, she'd want him to tell her it was okay first. When she looked back at him, the sleep was gone from his eyes.

"When you're ready, okay? - not a moment sooner. All right?" Cashell went on. James's eyes closed in assent. Agreed. She wanted to move past the subject now, because if management knew that she'd held something back from them, she guessed they wouldn't be particularly forgiving. But he liked her writing. That thrilled her more than she'd care to admit.

Suddenly nervous over him being right there in her office, Cashell went to stand up, but something caught her foot, sending her plopping back down so hard that the narrow wooden table on which she'd been seated wobbled, tilted and pitched her backwards in awkward slow motion. Riding a bull would have been more graceful. She landed on her butt with her feet in the air. Hastily, she rested her feet on the chair opposite her. That didn't make for a much more flattering position, and doubtless wasn't the manufacturer's intent for use of the chair. She lay still, mortified more than physically wounded. Right then, she longed for the carpet to swallow her up.

She saw James loom above her, looking enormous from floor level. He rolled up his sleeves, bent down, scooped her up and put her in the other chair as if she was a small bag of potatoes, before righting the table. His strength astonished her.

"Are you okay?" he asked with concern.

She nodded wordlessly, her tailbone and her pride throbbing.

"I can go get us something for lunch," James continued, as if nothing had just happened. "What do you feel like? I'm hungry. I haven't eaten yet today – and I need to go grocery shopping anyway."

Cashell smiled tightly up at him. "You're not laughing? Are you just trying to make me feel better? Didn't you see that clumsy splat I did a moment ago?" She was simultaneously glad that he didn't laugh at her expense and annoyed with herself.

"I'll be sure to tell the Olympic gold medalist Simone Biles how much you admire her work and that you will stop attempting to copy her because you've not been properly trained. Beyond that, I won't comment on your take on her floor exercise."

Cashell's eyes widened in sync with his before they both laughed out loud.

She stood and gave him a kiss on the cheek. "Thanks for not laughing at me." The longer she stared into his face, the more serious he seemed to grow. She took a deep breath and decided to tell him what she'd been thinking earlier about him and his Mom.

"If your mother was in her right mind, I have no doubt she'd be proud of all that you've become and that she'd tell you as much. I'm certain she regrets giving you away, and I'm certain that you can make her more comfortable by spending whatever time with her that you can. That's one thing you can do to show her you love her and that you forgive her everything."

Pushing aside her better judgment, Cashell stood on the tips of her toes to reach out and embrace him. The gesture was only meant to comfort: to drive home her point about his mother's love and the regret the woman might have shown if she'd been able to. She meant for the hug to be brief, but James hugged her back and she savored his arms around her just a moment longer than intended.

"I have some things in my cupboard here that I can put together for lunch." Suddenly brisk, she was the first to back away, making her way around the desk and busily shuffling some papers around.

"I'm sure I could eat cardboard if you put some mustard on it." James grinned.

Cashell nodded. "Just give me a few moments." She walked to the back of the room to wash her hands at the small counter. As well as the sink, her spacious office had a mini-fridge, a microwave and a small cabinet to store food items. She liked it a lot.

James was quiet as she fixed their food. Setting some soup in the microwave, it crossed Cashell's mind that they probably shouldn't be having lunch together there, of all places… but she supposed it would look OK to anyone who might look in on them if she claimed to be, say, interviewing him for a story. It didn't seem wrong, and it wasn't – not on a professional level, at least. Personally, though, her heart insisted that it was. She kept envisioning the consequences getting involved with James Parker could have on her heart and mind. She smiled wryly to herself. It was a little late for that.

Searching for small talk, she set out a plate of items to nibble while they waited for the rest of the food to warm up.

"How many children did you count at your brother's?" she asked casually as she rearranged papers on her desk to make room for their picnic.

James looked like he'd rather discuss something else – anything else. He shrugged.

"My step brother is just bad news. As far as children go, it looked like he has two - but, you know, wherever there's one there could be several more. There were two other people in the house. I guess the other kid could've been their child."

"Then you'd have another set of nieces or nephews," Cashell pointed out optimistically. "Hey, maybe they could all play together. There sure were enough toys in the yard to share around," she said, placing a tray in front of him.

James shook his head. He eyed the food skeptically. "I'd rather not have our little suburbanites Hannah, Kira and Jacoby becoming hood rats."

"Think of it as culture those other kids would be getting. Think of the things the girls could teach them."

James laughed at her wide, excited eyes. "If I took them within a mile of that place, Cole would never let me see them again." He picked up one of the crackers with some cheese, popped it into his mouth and crunched. She moved aside another stack of papers and set out napkins, a steaming bowl and half of a thick sandwich on a small plate.

"We're all a mishmash of different people's lives, you know," she pointed out. "Influenced by different things."

James raised an eyebrow. "You don't get to choose your mishmash. The mishmash is not the problem: it's the part where you have no choice in what's mashed."

"Well, speak for yourself. The Parker mishmash? Look at you: all five of you, lots of personalities, all different looks, but you act alike. You've been around each other, influencing each other, regardless of what all your respective parents gave you through your gene pools. David and Ms. Georgia gave you something else to use: the right frame of reference. What they passed on to you was something they received from their own parents, and they and God made it all work together for your good. Even many biological families can't make it look as good as your adoptive family managed. Look at Hannah - another transplant, if you will, who's fitting in... though I'll have to figure out a way to win her over. She's a tough one."

"She just doesn't know you. She's skeptical of everyone," James replied. "Unlike Kira – that girl's like a little puppy that goes with whomever brings her a treat. She'll get better. She gets jealous easily: gets annoyed if I give my affections to another girl."

James smiled as Cashell blushed and looked away. She wondered who there was in his life for Kira to be jealous of... but she didn't ask. It couldn't possibly be her, could it? No: that would be crazy. Flustered, she looked down at the desk to check she'd put out all the food. "Do you want some soda?" He nodded and she returned to the fridge, fetched a can and set it next to his food.

After a few minutes, she noted that he still hadn't touched any of the hot food. She looked over everything again, then walked around her desk and took a seat opposite him.

"I'm not as great as you are in the kitchen, but I have a few things I can make," she said, trying not to sound defensive.

"Do you always make lunch look so good?" he responded.

Cashell was surprised. Here she'd been thinking he was avoiding sampling her food.

"I try," she said simply. "You eat with your eyes."

"You eat with your eyes?" James repeated, as if he'd never heard that before.

"You did that summer work for Cole at his five-star restaurant: you have to heard that! It's gotta be part of Cooking 101," Cashell said with a laugh. "Hey, do you like crackers in your soup?"

"Yes."

She leaned over the desk, opened the sleeve of crackers and gently shook a handful into his bowl before doing the same to her own smaller portion. She'd made the soup at home last night and had packed extra to bring into work. She did this often, especially when it was cooler out, to hold her over in case her days ran long - which they usually did.

"Now what?"

She eyed him expectantly, spreading another napkin over her lap, and wrapped her hands around her mug as she blew gently over the top. She'd given him half of her provolone and turkey sandwich, and she took stock of what remained: some sharp cubed cheddar, saltine crackers, sliced apples. With a flash of inspiration, she set down her cup and pulled a jar of peanut butter from her drawer, spooning two heaping dollops next to the apple pieces. With all this combined with some plump green grapes, they had a pretty good lunchtime spread. But his watching her was unnerving; she felt a little self-conscious.

"I don't usually eat all this for lunch, but I wanted to gussy things up a little for my unexpected guest today," she said by way of explanation. "The crackers and fruit would usually be my snacks, but Brax's interview ran over so I didn't get to them today. One of my New Year's resolutions was to eat better. It's possible, if you set things up nicely ahead of time, but it's not easy, let me tell you. You, on the other hand, can probably eat whatever you want and burn it off with a quick run, unlike us mere mortals." Cashell raised her cup again and James scooted his chair closer to her.

"I'm hungry."

"Yeah, well, go ahead – why don't you dig in?" Cashell was confused when he took her hand.

"I want to say grace," he said.

"Oh," she said, finally sitting down and slipping her hand more fully into his.

One taste of the soup and James mentally stripped Cole of his chieftain title in the kitchen department. The thought entered his mind that he should get these two in the same room for a cook off.

"This is not homemade?" James continued to scarf it as if he hadn't had any nourishment in a week. The chunky pieces of chicken told him it was in fact homemade: he was pleasantly surprised. Additionally, the rich broth wasn't just brown salted water, but featured hearty vegetables that he actually chewed rather than letting them slither barely tasting, down his throat. Each hot spoonful was heaven: carrots, chicken, onions, celery and thick noodles, plus a mix of subtle spices he couldn't quite put his finger on.

"I take it you like it?"

"I'm in love with it," he said quickly, between heaping spoonfuls. He ate a few more mouthfuls of the cheese, crackers, apples and grapes as spacers, but this soup was everything. He wanted more.

"I want to come to your house to get more soup," he said breathlessly once he'd devoured a second bowl.

She laughed. "You know the way."

James put down his spoon and looked at his empty bowl as if there was something in it that induced pure lust. He looked at her, his eyes reviewing her with a new awareness.

"Did you eat all of your soup?"

"Yes, why? You liked it that much?"

"Yes."

He stood, picking up his bowl and utensils to clear the space for her, when her hand on his stilled him.

"This was nice?"

"Yes." Way too nice. So nice his brain felt scrambled. He was no longer hungry for anything to eat, but he suddenly missed her and he hadn't even left the room yet. Her laughter, her smiles, her eyes... everything about her drugged him. He didn't want to feel that way. He wanted desperately to be a grounded person. He ached to know how things played out, to find out the truth of his past, secure his mother, do well in the professional sports league that employed him. Sometimes, getting involved with someone could cloud one's ability to make sound judgments.

Cashell spoke up. "I was wondering if you'd go to this um, benefit event with me," she mumbled, feeling like a bashful highschooler asking her crush to the prom.

"What is that?"

"Just this... event. It's a fundraiser for the Heartfelt Foundation."

"Who runs that?"

"I do. I mean, I have a board and all, but I'm the chair of the fundraiser. You don't have to buy a ticket - you'd just be my guest."

"You can do that?" he said. He pulled the invitation from her hand and studied it. The thing was going to be at the Mandarin-Oriental - tickets were five hundred dollars apiece. His eyebrows shot up as he wondered just who would be at such an expensive plated affair, and questioned why on earth he was so ready to agree to it.

"Didn't Dexter go to this a couple of times?" he asked, stalling.

"Yes, he and Ellora used to go," Cashell said. "She made him buy an entire table, which I knew he wasn't comfortable with, but he still carried on supporting the benefit after she died."

James nodded. "Yeah – I forgot you know about all of that." That was the thing: there was something comforting about Cashell knowing his family so well. She was already familiar with the bad stuff that both Dexter and Cole had been through as well as the good, and he could understand many of her hesitations because she knew the truth. He could trust her. Still, whatever happened to "let me check my calendar" or "let me think about it"? It hadn't even occurred to him to pull out any of those old excuses.

James looked down, confused. His train of thought was removing him from the moment. Pocketing the stiff card, he said solemnly: "I accept your invitation, Ms. Bruer." Cashell beamed.

"Want me to pick you up?"

"No, don't bother. I'll be there super early anyway, making sure everything is okay," she answered. "You can just come later."

As Cashell turned to clear up the last of their lunch items, her hip knocked the stack of files she'd cleared off their eating space and everything slid to the floor. James bent with her to pick up the items. As he reached to gather up the scattered files, his eye fell on one thick folder with his name on it, bound with an elastic band. Stuck on the front was a yellow sticky note with a single word scribbled on it in small, rumpled handwriting. 'Banks'. His mother's name.

In an instant, the happy thoughts about trusting Cashell were crashing and burning so violently that the explosions were almost audible in his head.

"What is this?" he said in a low voice.

"What?" Cashell was on her hands and knees, rooting for a paper that had slid under the desk.

He pulled the fat folder off the floor and stood up so fast he felt dizzy.

"You don't know what this is? It's on your desk." His anger came easily. He'd known this was too good to be true. It always was. And here he had started to think he was getting better at identifying these people who meant to do him in.

"I - I don't know what it is," Cashell stammered. "My intern puts things on my desk without telling me."

"He puts things on your desk? Really? About your clients' parents - about my mother's medical history? Why on earth does that have anything to do with what you're trying to do here?" James leaned accusingly toward her. He held out the folder again so she could read the post-it, but her eyes didn't register. He opened it himself, flicking through it. It was almost three inches thick. He was saddened to read even one word written by one of his mother's many doctors.

"I would never dig up information on any of your family, James. Never." Cashell's eyes were wide.

"Really?"

"I asked my intern to get information on you – stats, that sort of thing," she admitted. "But I told him specifically no family: just about your career, nothing else."

"Well, looks like he doesn't listen too well, now does he?" She shook her head in agreement. "He doesn't, that's the problem. He's young, inexperienced... he's learning, but everything goes through me." She put her head in her hands. "I - I always manage to kill the stuff I want to protect, the people I care about... that's you."

"Is that so?" He'd heard enough. Brusquely, he returned the rest of the scattered papers to the desk. Why, he had no idea. Because he cared, that's why; but right then, his anger clouded the truth in his heart. He moved toward the door. It irritated him that his heart hurt when he saw a tear in her eye. It annoyed him that he cared.

"James, please know that I wouldn't hurt you. I have boundaries. I will only do so much, only go so far - and family issues, from your childhood to your extracurricular college history, isn't what I'm after."

"What does that mean?" he snapped. She knew about the college stuff, that's what it meant.

"Nothing! I - I'm telling you that my research for the stories is limited to sports and maybe some human-interest facts. Nothing hurtful or bad. As soon as I'd seen I had that folder, I would have given it to you, because I'd have known you would have wanted that information yourself. I want to do all I can to give you more about your mother." Her soft voice quivered, as if she were whispering a plea.

"Well, maybe this is just too good a story for you not to pursue. We all have our price," James said coldly.

"I didn't know it was here, or I would have given it to you right away," Cashell repeated. "More people have access to this room than just me."

James was done listening. He wasn't angry at her so much as mad at himself. Everyone was after him. Everyone seemed to need something from him to make their living and improve their own status in life. At the end of the day, he reminded himself bitterly, Cashell worked for the team. Considering all he'd been through back in college, he should have been more vigilant. Things didn't ever change, people didn't change; there were just different, prettier replacements, all with the same motive. Ultimately, Cashell's loyalties lay with the team's mission and goals, not his. Nothing was safe.

Cashell's eyes were full. "I wouldn't hurt you because... I love you."

He paused with his hand on the doorknob. If he didn't have a good reason to leave before, he had one now. Good news: now at least he knew for sure that it was time to go.

He glanced back as he opened the door and saw what he hadn't wanted to: the tears falling down her face. Everything in him wanted to hold her closer, to trust her... but instead he hurried from the room before he could yield to his instincts. The corridor felt cool after the office's warmth. His heart heavy with regret, he set off down the hall.

21

Home Visits

A WEEK LATER, JAMES SAT IN his truck outside Momma G's old-new house and studied it from the curb. For some reason, Bobby's house came to mind. There were people there, sure; but the love was hard to find. In stark contrast, the very foundations of the place in front of him emanated love, despite having been gutted by fire. Cole and Dexter had seen to the rebuilding and renovation of it and now there it stood, looking the same as it always had except for some minor wear and tear.

He hated that they'd had to cut down the old oak tree in the yard. It had provided him shade when he'd worked the garden's flower beds with Dave, and had held the swing that he'd seen Dave push Momma G in a time or two - before they got old and were seldom found outside at all. It was the same house, but everything else had changed. The mainstays of their family were dead and buried - long gone. He didn't like coming there anymore, without them around. As well as the architectural changes, the place really belonged to Dexter and Kira now. When Dexter's wife had died so tragically, the family had decided it was better for Dexter and Kira to move out of their old family home, considering the circumstances. As soon as Leedra was ready to walk down the aisle, she would join them in Momma G's comfortable old home.

One of the reasons he'd stayed away from this house before was the pain of knowing that his parents were gone. They had taught him so much.

The longer he sat there, the lonelier he felt. This wasn't Bobby's house, this was his, and he had always been safe inside his old home. The people inside this house were of sound mind, and they were his family. Tired of his trips down memory lane, he got out of his truck and made his way to the side entrance everyone used.

"I thought you'd never come inside."

Startled when the door opened before he knocked, James stood face to face with Leedra. With embarrassment, he realized that she'd been aware of him sitting out there for the last twenty minutes.

"I was just thinking, that's all," he answered a little defensively. "Things look nice... did you plant the flowers?"

"Kira and I did it," Leedra smiled. "She knows what all your mother's favorites were - we picked them out. I hoped you'd like them."

James stepped inside and took a seat. Leedra was dressed to kill. He couldn't believe how beautiful she looked: perhaps she and Dexter had a date night planned or something. "Why were you hoping I'd like them?" he asked.

"This is your home," she answered. "I wish you'd stayed over during Christmas. Kira would have loved it."

"Uh, yeah, but I have a house of my own now," James reminded her. Perhaps she had him stuck in a time warp in her head, still thinking of him as some young college kid. She must have been trying to make him feel better.

"Your room is still the same - we've kept it."

That surprised him. "Oh... well, I appreciate that, but it's not necessary." He hadn't expected to be having this conversation at all. The room thing seemed odd, yet a part of him itched to see it for himself.

Leedra looked at him fondly. "I know you're all grown up now, but I want you to know that once Dex and I are married and I move in for good, there'll still be a place for you here until you have your own family. I want you to feel like you can come and stay with us any time. That big house of yours must be lonely."

He looked at her. He'd never thought of it as lonely until the kids had come... and then gone again. He pretended not to have heard her assessment.

"Why are you all dressed up?" he asked.

"The question is, why aren't you? I thought you'd be going to the benefit ball with Cashell?"

Oh - that was tonight. Of course he remembered that disastrous conversation.

"Well, uh, I'm not," he said shortly. "Not anymore. I just found out about some stuff that... made me look at her differently."

"What stuff was that?"

He didn't want to go there, but once again he couldn't seem to help himself. "She had this secret folder at her office. About my Mom."

"I'm sure she wasn't going to use it to hurt you," Leedra said with concern.

"That's just it: how can I be sure?"

Leedra looked at him searchingly. "What does your heart say?"

He laughed.

"Don't laugh at me."

"I'm not laughing at you," James said.

"You know the truth deep down, don't you?"

He nodded.

"So you're angry. As sure as she got the information about your Mom, presumably she could get it again and use it right this minute to tell all kinds of things about you. What exactly did you find out, anyway?"

"Just a lot of medical jargon about Mom's different stints in various homes, and some detail on why she kept getting moved out of them."

"You should let Dexter take a look at it," Leedra suggested.

"I was going to, I just... haven't gotten around to it." Making that excuse aloud made him realize how unconvincing it sounded. Honestly, he really didn't want to deal with it at all.

He'd pored over the papers in the file so carefully, but what he most wanted to know wasn't there: what had made her crazy? Was it really postpartum depression? He still wondered if his birth caused it.

"Hey, what's up?"

The smell of Dexter's cologne drifted into the kitchen with the sound of his voice; then James's brother himself entered, with a goofy grin and eyes only for the woman before him. His hands were up at his neck, adjusting his bowtie. When Leedra hurried up to him and tapped his hands away so she could fix it for him, they immediately shifted to her waist. James studied the slate tiles of their kitchen floor.

"Are Cole and Allontis watching Kira?" he asked.

Dexter nodded. "Cole's taken off for a few days. DC Restaurant Week is just wrapping up."

"How is Allontis doing?"

Leedra got the tie to a satisfactory state and turned to the sink, while Dexter turned to face James. "She's doing better with the kids being out of school, but still up and down. Hannah sticks to her like Velcro." His brother did a double take. "Sorry, I must've missed something... why aren't you dressed for Cash's benefit?"

James was caught off-guard. He looked to Leedra for help and, sensing the awkwardness of the situation, she gave her fiancée a meaningful glare. "None of our business, honey."

"Seriously?"

"Yes, seriously. Now, we gotta get ready to go. Do you have your phone?"

Dexter patted his pockets and shot out of the room once more. James addressed Leedra again.

"I have trust issues that I need to work out, Leedra. As in, I need to get better at spotting people who are gonna hang me out to dry."

"And why would she do that?" Dexter said, walking back into the kitchen. "By the way, might I add that if you have to ask, you're dumber than you look."

James bristled, eyeing his brother. It was as if Cole and Dexter had merged: they sounded so alike it was scary.

Leedra snapped her purse closed. "We're going to go now, sweetie."

James stood as Leedra gave him a parting hug. She smelled like flowers, and her ball gown was a pretty blush color that set off her brown skin perfectly. He returned the hug briefly and took a step back as Dexter helped her into the coat he had plucked from the hook on the back of the door. The season was getting significantly warmer: only the nights were still cool.

Before Leedra followed Dexter out, she spoke quickly and quietly to James. "There's some of your old clothes in the closet: a suit jacket should still fit, and some slacks. Look in Dexter's drawer for black socks. Cole's home – you could borrow his Lexus just for tonight, instead of that outsized gas guzzler you drive around. If your heart tells you to change your mind, you listen, okay?"

She gave him a quick peck on the cheek and closed the door behind her. Through the window, James watched Dexter open and hold the car door for her, but not before they kissed each other liked they hadn't just been together in the house moments ago.

Alone at last, James turned from the window to look over the kitchen. Being back in here felt a little like meeting up with an old friend after a long time apart. Slowly and thoughtfully, he mounted the stairs to check out his room. If Leedra could read his mind so easily he'd have to start wearing his football helmet around her, he thought with a wry smile: maybe that would help. The accuracy of her read on him was scary. Perhaps he'd go along to this benefit just to hang out with the girls… only, he quickly remembered, there would be no girls there to hang out with. Leedra's dress and Dexter's suit and tie meant they'd hired a babysitter. They were going to have fun as they supported someone that had done them a helpful service at a painful time in their lives. James knew that at key moments, Cashell had served as the family's figurehead and the point of contact when they were overwhelmed: she bore the brunt of the calls, the media queries and the unscrupulous reporters digging for personal information.

What Leedra had said was true: by anyone's estimation, Cashell likely had tons of data on the entire Parker family. She'd only come to know James recently, but she'd known the rest of them for years: as long as she'd been in the business. One way or another, a single little tidbit about his mother could have been sold to TMZ by now, if they were willing to pay for it.

Maybe they would if you were more popular, an inner voice chimed in. It was just medical records, after all - nothing to do with what had happened in college, or any new scandal. Nothing about some secret illegitimate lovechild, or lack of child support from his multi-million-dollar contract for said illegitimate child, for example. He'd seen some of that sort of thing dished out about other players, way before he'd known Cashell. Not to mention the made-up stories were usually far more salacious than someone's aged mother's mental health issues. Get over yourself.

What might have bothered him most of all was the fact that someone, whether it was Cashell or her sneaky intern, had gotten hold of information he couldn't - not even after he'd paid several thousand dollars for a stupid summary report that turned out to be shorter than his current contract. The summary, he reflected glumly, had merely told him where to locate his mother and where she used to live, then had basically instructed him to do the rest of the digging on his own. No medical records; not even his wayward brother's criminal record.

Why he would even consider anything that Leedra had said irked him no end. Why was that? Because you've thought about Cashell all week, and telling Leedra the story out loud made you question your own judgment. Because, truthfully, Cashell Bruer is not the evil and conniving woman you've made her out to be - that's why.

"Thanks, conscience," he said out loud.

James surveyed his room. It was freshly painted, with a large modern bed that would fit his large adult frame better than the one he'd had as a teen. Dexter and Leedra had also updated his furnishings, including a new nice-sized television, new dresser, matching end tables and a bench at the end of the bed. It looked like more of a guest room than his room; but he could stay there, he reasoned. It was good enough – nice, even. It certainly didn't make him feel like a kid, and for that he was grateful.

James sat on the bed and opened the bedside drawer. There sat the Bible Momma G and Dave had given him when he was baptized. He stroked the cover's monogram with his fingers. He remembered how excited he'd been that the book had his new name on it: it showed he was a Parker, not a Banks, and definitely not whatever his father's name had been - he wasn't even sure about that. Now, he opened it and read his favorite passage: Philippians chapter four, verse eight, heavily marked with childish marker pen. He read the familiar words quickly, then closed the book to stare at the cover, noticing that his fingers left a mark on the dusty cover.

Also on the nightstand was a photo of him with Momma G and Dave. He lifted it carefully to look at it more closely. Instead of remembering the good things, sitting there in his old room, he gave in and let all that was bad crowd out the wonderful homey happiness he normally felt in this house. The more he sulked, the more frustrated he grew. Dexter had found love, Cole had found love, so why couldn't he? The woman of his dreams had straight-up proclaimed her love for him, yet he couldn't do the same. He'd walked out, as if she'd said and done something terrible.

Brooding, James set the picture back down but kept the Bible close to his chest as he stood. All of a sudden, words that his adoptive father might have said entered his mind, almost as if David was in the room with him: "Boy, sit there feeling sorry for yourself because you're sorry, or do something to make a change. Get on with it, now!" James had to smile at the memory of the old man. David had been a lot like Dexter: calm, straight-talking, sensible. Even if he called you a dummy, you couldn't be all that mad about it - because you were no doubt acting like one.

James checked his watch. He wouldn't borrow Cole's car, but he resolved to get himself over to the local men's store and pick up an appropriate outfit off the rack. He was going to this benefit and that was that.

Down in the truck, he found Cashell's memo from a couple of weeks ago with information about the benefit ball in his phone. He pulled up the site he'd been browsing for suits to show the sales rep. James had never been a fashion person, exactly, but knew just enough to make it look like he was. Selecting a sample outfit to show the sales guy for inspiration, he clicked his seatbelt and started the engine. He'd get to the ball a little late, but once he got there, he hoped that Cashell would accept his apology.

22

Spiffy

"NOW, WITHOUT FURTHER ADO, IT gives me great pleasure to present this year's special Humanitarian Award to... Cashell Bruer!"

Rising from her seat with a gracious smile, Cashell carefully lifted the hem of her gown and made her way toward the stage as the whole room burst into applause.

Somehow audible above the sounds of cheering and clapping, a small noise from the rear door of the ballroom caused Cashell to glance in that direction as she mounted the steps to the stage. She did all she could to remain upright. Her mouth was suddenly dry. Her hands turned clammy, and her knees felt like they might give way and melt her into a heap of cobalt-blue chiffon right where she stood. Reaching the stage with a heroic effort, she could no longer take in what the presenter was saying. She registered that her brother was recording the presentation from his table near the stage, his phone trained on her; but otherwise, her mind was a blank.

The older female presenter loomed before her, holding out a beautiful clear glass award with her name engraved on it in gilded lettering. Doing her best to remain calm, Cashell smiled as myriad flashes burst on her occipital lobes. Through the glitz and glare, she kept her eyes on James, who was now moving through the crowd to sit down. He was dressed to the nines, sporting a perfectly fitted slate-gray vest over a crisp rose-pink shirt, with a necktie checkered with subtle traces of pink and white tied into a trinity knot. His tailored pants were freshly pressed, and the whole ensemble demanded that people sit up and take notice - which people were certainly doing. As Cashell stood frozen to the spot up on stage, heads turned from the featured presentation to watch James join Dexter's family table, pulling up a seat right next to her dad.

Before Cashell could get off the stage, people were clamoring for her attention. She was being ushered off the stage to take her seat. Cashell stepped mutely down, saying an inward prayer of thanks that her welcome address had concluded well before she'd seen James enter: she wasn't sure she could have made it in her current emotional state. Thankfully, she wouldn't have to speak again until it was time to close the night with the traditional big announcement of the total donations received: unfortunately, that total wouldn't be very large this year. Donations were just down across the board. In any case, when that time came, she hoped the butterflies in her stomach would flutter away and leave her alone. She knew that was unlikely, because first she needed to talk to James.

Her heart was full of hope that now he finally believed she'd never wanted to hurt him. The memories of their last encounter saddened her: she recalled his look of disbelief as he'd assumed the worst about her and her motives. The agony had been compounded when she'd laid it all on the line and told him how she really felt about him – and he hadn't responded at all, except to walk out of her office – and, she assumed, out of her life. What she'd said was true, but saying it at that particular point was probably a mistake. She was in love with him, and, she reasoned, that was likely very scary for him.

It was time for the benefit's musical interlude. The live jazz ensemble made their way back to the stage and started right away with an up-tempo number that Cashell immediately recognized, by DC's local artist and VJ Angela Stribling. As she weaved a path through the tables cramming the large ballroom, people were congratulating her left and right. She set her heavy award down on the family's table hastily as she passed, causing the fine china to jangle precariously. Her brother gave her a curious look as she rushed by him without a word of greeting, and she was aware that he was following her as she finally made her way over to the man she wanted to talk to more than anything.

"Hello," James said.

"Hi," she breathed, in fresh amazement at seeing him there in the flesh.

"Can we talk outside?"

"Yes."

She was surprised when, rather than hold out his hand in greeting, he grasped hers in his own and pulled her gently outside onto one of the balconies flanking the large room. She followed willingly where he led, then moved ahead of him to the railing. She took a moment to admire the gorgeous view – the Washington Monument, seemingly just yards away from where they stood, and the Capitol dome lit up and beautiful in the distance as the night descended and covered every speck of iniquity. Much as she could have stood and stared at the beauty before them for hours on end, she knew that she had to face the man before her – even as her thoughts leapt off the terrace at his mere presence.

"You look beautiful." James's voice was honey in the dim evening light.

Okay, she'd take that. "Thank you." She managed a small smile. "You don't look so bad yourself."

"Thanks."

"What made you come tonight?" She sounded stiff and formal, she knew. After all, she was trying to protect her feelings; but deep down, she knew it was no use.

"I wanted to support you," he answered simply.

"Oh… I see."

"Also… I wanted to say that I'm sorry I walked out on you so abruptly, Cashell. I've got a lot on my mind, you know?" James looked down, shamefaced.

Cashell sighed and turned to face him. "I know you do, James, but I need you to understand beyond a shadow of a

doubt that I wouldn't do anything to hurt you."
James was thoughtful. "I believe that now, I guess."
"You're still not sure?"
"I'm sure that my feelings for you grow all the time. I'm sure that I enjoy spending time with you. I'm here now, aren't I? I came to support you, Cashell. I care a lot about you."
She nodded. Caring and love were two different things.
"Could we just try to enjoy these moments?" he continued.
Cashell grimaced. "You say it like you have a terminal illness or something."
"I'm just trying to live for this moment, right now." James grasped her hands. "I want to be here with you right now. You look so gorgeous - and I'm not terrible-looking either," he finished.
She laughed.
"Now," James went on, "we've got food, other people's expensive champagne, a live band, and one of your favorite activities awaits. Dancing." He raised an eyebrow in invitation.
Cashell smiled. He had her there: she did love all of those things. Maybe James was right: she shouldn't waste time trying to figure out what the two of them were to each other and should just enjoy the here and now instead. She believed it would all work out. She had said her prayers and that's all she could do: the rest was up to God.
Plus, James had a point: he was impeccably dressed, all the way down to his honey-colored oxfords... and no socks. She smiled when her eyes reached the bare ankles peeking out. He turned and did an exaggerated twirl, modeling for her. She laughed again. He caught her hand and she twirled for him. Her dress caught the evening breeze as it swirled around her legs.
"We're a good-looking couple," he remarked, but she kept quiet. To her surprise, he spun her back into his arms and held her close.
"I'll always protect you," she whispered.

He reared back at her words, regarding her strangely, and for a moment she was afraid that he would flee; but she held on to him and looked down, laying her face against his chest and wrapping her arms around him hoping never to let go. When she looked up at him, his breath caressed her face just before his lips met hers.

James couldn't figure out why he was holding so much back. Yes, he'd been hurt; but despite all his desires to have his own family someday, he seemed to recoil whenever a potential opportunity presented itself – herself. Whenever Cashell was in his arms, though, he was always reluctant to let go. An unfamiliar feeling cascaded through him every time. Everything within him wanted to love her.

It had to be lust. That's all he could think of as he moved his lips against hers, and it was scary. Her dress, more revealing even than her birthday cocktail dress, felt like pure silk. It was blue, like the prettiest coastal water, and slid cool and inviting against his fingers.

To bring his mind back to the present moment, he moved back slightly – not out of her embrace entirely, but enough for their lips to be forced apart – and summoned some small talk.

"This is, uh, swanky. I didn't expect there would be this many people, or that it would be so upscale. Is that…?"

Cashell turned to follow James's line of sight. "McIntyre, yes." She rolled her eyes at him. "Typical male: you would spot the model type straight away, now wouldn't you? I'll just point out her boyfriend right beside her there: a heavyweight boxer, for your information."

"All right, all right," James said, raising his hands in mock surrender.

"Hey, player, I'm all the eye candy you have room for tonight," she smiled.

"That's the truth." When her jaw dropped slightly, he couldn't resist kissing her again. "I only have eyes for you."

"Be careful with that."

He nodded. A very true warning. From hour to hour, James went from running away to running back to her. That's how his thoughts went every single day.

Cashell adjusted her dress. "Let's go inside and have a dance before I need to make the tally announcement."

"How are the donations this year?" James enquired.

"Paltry. I've been looking for someone to take over the fundraising: I have to make some changes to the Board. I've been talking with Leedra – I'm hoping she can help me with some strategic planning. Oh, and there they are now. Let me go say hello."

James followed as Cashell led the way to join Dexter and Leedra on the dance floor. Before James could protest, Dexter put an arm around Cashell and they started dancing as Leedra turned to him. To his surprise, James actually felt a stab of jealousy. He'd come especially to see Cashell and now here she was dancing with his brother! Dexter winked at him.

"My partner is taken at the moment - want to dance with me?"

Leedra's eyes twinkled mischievously.

"Uh, okay," he replied dumbly.

"Well, don't sound so excited about it," Leedra teased.

"I didn't mean it like that - not at all. I just, uh…"

"I'm glad to see you here," she said, cutting off his mumbling. Unexpectedly, she leaned in and embraced him fully before assuming a dancing position, planting a kiss squarely on his cheek.

"Do you need the love talk, too?" Leedra asked, after a few moments of witnessing him staring wistfully after Cashell. She narrowed her eyes at him playfully.

"No! I mean, not, uh, not right now." He didn't really know what 'the love talk' was, but the title scared him: it would, he guessed, be similar to the talk that had persuaded him to attend this very function in the first place. Well, here he was: that would have to suffice for now. Nevertheless, he found himself continuing the conversation against his better judgment.

"It's hard," he sighed. "I don't think I've been in love before. A long time ago someone I really cared about got badly hurt, and it wasn't..."

"Pleasant?" Leedra nodded. "Of course it wasn't. Well, you should just know that Cashell is different. She's loyal - she has integrity. Stick with her, and you're saving yourself from possible pain. Believe me: I've been there, done that. Once you get past the thought of something awful happening, past the fear of losing anything, the gain is so much greater than the fear. Love is worth the fight."

James stared at her as they moved together to the music. "How did you get to know all this? You've only been engaged for a hot minute."

"And I've been in love and running for twenty-five years," she retorted. "It's exhausting. I know."

James didn't know what to say to that. Leedra had carried a torch for Dexter for twenty-five years? That was a long time.

"Listen, I, uh, wanted to ask you about Family Weekend," he began.

"I see you, trying to change the subject," Leedra laughed.

"No, I'm serious," he said. Sure, who wouldn't want to get off the subject of one's own lackluster love life; but he'd heard everything she'd said and had honestly taken it all to heart. He couldn't believe that she'd been in love with Dexter all those years. He also knew that he wouldn't ever forget Cashell, even if she were to disappear from his life completely. His hesitations weren't about her health, but about him and his past - about his mother's abandonment. The one woman he loved, for no real reason other than the fact that she'd birthed him, had let him down. He was still mourning the mother he'd hoped to come to know but now knew he couldn't. Momma G was awesome and loving, yes - but she was gone now. He didn't think he could take the pain of yet another woman leaving him, regardless of the circumstances.

He looked back at Leedra as they continued to dance. "Kay-Kay is worried that you aren't getting married," he told her.

"She was sad about that when she stayed with me."

"I know. My precious girl." Leedra said it as if Kira was her biological child. "James, I love your brother more than anything, you know."

"Then marry the fool already."

"Listen to you! I'm getting to it, James, all right? I want to go slow - I can't rush this. Things with Allontis have been... tense. You know. She's trying a couple of different medications, and until she gets her dosage right, I just come home and take care of the kids - make sure everything is okay."

"Why didn't you call me?" James asked.

"You're busy," she replied.

"It's the off season. I'm not that busy. Tell you what: the kids can stay with me again - for two weeks this time. You talk to Cole and Allontis and let me know."

"Okay, but you talk to Cole too," Leedra replied. "He's worried about Allontis. I think she'll be fine, but it takes time. I've seen depression like this before."

Leedra kissed him on the cheek again and he glanced up to see his brother staring daggers at him. Maybe their dance had gone on a little too long for Dexter's comfort. James ignored him for a moment longer while he spoke to her:

"I'm glad you'll be joining our family."

"Me too." Before the words had left her mouth, she was back in Dexter's arms, as if drawn by a magnet. Then they were kissing, and instantly James felt like a third wheel.

He hurried away to find Cashell, who was off to the side now, talking with her father. They were flanked by a tall man whom James recognized as her brother, Malcolm, and a woman of similar height, presumably his date. Taking a deep breath, James approached the group. The older gentleman noticed him before Cashell did and addressed him first.

"Mr. Parker?"

"Yes sir. Hello." James extended a hand to both of the men.

His shake with Malcolm was rougher than the one with Cashell's father: almost brotherly. Thankfully, Malcolm was out of his police uniform now, making things a bit more relaxed then when they'd first met.

Cashell's father scrutinized him. "So, we meet again."

"Yes," James acknowledged. "How are you?"

"Good. Do the suits you buy no longer involve socks?" Mr. Bruer's face was cold and impassive.

"Daddy, stop it!" Cashell broke in. "It's a youth thing - something people in your age bracket wouldn't understand."

"Is that so? Well, young man, have you signed that deal yet?"

"Yes," James replied, a little nonplussed. "It – it should have been all over the news."

"That so?"

The way her father stared at him was more irritating than intimidating. Thank goodness they didn't meet more often, James thought.

With a final glare, the older man turned his attention back to his daughter. "Your mother and I are retiring for the night, darling. Be nice if you'd come visit us sometime."

"I'll be over soon, Daddy."

"Yes, we seem to hear that a lot sweetheart, but we're still waiting."

James smothered a grin as Cashell rolled her eyes, looking every bit the petulant daughter. She grabbed his hand as her father moved to depart.

"See you, Mr. Parker - Malcolm."

"See you, sir."

"Take care, Dad."

When Mr. Bruer had left, Cashell and James finally had the opportunity for a dance. Soon she would have to make the tallied donation announcement and the night would be over. A slower song started playing, making this dance a little more intimate. Once again, James found that she fit perfectly in his arms. Quickly, they found the rhythm that only they knew and swayed comfortably to the beat.

"Was that your brother's girlfriend?" James asked.

She laughed. "For the night, maybe: who knows? My brother needs to settle down. He likes lots of flavors. He's older than I am."

"Nothing wrong with sampling the buffet until you settle on an entrée," James remarked with a rakish wink.

"Until something from the buffet gets you sick," Cashell shot back.

James wrinkled his noise at their food-poisoning analogy. "Yeah, sampler trays are like that." He smiled down at her. "I think I'm pretty much settled on the dish I want. I've been looking at it for a long time."

"You have? Well I hope it doesn't melt - or get snapped up by someone hungrier," she returned, cool as a cucumber.

He nodded. He sort of liked this code-speak. Cashell lifted her head. Her eyes could not have been any more beautiful, he thought. "That brings about an important question."

"What's that?" He had to stop swaying. Her lips beckoned his and he was feeling dizzy once again. Sheesh – he'd always thought that only women felt this way. Leedra's words from earlier played on repeat in his mind: why be afraid of love? The more he considered the package he was currently holding in his arms, the more he wanted to keep her forever.

"Well, what exactly will we be calling me at this Parker Family Weekend? I mean, if the girls were to ask - if Leedra or Dexter, or Cole or Allontis were to ask?"

"First of all, the girls might ask, but Leedra, Dex, Cole and Allontis are all grown-up enough to mind their own business and draw their own conclusions. As far as what to call you?" He continued swaying thoughtfully. "How about Filet Mignon?" He smiled mischievously and she chuckled at his silliness. Impulsively, he kissed her once again before the music changed, and they danced as long as was socially acceptable.

23
Parker Family Weekend

NOW THAT THE LONG-AWAITED WEEKEND had finally arrived, James wasn't sure what had possessed him to invite Cashell. He found himself stressing about everything and everyone involved with this 'little shindig'. James ran the vacuum distractedly as he reviewed his mental to-do list once again and remembered that he hadn't put together the ping-pong table for the girls downstairs. At least all the televisions were hooked up - including the new seventy-two-inch screen he'd bought last week.

Now, as he worked, the nervous questions began niggling him again. Was there enough to do over the course of three days? Were the chemicals in the pool just the right ones? - would the weather heat up enough to go for a dip at all? - did the girls even like that sort of thing? And just how old was the other child who'd be coming - Sharon's kid? Sharon was the long-time girlfriend of his other brother, Adrian: they'd been dating forever.

It seemed like eons since his family had all been together under the same roof for more than one night. As far as James could remember, the last time had been when Momma G had passed away. That was a lifetime ago, and a depressing one at that. Although he thoroughly enjoyed having his brothers under one roof on whichever rare occasions it came about, the circumstances of that last reunion had not been happy.

The whole gang would be staying at James's new place for two nights and three days. Truth be told, that had him a little on edge. A part of him wanted to come out with it and tell them all about how he'd found his mother and wayward brother, while another part of him wanted to keep his two families separate, hoping beyond hope they'd never have cause to meet.

When the doorbell rang, he jumped up with a start and promptly banged his head, forgetting that he was on all fours under the very Ping-Pong table he'd remembered to fix up earlier. The instructions lay on the floor, hardly legible, with complicated steps describing how to attach a simple net that should have divided the table in half. He crawled out from underneath, rubbing his head, and bounded up the stairs two at a time. It was probably Leedra or Dexter at the door: maybe both. When he reached the door, he discovered it wasn't either of them.

"Hey," he said , surprised and gratified to see Cashell standing on the doorstep.

"Hello. Uh, I just thought I'd stop by early, see if there was anything I could help you do?"

"Yes, okay, that's great," he said absently and gave her a bright smile which faltered after just a few seconds. He hugged her tight and kissed her on the lips.

"James?"

"What?"

"What's the matter?"

"Nothing," he said as he led her in, noting that she lifted not one but two grocery bags from the top step. He took them from her hands and set both on the kitchen island.

"You're not nervous, are you? This is your family, she reminded him gently. "Your family that's been there through everything... They love you. What's the matter?"

He shrugged at her questioning gaze, taken aback that his anxiety was so evident. Either that, or maybe her time spent reading and questioning others had just made her a better judge of mood than he'd previously guessed. He knew that they loved him, of course he did. It was just... different this time around. This whole weekend felt like it crossed new frontiers of 'adulting' that he hadn't even considered. Until now.

"I just – uh…"

"You want everything to work out?" she supplied.

He nodded, somehow relieved. Cashell had moved closer to touch his arm.

"It will. Don't worry so much."

James nodded. Her hand left his arm and he resisted the urge to touch the spot.

"Can you spare a couple minutes to help me get some stuff out of the car?" she asked.

"What? Okay… what did you bring?"

"Just some goodies."

After two trips to her car and four more grocery bags adorning his kitchen island, James began to wonder about the exact amount of food that 'just some goodies' might entail. He peeked into the bags. "This is a lot of food, Cashell… Oh but say, is this the stuff to make that amazing soup?" he asked hopefully. Not that he'd know what exactly was in the soup: he only knew that he wanted more of it at any opportunity afforded to him.

Cashell smirked. "No! It's too hot for soup."

"I liked it, when can I have some more?" he demanded.

"I'll, uh, make you some next week."

"Maybe we can have lunch together again?"

"What?"

"Lunch together, or… dinner?"

"Dinner, what…? I mean - okay."

If she found his desire to have lunch with her again - or dinner, for that matter - a little odd, she didn't comment, but he did see the doubt cross her face momentarily. She seemed unsure of what to make of his thoughts, and certainly what came out of his mouth. He helped her unpack the items from her grocery bags. If she was uncertain, welcome to the club: he found himself just as dumbfounded.

"Hey, check out these pots," he exclaimed suddenly. "I bought these for Cole: this is the brand he uses at his restaurant."

James pulled Cashell over to the stove, where he'd set up the new cooking utensils. Stainless-steel pots and pans glistened, with copper bottoms and spotless finishes that brought to mind a line of shiny new cars sitting on a lot. She picked one up and weighed it in one hand.

"Wow, this is heavy - nice."

"Yeah. I hope he likes it."

"I'm sure he will, hon. That was very thoughtful."

James swelled with pride. Having Cashell here early seemed a good test run for his own family's arrival. He was glad they were coming. Plus, her presence made him feel unbelievably good. Little did Cashell know that having her there was just another part of what he had always wanted. He could get used to her presence. Admittedly he loved her too - he would just keep it to himself for now.

James eyed Cashell as she began to open various packages. She unwrapped and washed a huge wooden cutting board before using it as a base on which to arrange all the deli items she'd brought. There were all sorts of meats: salami, herbed sausage, prosciutto. He only recognized that last one because Cole had made similar snack trays, but James always arrived just in time to eat: he'd never seen his brother actually put one together. Veggies were arranged in an elaborate arc - cherry tomatoes, carrot sticks, olives – interspersed with four different cheeses with lots of different crackers, from Ritz to fancy sea-salt water biscuits. She sliced some cheese and opened a jar of jelly, spreading them in equal amounts on crackers before turning to offer him some. He leaned toward her, opening his mouth.

"You have hands, don't you?" she giggled.

"Yes, but I like yours better." Before she could protest, his teeth grabbed the entire cracker from her fingers like a horse and devoured it, chewing noisily.

She turned away from him and James closed his eyes thoughtfully.

"That was so good." He made a move to grab more, but her quick hands smacked him away.

"Hey, don't mess up my masterpiece!" She continued to fuss with various items, adding handfuls more on the round board. The colors of everything were bright and vibrant: reds, greens, oranges, whites and golds. The sight of it made him suddenly ravenous – not just for the tray, but for the domestic goddess that was reigning supreme in his kitchen, moving around it as if she belonged here.

"Now, I'm going to put this in the fridge for the moment. I'll add the breadsticks and cranberries in a bit, so it looks fresher. Do not touch." She held out a finger in warning and James put his hands up before crossing them over his chest.

"You're a tease."

"You're greedy," she returned with a smile.

James was disappointed, but he reassured himself that he'd get more later. Heck, he had half a mind to spirit the entire tray up to his room now to share with just her later. His family would be none the wiser of its existence.

They continued to work together, putting things out, making everything easy to access and wiping down the kitchen, in preparation for Cole the master chef's arrival. It was the only time they had alone together before his brothers and their families started to file through the door, ready for Family Weekend.

24

The Unintended

IT WAS DAY TWO OF the three-day weekend and James's anxiety was nowhere to be found. As he surveyed the living room and saw that everyone was content, he felt himself relax: something he hadn't felt in a really long time. The people around him were happy, and that made him happy.

Cashell fit in like she'd been there forever. The girls adored her: their newest and "bestest BFF of all time." They'd hated saying goodnight when she'd left last night, after her beautiful antipasti tray had been demolished by the hungry group. The thought had snuck up on him that if they were married, she'd be their real aunt — and, more importantly, she wouldn't be leaving his house at the end of every evening.

Unfortunately, Leedra had had business to attend to so hadn't arrived Friday night with the others, but she was due to show up any moment now. He finally realized what she had meant at the benefit the other night. Dexter seemed hypertense when he'd arrived without her, but James knew that all tension would disappear as soon as Leedra appeared at the door: Dexter would visibly relax, and Kira would finally stop moping around as if she'd lost her only friend. James couldn't wait — mostly because then Kira would finally stop clinging to him and inserting herself between him and Cashell at every turn.

It was amazing to witness the closeness and love between Dexter and Leedra, and to reflect that it was once buried for so long. James wondered whether his feelings for Cashell could ever develop into something like what Dexter and Leedra had.

At this rate, he reckoned, they could get there pretty quick.

James continued to watch his family preparing breakfast around the table. Even though it was only ten o'clock that Saturday morning, the people he loved most were all there and ready for a full day of Parker family fun. Cole had already fired up the grill. Because he was a professional chef, eating was a major part of their days and nights. The weather was perfect. James was relieved that he'd bought extra folding chairs for the patio, and the pool had been checked out and readied for swimming. He'd been for a swim early that morning to check it out.

The doorbell rang, and when Hannah bounded to answer it, there stood Cashell in the doorway. James's breath caught in his throat when he saw her. She was wearing his old college jersey, tied at her hip to make it fit more snugly, and she'd fringed the oversized sleeves, making her look like she belonged in some college dormitory.

Despite not being even halfway through the weekend, he was beginning to dread the start of training camp in just a few weeks. At that point, his time there with Cashell might be over if he didn't make a move to declare his feelings: some sort of bid to keep her as a part of his life. He caught himself in the thought and chuckled. The heavy dose of family time was obviously warping his mind.

"What's up? Every time I look at you over the last twenty-four hours you're deep in thought. Something on your mind?"

James squinted up at Dexter, who'd brought out a pitcher Cashell had mixed for their outdoor brunch. He set the jug on the picnic table and took a seat next to his brother, as James crossed his feet one over the other.

"Cashell and the girls are already planning some kind of spa night – they all seem pretty elated." Dexter smiled.

"Is Leedra here yet?" James enquired.

"Almost, she said last text." James noticed that his brother was holding his cell phone in a deathlike grip.

"You really love her," James observed.

"Leedra?"

"Yes, who else?"

"Just making sure." "I was just thinking that I've never seen you so affectionate with any woman – not even Ellora," James remarked, saying Dexter's late wife's name aloud.

"I loved Ellora very much," Dexter shot back.

"I know you did. I just..." James trailed off.

"Leedra is so different," Dexter sighed. "She doesn't act needy or want anything. I missed her for so long... I guess I feel like if I stop touching her, she'll disappear again."

"That's heavy," James said.

"You'll feel that one day," replied his brother.

"It's scary though, ain't it?" James asked quickly. The words took him by surprise as they left his mouth. He sat back a little, wondering how he'd already managed to steer the conversation this far down the road of love. He'd never really talked to his brother about relationships before, beyond a little light banter at sixteen or seventeen about impressing girls. This time around, he was serious about trying to start a relationship: not serious-serious yet, perhaps, but definitely far past the point of a sixteen-year-old crush. When the time was right, he knew he didn't want to play around.

"Yes, scary... but worth every gray hair, every heart-hurt, every kind of fight."

James nodded. His brother looked down at his phone and stood up abruptly. "Leedra's here." Dexter's thumbs worked quickly in reply, and a moment later Leedra walked around the side of the house, shielding her eyes with her hand against the morning sun and smiling as she approached.

"Hello, sweetheart."

"Baby, come here. How are you?"

"Fine."

James watched the exchange. Even when Ellora had been living, James hadn't seen Dexter – whom he'd always seen as his more serious and quiet brother - react to a woman this way. Sure, Cole was quiet too; but Dexter normally didn't say much of anything at all. After Ellora's death, he'd become even more reserved.

Leedra had changed all that. She was special, different, softer: clearly the only one who could quell the tangible nervousness Dexter exhibited until she was by his side.

"I didn't want to wake anyone – I thought you all might've slept in."

"You wanted a few moments with Dexter, you mean, before Ms. Kira descended?" James teased.

Leedra chuckled. "She's fine."

James sat back down as Dexter pulled Leedra onto his lap. He knew he should excuse himself, but he couldn't deny that he was curious about these two. How and when did they know they wanted to spend the rest of their lives together? And what was it that made them carry a torch for each other for so very long?

"How's everybody doing?"

"Good," James spoke first.

"Better now that you're here," Dexter interjected.

Leedra smiled. "I made a little detour to the store to get a few things on the way here. Are Allontis and Cashell around?"

James nodded, and Leedra smacked her forehead with her open palm.

"I'm sorry, by the way - if this one would let me go, I could properly greet our host, my future brother-in-law!" Leedra tapped Dexter in mock aggravation as he nuzzled her playfully. "How are you? This place is nice: quiet, a bit out of the way. I like it a lot. The drive over here was so relaxing, too. It's beautiful, with the mountains just beyond your yard. They look so close you could touch them."

"They're pretty far away." James stood again as Leedra finally extricated herself from Dexter's lap. She held out her arms, hugged him close and kissed him on the cheek.

"Watch your hands, future-brother-in-law. After you're

done drooling over my intended, why don't you get us some coffee?" Dexter quipped, not entirely joking.

"I got it." James kissed her cheek, just to annoy Dexter, and left them alone. His brother didn't really want coffee: he just wanted a few minutes alone with Leedra. James could understand that. He smiled to himself. He felt silly for interrogating their love. What was there to wonder about? Leedra was kind, almost like a mother. Dexter was a completely different person around her and James rather liked it, even if he was bossed around a bit more as a result.

As he entered the kitchen, the smell of his favorite breakfast meat wafted past his nose. Bacon. Cashell was standing with Cole, learning some culinary tricks and stirring a pot of something delectable. Thinking he was undetected, James hung back to watch. He was still musing over his other brother and his bride-to-be. How could two people have carried the torch unrequited for so long, then require a full-blown passionate reunion after every 24-hour separation?

"You just gonna stand there, or wash up and help the girls set the table?"

Embarrassed that he'd been spotted staring off into space, James smiled. "My family is so bossy." He winked at Cashell and she moved nearer to him to help. Their arms touched as he handed plates to her. "Stop making my girl your sous chef, Cole - get Hannah in here to do your bidding, why don't you? This one is mine."

James liked her nearness, he liked how well she fit in here and he liked her, a lot. He bent to kiss her cheek before moving to the table to set it. They worked well together in tandem, and when the doorbell rang again, James moved to answer it, the eyes of the kids on the sofa following him to the door. Without bothering to look out the small side windows first, he swung the door wide, with the genial feeling that right now he would welcome anyone... then he saw who stood there and quickly amended his list. Anyone except him.

James's smile vanished. His beneficence and cordial friendliness escaped out of the door with the draft of warm air, as if snatched away by the man in front of him.

"What's up, Slim Jim? You're having a party and your own brother didn't get an invitation?"

25
Watched Pots Never Boil

"WHAT ARE YOU DOING HERE?" James snapped.

"Is that any way to greet your brother? Gee - tough crowd, man." Bobby leaned on the doorframe with a sneer.

James stepped outside and snapped the door closed behind him with an air of finality. All he could think about at this moment was how he could possibly keep his biological brother as far from his adopted family as possible. He couldn't delay the meeting indefinitely, perhaps; but he certainly didn't plan to make it easy for Bobby.

"I'm not going beat around the bush, Jim. I need some help paying Ma's bills and some... other stuff out at the house. Can you help me? Her Long-Term Care insurance should be called short-term, cause it ain't long enough - you know what I mean?"

"You expect me to pay to look after someone you won't even let me see?" James returned levelly.

"Now, just a minute, I ain't say you can't see her," Bobby said slyly. "I just don't want her upset, that's all. She be displaced, nowhere to go, you know?"

James knew he couldn't keep his family from coming out to the porch eventually to see what was keeping him, but he really, really didn't want Cashell or Allontis to set foot outside. Of course, because he didn't want that, it would be exactly what he got.

He heard footsteps and the click of the door. Sure enough, Allontis emerged first.

"You okay, honey?"

"Yeah, fine," James said curtly. Allontis looked at him quizzically before turning to see who he'd come outside to chat with.

"Hello...?"

Although he tensed up, James didn't look at her: he was too busy watching Bobby's interest rise to new heights right before his eyes.

"Well, hello to you! Please say you're not married."

"She is, to my brother," James said quickly.

"Well I'll be darned. I was hoping you were married to Jim here - I'd feel a lot better about stealing you from him instead," said Bobby, syrupy sweet.

Allontis laughed, but James kept a straight face. He didn't like jokes, especially not with people he didn't know that well. Bobby should have the same kind of restraint, he thought angrily, considering he'd never even met Allontis's husband, Cole. He glared at Bobby, who was still eyeing her up lecherously.

"Allontis, this is my brother, Bobby. He just came by to say hello. He's leaving in a minute - aren't you? I'll be inside soon," said James.

"Okay..." He felt the admonition for his rudeness in Allontis's stare, but he knew she'd understand when he explained things to her later. She went back inside, murmuring politely to Bobby that it was nice to meet him. James ensured the door was closed firmly behind her.

"Good God almighty - what you call her again? Londis, Lonnie? She'll put a hitch in your git-along, won't she? She superfine. Her man real big?" Bobby leered.

"What?"

"You know, a big guy?"

James annoyance grew. "What difference does that make?" he snapped.

"Aw man, calm down."

James's patience was coming to an end. "No, you chill out, Bobby. Allontis is like a big sister to me. I've known her since

I was a baby."

"Big sis hell, sign me up little brother!"

James rolled his eyes. To his annoyance, the door opened again and this time Cashell came out.

"Hello."

James stood and moved to talk to her first. He tried to whisper a warning as quickly and as nicely as he could; but although she nodded, she didn't heed his advice. No doubt Allontis had told her who was out there and Cashell's curiosity was well and truly piqued.

"Well, well, well. Hello my dear. What be your name?" said Bobby.

"I'm Cashell. I'm a friend of James. Who are you?"

"Bobby."

"Yes, okay. Nice to meet you."

She reached her hand forward. James stood right by her side, crowding her. He wanted to protect her somehow, but he was unsure of what else to do.

"The pleasure is all mine." Bobby proceed to pull her closer when their hands connected and James resisted the urge to help him let go. Cashell managed to stand firm despite the yank on her hand, freeing her hand from his as gracefully as she could. James was thankful.

"Did you want something to eat? We're having brunch," Cashell asked politely.

"Don't that beat all! This girl got some manners, how about that Jimmy? Don't mind if I do, young lady. Brunch? What now, ain't that like breakfast and lunch joined together?"

Cashell chuckled, "Yes, it is." James shook his head and followed them around to the back where Cashell led Bobby, hanging back and watching his brother closely. In the backyard, he saw the lovely tableau of all his family together, eating their breakfast - the same meal he should have been enjoying with them, he thought with some irritation. Still, he let Cashell take the lead with introductions. He knew what she was trying to do and that she had the best of intentions, but he had a sinking conviction that it wasn't going to work out - not in the way she hoped. He didn't know for sure, but he had a feeling. For now, he decided it was best not to say anything else.

"Everyone, I'm Bobby. Mighty glad to meet you. James and I are just getting to know each other. He needs to warm up to me, is all." His brother was turning on the charm full blast.

"Well, have a seat," Leedra offered.

The family welcomed him warmly and returned to their meal without much comment, but James could barely eat. He stared at the intruder, worried that all this charm was some sort of act and that Bobby would eventually hamstring them all. James wasn't about to let any of that happen. He had met people like Bobby before, and he resolved that it would take more than just a few cordial introductions to get him to change his mind.

Brunch continued without incident. The kids swam, ate, watched a movie and played ping-pong, liking it all as much as James had hoped they would. Bobby hung around and did little save gawking at the people around him, grinning especially mischievously at Cashell. He did nothing particularly out of line, but then it had only been a couple of hours since he'd arrived. James was perpetually on edge, worrying that at some point Bobby would figure out the very worst thing to say and that would be end of niceties. From his stance next to Cole, who was working the grill, James had a clear view of the entire backyard.

"Did you want to sit by me?"

Suddenly, Cashell stood in front of him. In his private funk, he hadn't noticed that she'd changed into a one-piece swimsuit. It was pink, with a purple stripe down one side that elongated her short stature. He looked at her like a starving man regarding a meal. His mouth was dry and his palms grew instantly sweaty.

"I... uh, yeah, in just a moment. You wanna go for a swim?" James fumbled for the right words.

"Yes but the kids splash a lot. I was hoping you could run some interference," she smiled

"Okay, yeah - in a minute." He wasn't trying to blow her off, but even Cole looked over at him disapprovingly. As she sauntered away, he regretted the inability to reign in his sour mood.

"Jimbo, you need to chill out." Dexter dragged a carrot through some cheese dip Cashell had thrown together and popped it into his mouth. Cole nodded in agreement as he turned over the peaches on the grill with metal tongs. The cut fruit, featuring picture-perfect black hash marks, looked good enough to eat right off the hot grill. Cole slid them onto a plate grilled sides up, sprinkled them with brown sugar and placed dollops of yogurt in their centers. They would go perfectly with vanilla ice cream, or they'd probably go down wonderfully on their own. James's mouth watered - not at the peaches, but at the sight of Cashell in her swimsuit. He'd told her to have fun and feel like a part of the family, but he'd forgotten that meant swimming – and that could be with him, if he would just snap into a better mood.

Bobby was well-behaved. He engaged with the kids, even playing with them a little as he sat on the edge of the pool, but James could see plainly how he kept looking over at Cashell and the rest of the women off to the side. Everyone, James finally noticed, was now wearing a swimsuit of some sort. Setting the peaches down, James looked back at his foster brothers.

"I just don't like him," he declared.

"Well, you're about to tell him as much - keep your voice down!"

"Well, maybe he'll leave if he hears me," James retorted.

"Doubtful," observed Cole, turning down the grill.

"Did he have a reason for coming by? How'd he know we'd all be over here?" Dexter asked.

"Yes, he asked me for money to pay Mom's bill at the nursing facility. I don't know. He's bad news. I think he's into drugs or something."

"Well, I could get some information on him. What did your detective say?" Cole asked. He closed the grill when he'd retrieved the last of the peaches.

"He has some convictions - what for, I don't know. He did some time," James told his brothers under his breath.

"At the end of the day, he's your brother."

"Half."

"Kinda like us," Dexter pointed out.

"No way! Not at all like us. We've grown up together since we were children," James defended.

"And we have no blood relation," Cole added.

"And we don't need that." James was annoyed at the turn their discussion was taking. For all his grandstanding about their blood relation not being an issue, he was uncomfortably aware that he was the one that had started this stupid hunt for his quote-unquote real family for just that reason. He just didn't like what he'd found, and that was the problem.

"Where's Cashell?" James turned around and scanned the yard. As he searched for her, Bobby approached him.

"Nice family you got here. Everyone seem real friendly," he said softly.

James drew himself up to his full height. "Thanks."

"Cashell your girl?"

"What?" James turned around to face his brother head on, his guard and his radar now fully up. He couldn't help the instinctive way his fists balled up when Bobby said Cashell's name. He eventually spotted her, sitting with Allontis and Leedra under a sun umbrella enjoying the shade. He looked back at Bobby. "Who wants to know?"

"Just checking, man. It's a yes or no question." Bobby picked his teeth. "Territory 101, brother: if something is yours, you put your name all over it. Regardless of any rank, relation, age, size, and even gender, you let everyone know. Ain't that right, Cole? You put your name on Allontis, I bet?"

"Women aren't property, Bobby," Cole returned coldly.

"Or cattle for that matter," Dexter interjected.

"Sure they are – y'all have just been Northern-ized," Bobby said mischievously. "Now Jim Boy, I saw her looking at me. Saw you get all tense. She wanted to greet me, now ain't that real sweet? She know the real good-looking McCoy when she see it," he crowed.

"She doesn't know a thing about you - and she never will," James returned hotly.

Neither Cole nor Dexter commented further: that's how they were, James knew. They didn't argue, they just stopped looking at you and moved on, demonstrating that they were done talking with you. James was done too, but he clarified just in case Bobby still didn't understand. "She's my girl, yes."

"Right," Bobby chuckled, as if relishing a private joke. James didn't like it. Bobby looked around and raised his voice.

"Everybody, it's been a pleasure. I'm about to go. Oh, hey James, I was hoping we could talk about that… thing I mentioned earlier?"

"Whatever you want to say, you can say in front of my brothers." As soon as the words left his mouth, James realized how that sounded. He hadn't meant to make it so blatant, that Cole and Dexter felt more like his brothers than Bobby did. It just came out wrong. He rushed on before Bobby had a chance to get his dander up, which seemed almost inevitable before this day was out.

"If I can visit Mom, I'll pay it when I come down," James said.

"Oho, you don't trust me with the money?"

James knew it would come to this. He wasn't that good at diffusing a situation, but he could see when one was escalating and getting out of hand.

"I would pay them directly. I don't really know you, so I guess you're right, I don't trust you yet - but I will take care of our mother."

"Oh, but I can't, right?" Bobby goaded, his eyes glittering.

"I didn't say that. I'm saying I'll support her too, now that I know her - and you."

"You do that."

With that, Bobby left the way he had arrived, sauntering away around the side of the house. They heard a car roar off down the street and James listened intently, hoping that Bobby had finally left them the heck alone. He had said he would pay, James reflected, so why would his brother be upset unless he wanted cash to use for something else?

Relieved that Bobby was gone at last, James decided to take a dip and cool his jets in the pool. He removed his shirt and gave a yell, then when all the kids looked around he took off running to jump in. He let the cool water shock his system back into a right attitude and a better mood. Delighted, the shrieking kids descended on him, but not before his eyes met Cashell's briefly in silent communication. He mouthed the words I'm sorry and did a little twirl of his finger against his temple, hoping she could read his signage for a temporary moment of insanity. When she smiled back and blew him a kiss, relief surged through him and, in that moment, he knew he loved her.

———

Cashell watched, mesmerized, as James took off the sleeveless shirt he'd been wearing and dived into the pool. When he surfaced, water up to his chest and attempting to apologize to her, she couldn't help but forgive him. She had seen that he'd been trying his best; she knew how hard it was for him to connect with the brother he'd never known. Perhaps she'd been presumptuous by inviting Bobby to the family meal, but it seemed the right thing to do at the time. If she could help foster the relationship and attempt to build some sort of bridge between them, she wanted to try. All she could do was help extend a tiny, withering olive branch. If it broke in half, well, that was on them, but she'd been intent on at least trying. James didn't need another brother per se: he just needed peace about his family. More than anything, she wanted to help facilitate that in some small way.

His body, however, didn't need any help at all, she considered as she looked at him moving in the sun. Not another workout, barbell or sprint - not even suntan lotion could make him look better than he already did. Sure, the outfit he'd been wearing before hadn't done much to conceal his impeccable arms, taut stomach and the long legs that used to run the 400-meter dash in high school and sprints in college: the perfect combination for his current position on the field. But when he dove into the pool, it was another level altogether.

"Cashell, you're sweating," Allontis observed.

"It's hot - it happens. I'm fine." She waved off the comments, nearly forgetting that she was holding Sophia Renee. The baby was just a warm weight in her arms as she dozed off. She made not a peep, resting comfortably while Cashell continued to ogle the child's uncle. If only the little girl knew...

Leedra came over and handed her an icy drink filled with mulberries and peaches.

"It's good: not too sweet, just right," Leedra said, sitting down opposite her.

Cashell thanked her and took a long sip before setting it on the small table between their lounge chairs. "It's good. Cole made this?"

"Yes," Allontis said. "The kids really like it, too."

"It's nice that it's all-natural for them," Leedra said, crossing her long legs. The woman was tall, full-figured and beautiful. She wore a colorful sarong tied around her waist over a sleek swimsuit.

Cashell looked down at the baby. Her eyes opened to stare at her surroundings and momentarily at James before she closed them again. "Where did Jacoby and Sophia Renee get these eyes?" she wondered aloud.

"From Allontis, of course," Leedra answered. Cashell smiled.

"I had to give them something of mine. They'd both look just like Cole otherwise," Allontis added drowsily from her nearby sun lounger.

Cashell barely heard what they said as James did something in the pool. A small sigh escaped her lips. So beautiful...

"Beautiful, huh? Are you talking about James or my baby?" Allontis giggled.

"What?" Cashell looked over, alarmed that her inner monologue had gone rogue - and that her gaze had been so easily followed by the knowing women beside her. Even Allontis had rolled over onto her side to stare at her, regarding her with renewed interest. Cashell smiled shyly, not even bothering to protest because, in all honesty, they were completely on target. "Busted."

When they all laughed, the baby was startled out of a doze and started crying. Cashell laughed too as she stood and handed the child reluctantly back to her mother. The spell had broken: she'd loved the weight of the child against her, but staring at James just seemed to do something to her, especially when he stared back. Now, the crying baby had changed the atmosphere. "Um, should I get a bottle?" Cashell offered, turning toward the house.

"Would you please?" Allontis cuddled Sophia close.

Cashell stepped through the terrace doors. The chill from the air conditioning after the unseasonably warm weather in the backyard gave her instant goosebumps. She wiped her damp feet on the mat inside, went to open the fridge and grabbed the bottle, wondering if she should warm it up or if the baby drank it cold - she wasn't sure.

As she closed the refrigerator door, she almost dropped the milk. There behind it, staring at her, stood Bobby.

26
Boiled Over

"HEY BEAUTIFUL. I SEE MY brother like his women thick."

She would ignore that. "Um, hello Bobby. How are you? You enjoying yourself?" she said with a forced air of cordiality. Her hand tightened on the bottle she held. The coldness of the bottle combined with the blank, dark stare from the man in front of her somehow made the room feel much chillier.

"Yeah... you know what would be great though, if we had a little Cristal, Bacardi, Patron -you know- up in here."

"Oh... well, other than a glass of wine every now and then, I don't think the Parkers drink much. I kind of like that about them. Don't have to worry about any alcohol-induced family brawls."

She laughed nervously. The suggestive way Bobby's eyes looked her up and down, the thought of him touching her, caused her skin to crawl. Her swimsuit wasn't revealing - she'd deliberately chosen a conservative option - but by her estimation, she could be wearing her dad's courtroom robes for all the difference it would make. This guy would find a way to make anything feel explicit.

"Strong drank is good - loosens people up." Bobby moved closer. "You like my tats?" he leered.

If I could make them out, she thought silently. She looked a little more closely just to be polite, and resisted the urge to shake her head. He moved closer still and she took an involuntary step back. "You certainly have a lot of them," she said aloud.

"How serious are you and Jay?" Bobby asked.

"What? Oh, uh, I'm quite fond of James. He's a good person," Cashell responded.

"He that good, you know, when it counts?" Bobby said softly.

"I don't know what you're speaking of."

"Oh, look, now you're being - what they say? - coy. Well, let me just tell you, if you ever get tired of my slow-as-molasses brother, I'd be happy to…"

"Cashell, I'll take the bottle to Ma-Allontis." Hannah had appeared at Cashell's elbow. "The baby just started crying again. Oh, hey Uncle Bobby."

"I'm not your Uncle, girl," Bobby snapped.

"Well, s'cuse me," Hannah said, making a face, as Cashell hastily handed her the bottle. As she was leaving, Hannah turned back once more, hesitating. "Are you okay, Cashell?"

"Of course – I'm fine," Cashell lied.

With a final look of concern, the girl turned to head back out of the double doors, but a firm hand pulled her back. Alarmed, she tried to wriggle away, but the grip only tightened.

"What do you mean, is she okay?" Bobby hissed. "We grown folks in here talking. Why don't you mind your own business, Hannah Banana?"

"Don't call me that."

"Go on ahead, Hannah. I'll catch up," said Cashell, trying to keep pretending that the situation was normal.

"Why not? Hannah rhymes with banana," Bobby spat.

"My mom used to call me that," Hannah said quietly.

"She said don't call her that." Cashell's eyebrows rose. "Bobby, why don't you just stop? I'm gonna go outside."

She was shocked that he would act in such a way, with all the family so close by, plus the fact that Hannah would doubtless report back to the family later on. "I think it's time for you to go," she added. "James is trying to be nice to you, Bobby. You're a guest in his house, and I was only trying to be nice to you by inviting you to join us."

"Oh really? Ain't that nice? Everybody here nice but me, is that what you saying? And this little rug rat..."

What was he, two years old? She couldn't believe her ears.

"You don't know her at all," Cashell snapped. "She's a child, you're an adult. Why don't you act like it?"

"Why don't you come here? I'll show you how adult I can be."

Before she could get away, he'd grabbed her. His arm around her waist, her own arms pinned to her sides and unable to get free. He was crushing her to him while his other hand reached for her swimsuit, yanking roughly at the elastic fabric. She managed to break away and slap him, only for him to return a leering grin.

Out of the corner of her eye, she saw Hannah sprint from the room. She was certain the child wasn't rushing for another cannonball into the pool. James would not be happy.

"I asked you to leave, Bobby – please, just..."

"Oh, you begging me now? I like that," Bobby said. "Why don't you get down on your knees?" He grabbed himself suggestively.

Repulsed, Cashell moved away again. Bobby lunged for her, pulling her back into the kitchen, his hands everywhere and his lips pulled back over his teeth like a snarling dog. As he hovered near her face, his breath was so foul it made her want to gag. She saw teeth, moments before he bit her chin. She screamed... and then other hands were holding her, strong arms pulling her away. In a blur, James made sure she was on her feet, but his eyes never looked at hers: they were trained on Bobby. She saw Cole, too; but James had been the one to wrench her free, she was sure of that. She was relieved to be out of Bobby's grasp: she wiped her chin in disgust.

Staggering, Cashell's knees buckled and she staggered backwards into the corner of the kitchen island. Leaning against it, she watched as James punched his brother in a way she'd never seen before grabbing his loose-fitting shirt around the collar, pulling him as Bobby struggled to get back on his feet. The shirt seemed to cut into his neck and she prayed he wasn't being choked - not that anyone seemed to care but her. As James dragged him, Cashell saw Bobby try to topple everything as he went, including a very pretty vase that crashed to the floor.

The door opened as James neared it, and Dexter held it wide for James to get out with his brother in tow, then closed the door with finality.

In shock, Cashell hurried to the door. "Shouldn't you make sure he's all right?"

Dexter turned to her calmly. "He's all right. Are you?"

She nodded absently. She was fine: wasn't she standing there, fine? She was worried about James, that was all; but she seemed to be the only one. She glanced up and saw Hannah watching through back door. Cole quickly closed the blinds before starting to clean up the chaos that was left in the kitchen, as if this sort of thing happened every day. Cashell's hands shook. She was nervous for James; although, despite Bobby's muscular appearance, James's anger would surely have given him the edge in any fight.

She touched the fresh graze his teeth had left on her chin. The foul smell of his breath came back to her, and the memory of that particular odor made her think that Bobby had been smoking something other than your standard cigarette. She couldn't be sure: she didn't know anything about illegal drugs, as she had a hard enough time keeping up with all the legal ones she herself had been prescribed over the years. Why would anyone dabble in substances that even doctors were unfamiliar with? She'd never understand that.

Her head snapped up as more yelling came from outside, followed by... nothing at all. Long moments passed before the door flew open and James reentered, slamming it so hard that the few pictures he'd managed to hang rattled on the walls. Seeing that he didn't have so much as a bruise on him gave her a modicum of relief. The look in his eyes, however, was another matter; and they didn't soften when he laid them on her.

She watched him survey the room, taking in the swept-up shards of the vase and all the other damage. He pounded a fist into his hand with a cracking sound. His stormy anger scared her. She felt embarrassed – responsible, somehow, though she knew it really wasn't her fault. She simply hated fighting: hated the rage that she saw in James's eyes, and hated that his relationship with his own brother, new and fragile to begin with, was probably now completely severed by a few moments of utter stupidity. She was also concerned that Bobby seemed the type that would happily use his mother as a pawn in this situation, somehow. He would find some way to keep James from seeing her, when in fact this whole ugly episode had been of his own making entirely. The little voice of conscience piped up again. She had invited Bobby in. Now she knew why James had so resisted it.

Embarrassed and heavy-hearted, she stood there, waiting for James to talk to her, to say anything. He was silent. He probably did blame her.

She knew she needed to leave. She was exhausted. There was dinner and a movie still to come, with Cole's savory three-cheese popcorn that she'd been dying to try… but she knew it was time for her to go home. Before she could say as much, James spoke.

"I'll be back in a minute." He disappeared back out of the kitchen door.

"He needs to cool off, that's all." Cashell looked over to see Cole hunting for some rubber gloves under the sink. In all honesty, she'd forgotten he was there at all. Sad and deflated, she went to locate her travel bag. She would be gone before James returned.

Later, Leedra herded a pair of clean, damp and excited girls from the bathroom. Before she could tell them to settle down, they'd scampered off in a whirlwind of giggles and towels to find their pajamas, although in all likelihood they would be awake for the next few hours.

In the sudden calm that followed their exit, Dexter gave her a meaningful look. Admittedly, Leedra was nervous about how the two of them would spend real 'alone time' together. Though she and Dexter were often together at his house or her apartment late into the night, there were always other people around. Never before had she felt her desire for him come on so strongly as it had over the last twenty-four hours. It scared her.

As if reading her thoughts, he held out his hand. "Come talk to me."

"Okay... but, uh, did you want to make sure Kira was tucked in first?" she asked, stalling.

"Nope," Dexter answered decidedly. "Cole and Allontis are here, and we all know those girls won't be going to bed any time soon anyway." He grinned. "They might as well be at summer camp with the amount of sleep they're getting, up giggling all night with their tablets."

"Okay, uh..."

Before she could think of anything else to distract him, his hand grasped hers and pulled her toward one of the rooms at the furthest part of the hall, set back away from the others.

"Are you sure this isn't... someone's else's? It - it could be James's bedroom," Leedra stammered.

"I'm sure."

When she entered the room, she gasped. An array of lighted candles was already flickering on the hearth, and the only other light, from a small lamp off to the side, gave the room a cozy glow. A blanket was spread out on the floor, with numerous pillows arranged on it. The room had a fireplace too, but with the warmer days still nearing ninety degrees it was still too warm to start that up, even for show.

Listening closely, Leedra could hear Roberta Flack's low, melodic voice setting the mood. Unbeknownst to Roberta

Flack, Leedra had been in that mood for most of that day already, gazing across the pool's shimmering turquoise water at her intended. She wanted to giggle out loud at her internal monologue, but then she'd have to explain her thoughts. She guessed that Dexter was having the same thoughts, and probably needed no encouragement whatsoever. Significantly, she noticed that the bed had no frame, not even a headboard or covers - yet somehow it looked quite comfortable all the same.

She knew that Dexter, being the gentleman that he was, would not intentionally set up this ambience for purposes of seduction when they weren't yet married. Her guess was that he had arranged the blanket, pillows, soft music and candles like this simply in the name of romance. With some trepidation, Leedra continued to stare at the set-up around her. She was still a little hesitant, but it all looked so inviting that eventually she followed Dexter's lead and removed her flip-flops to join him sitting on the blanket.

He had set this up out of sheer thoughtfulness. This amplified gesture of super-romance made her just giddy with love. Cuddling instantly shot up her favorites list: just as important for any marriage as the act of making love itself. She settled down among the cushions as the vanilla scent of the candles wafted around her.

"When did you possibly have time to do all this?" she breathed.

"Not long ago," Dexter replied softly. He pushed pillows behind her back as she crossed her ankles in front of her. Despite her initial nerves, she reminded herself that she loved the man sitting next to her. He was the least pressuring person she knew. With those thoughts in mind, the tension began to roll out of her. It was just the two of them, and he always put her at ease. She was peacefully silent.

After a few moments, he reached under the pillows behind him and retrieved an ice bucket. Pushing some of the ice aside, he pulled out a spoon. Leedra's mouth formed an O shape as awareness began to dawn on her, and she smiled at him in delighted surprise. "What kind is it?" She knew he'd brought her favorite ice cream. She tried to reach around him to get a look, but Dexter dragged out the reveal in old dramatic fashion. Next, he pulled out the familiar brown-and-yellow carton with a flourish. She wanted to squeal, but remembered the other houseguests and the hour of the night and tamped down her excitement just in time. It'd been a favorite addiction since her return to the states. Being away on a Mercy Ship for so many years, she'd rarely gotten to enjoy any kind of frozen treat, let alone her favorite ice cream. Nowadays she was all but a connoisseur of the stuff.

"I snuck this into the grocery run and bought the kids the cheaper brand so they wouldn't eat yours," Dexter smiled.

He opened the carton, pulled off the protective film and handed it to her, but not before playfully reminding her: "You have to share."

"Oh really? Who with?" She laughed at the look he gave her. "Can't you go get yourself some of the kid's stuff?"

"No, I can't," Dexter replied. "It's cheap and tasteless and I want yours."

Leedra laughed. "You're right about that. You know, I'm surprised these kids of all people like it: their palates are usually pretty mature from all Cole's amazing cooking. It's kind of scary, really. They know when the salt is missing or when something's burnt on the bottom without even seeing it. It's kind of a lot of pressure."

After running her spoon around the edge of the carton and savoring a few creamy bites with deliberate slowness, she finally fed him a bite, laughing at his frown over the painfully small amount she'd put on the edge of the spoon. Watching his lips as she ate did something to her.

She looked back down at the carton thoughtfully, taking a final-for-now spoonful and setting it down a safe distance from her.

"Is that why we're not getting married: because of... pressure?"

Dexter sat up straighter. "I want to marry you tomorrow."

"Sounds good to me," she replied, smiling. "The thing is, I want a certain something, but I don't know how to put it together. I just, uh... well, it's a lot to plan. Don't you want something formal?"

Dexter hesitated. "I had that the first time around... but I know you've never experienced it. If that's what you want, then let's hire a wedding planner."

Leedra was pensive. "I thought about that, but it seems so impersonal..."

"You pay to personalize to the level you want. They source things for you, make suggestions, recommendations. All you have to do is pick and choose."

She nodded. She knew that, of course; but she also knew that the charge for such services would be quite embarrassing. The average fees raked in by pro wedding planners could buy important equipment for the Mercy Ship, her former home.

"Leedra, I did have something else to tell you. I want you to know that I can no longer say children don't matter to me."

Leedra bit her lower lip. "Oh? Because you've changed your mind?"

"No, I haven't changed my mind. It's just that no matter what I say, you don't believe me. Whether our children come from your womb," - his hand reached out and tenderly touched her stomach - "or someone else's who has given up on them, it makes no difference to me."

"I - I..." Leedra looked down, hoping she didn't cry. "I wanted to be able to give you a gift. The best gift. I want a child born out of our love."

Dexter gently touched the jagged scar concealed by her sheer skirt, thinking of her thousand other invisible battle scars that had yet to heal. The least he could do was to be patient. She'd overcome so much, and he loved her more than anything.

"You have given me two precious gifts already," he murmured. "My daughter, for one, when you saved her from being sold away like a piece of real estate. That is the ultimate gift."

Leedra nodded, smiling. She loved his little girl. Having both the two of them around her was more than she could have hoped for.

"And the second gift?" she whispered.

"The second gift is you. You brought yourself clear across the continent to confront your past. That was no easy task, and I benefited from it all."

"You're worthy," she said in awe.

"You are worthy," he replied. He caressed her face and she leaned into his palm. "You are the gift, spared one fateful night when everyone else wasn't so fortunate."

Leedra smiled, tears in her eyes. When they fell, Dexter leaned over and kissed them away.

"I want to be a good wife."

"You have to actually get married to be a good wife," Dexter reminded her.

Leedra laughed. She turned and leaned herself into Dexter's waiting arms, resting her face against his strong neck and shoulder and inhaling his masculine scent of warm skin and cologne. In every moment like this between them, she felt her resolve to wait slipping a little more. Impatiently, she wished to be married right then.

She looked into his eyes as he looked down at her. "I don't know who's a better advocate: you or KayKay."

"If she's pressuring you, you tell me. Is she? I can speak with her."

"You'll do no such thing! Of course she's not pressuring me. She only wants what's best for her daddy - she's a staunch advocate for you, and a gosh-darn good one at that. I can understand how eager she is to have her family whole again."

"We're advocating for your happiness too," Dexter pointed out. "We hope that we – the two of us - are what you really want, just as much as we want you."

"Please don't doubt that. I do. I want you both. Right now, I want this more than anything." She placed her arms around his neck and kissed him with all the pent-up longing she felt in her heart. Nestling her head back onto his chest, she listened to his heartbeat. It lulled her as his comforting arms soothed away the bad as they always did. She felt the safest in his arms.

"What about an early fall wedding?" she whispered, thinking about all the fall colors: burnished reds, golds and warm oranges.

"I like that."

Leedra smiled dreamily. It would be a beautiful time of year, and would allow just enough time to plan something small. Plus, she could start preparing to host Christmas dinner at their house, instead of Cole cooking everything on his lonesome. It had been nice this past Christmas, but because she wasn't yet married to Dexter, there was still a hint of disjointedness. She understood Kira's confusion. After their previous Christmas day together, the girl had watched her pack up her gifts, load up her car and head back to her apartment. Looking back, Leedra realized that of course some form of departure happened each and every night. She hadn't considered until that moment how sad that must have made Kira.

It was time to be there for good. The thought actually soothed and excited her. She nuzzled closer into his chest. "You find me a venue and a pastor, I'll do the rest; but small, intimate, just family and some of your friends, okay?"

He nodded against her forehead. "I love you, Leedra."

"I love you," she answered.

27
Unresolved Issues

JAMES WAS GONE FOR LESS than an hour, but with the house so quiet and everyone back to doing their own thing, it felt like he'd been away for an eternity. By the time he returned, Cole had cleared away the chaos and was apparently prepping the kitchen for dinner. The savory smells that met his nose represented all that James wanted back in his home. Momma G had been the first to create such divine aromas, and now Cole was tasked with similar mastery, using fire and oil and whatever food he'd selected at the grocer. It was as close as any of them could get to Momma G's legendary cooking these days. Having all these people together in his house, James reflected, was as close as he was going to get to being a teenager again.

Hannah sat at the island reading her book and James gently touched her head and the dampness of her hair and shampoos from her bath wafted to his nostrils. "I'm sorry about what happened today, sweetie. Did Bobby hurt you?"

She shrugged. It wasn't her style to show emotion that overtly. She turned in her seat and reached out a reassuring hand, laying it on his shoulder and patting gently. James smiled, swallowing the urge to laugh at this quaintly adult gesture. He took a deep breath. "Anyone picks on you, ever, you come get me."

She nodded, but she glanced at Cole, working wordlessly just over James's shoulder. Cole was more like her father than a big brother, and he'd obviously be the first line of defense, if it ever came down to that. She'd always get him first, as she had that afternoon. Heck, James would probably go to Cole first, too, if he were ever outnumbered or outmuscled. Bobby was strong, but James's anger today had made him invincible. No-one was going to come up into his house and disrupt his entire family. James tried to banish his surging anger back down to wherever it rose up from. He took a deep, steadying breath.

"You can't choose your family, Uncle James." Hannah's voice was clear and calm. "They choose you. You just try to work with it as best you can."

James smiled fondly, a little bit in awe of the young girl's preternatural wisdom. He squeezed her shoulder and gave her a kiss. As he walked away down the hall, he thought about what Hannah had said. The undeniable truth of her comments was bittersweet. His real family wouldn't even have been around to hurt his adopted family if he hadn't gone looking for them.

"Hey." Allontis emerged from the room just off the kitchen as he passed, closing the door somewhat furtively behind her. James gave her a suspicious look.

"Is Cashell in the library?"

Allontis looked skeptical. "That's the library?" she asked, evidently unimpressed. "Man, have you got a long way to go." She shook her head.

"Very funny," James replied. "Um, how did Cashell seem?"

"She's okay, honey - she fell asleep. She's had a long day. She's, uh, probably just waking up now."

"What's the matter with her?"

Allontis gave him a look. "She's probably scared to death, James."

"Why?"

"Well, from what I heard, you turned into an animal earlier today: you dragged your own brother out of the house. She's never seen you act that way - I haven't either, for that matter. Hannah ran out to get us. She was scared, too."

"If you'd have seen what my brother was doing to Cash, you'd understand!" James blustered. "Cole would have killed him if it were you."

"Okay, sweetie, I know... but when you came back, Cashell said you didn't even talk to her. You just left. She feels bad too: she knows you're trying to make things right with your family."

"I just needed to cool off... Besides, ain't nothing gonna be right with that side of my family."

"Okay, then tell her that and be calm about it."

"I am calm," James snapped.

Allontis raised her eyebrows. "Why didn't you tell us you went looking for your family?"

James shrugged, feeling even guiltier than before. "I just wanted to find them on my own."

Allontis nodded. "We are here for you - you understand? We love you, no matter what." She put her hands on his chest and moved closer. "I'm glad that Cashell was there for you. She's very kind. The family likes her a lot. It's been a while since you had someone in your life, and I want you to be happy. Be nice to her, OK?"

He nodded glumly. Right now, happiness seemed impossible. Peace was all he was striving for at this point: a drama-free life.

"Lonnie?"

"Yes, James?"

"Are you, like, okay? Like... back to your old self?" He wouldn't admit how worried he was about her. She seemed fine, yet he was starting to realize how much went on in the family that he didn't know anything about.

"Praise be to God, I've been feeling really good," Allontis answered. "I got a doctor to change my medication a little. If I can just keep it together, with my family intact and safe, I'll be fine. I'm talking about you, too," she added, eyeing him beadily.

Relieved, James nodded his understanding. He hated that she was on medication at all, but he thanked God nevertheless because they all needed Allontis around just as she was, medicated or not. She and Cole were becoming the new core of the family.

As she walked away back to the living room, James considered that this version of Lonnie did indeed seem more confident and less fragile than the scattered and distracted woman who had come to visit him with her newborn daughter just a month ago. After witnessing her uncertainty and fretfulness that day, coupled with the crying and fatigue, he'd prayed for her every single day.

He thought of his biological mother once again, sitting in that awful nursing home. Especially since experiencing her behavior first-hand, James had often wondered about exactly how a person slipped into a serious mental health issue. How did it start? A piece of his heart would always yearn to know his mother, but one thing was for sure: he was cutting his brother loose today. Blood or not, he could never risk his adopted family in the process of trying to make some biological connection. It just wasn't worth it.

Allontis was going to be fine and he was so thankful. He was just glad she was back to her old self. He resolved that he would fight to keep this side of his family whole and together, even if the other side was a different story.

Now that Allontis had left him, he remained in the hall for a moment, staring at the closed door in front of him. After a few moments, he opened it slowly to check on another lady whom he'd realized that very day just how much he loved.

James was quiet as he entered the room. Cashell lay on the lone sofa, a blanket pulled up to her chin, eyes closed and one hand holding the blanket in sleep. Her breathing was even and quiet. He sat on the floor next to her.

Unfortunately, Allontis's assessment of his would-be 'library' was right. Looking around the room as he sat, he had to admit the space needed work. Cardboard boxes still lined the walls in teetering stacks: old books, mostly, as well as some things from Momma G's house and a bunch of other stuff he'd forgotten about. There were a couple boxes of old trophies he'd planned to hang when he got around to it, and a desk he'd ordered but hadn't put together yet. He agreed with Allontis's estimation: some library. The only sign of the room's purpose were the custom built-in bookshelves that he'd had installed, and even those held just a few books, alongside a handful of knick-knacks and a fake plant.

"Mmm... What time is it?"

Cashell was stirring, her eyes groggy with sleep. "It's almost seven," James responded.

Cashell gasped. "Oh, wow. I had fun today, but I should go now."

"You had fun? Really?"

"Yes, I had a lot of fun. Thank you very much."

"Don't you want to stay for dinner?" James wheedled as she sat up. He didn't get up from his seat on the floor; he simply stretched out his legs and leaned back on his hands. He noticed that Cashell kept the blanket clutched tightly to her as she sat up, holding her arm at an awkward angle and bringing the blanket over her as she crossed her legs Indian-style and stared at him.

"Are you all right?" he asked, concerned.

"I'm tired."

James sighed. "I'm sorry that I left earlier, Cashell. I just needed a minute to chill out."

She nodded but didn't say anything. The noncommittal response drove James mad, but outwardly he remained calm. He wasn't angry, only frustrated that his feelings for her were catching up with him. He didn't want her to think of him as that guy who disappeared at the first sign of an emergency, especially when it involved risk to her – at the hands of his own brother, no less. Unbidden, a similar incident from his college years came to mind.

"Are you hungry? Cole's probably almost done. He's making you a veggie burger."

"I'm good," Cashell said quietly. "I just want to go."

"Please don't leave."

Cashell moved to stand and as James stood up to help her, he bumped her arm. She winced at his touch and moved hastily away from him.

The reality of what had happened dawned on him and he tried in vain to keep his anger at bay. Silently, his gaze shifted to the hand that held the blanket. "Let me see it, Cashell. Please. I would never hurt you."

"I know that. I'm not afraid you would hurt me, James - I'm afraid for the person who did. Please don't be mad. Please don't. I'm all right," she pleaded. Sensing that the jig was up and that she could hide no longer, she let the blanket fall. What else could she do: wear a blanket all the way out to her car?

When he saw the stormy-colored bruise, the shift in his temper was palpable. Cashell had never witnessed it in him before. She thought she even saw tears in his eyes: unexpected and almost unbelievable.

"Are you serious?" James whispered.

"It was an accident. He... didn't know he was hurting me. I bruise easily because of m-my heart medication and the blood thinners I take."

"So now you're defending him?" His tone, steely and low, told her he was on the verge of getting angry. Again.

"Please calm down."

She leaned into him and put her arms around his waist, relieved that he didn't pull away even though he felt rigid in her arms. The smell of chlorine mingled with faint traces of his cologne.

"What happened a long time ago? Please tell me." She felt sad because he was sad. This went beyond her stupid bruise. The truth was that she could merely bang into a door and have a bruise for weeks at a time. It had hurt, the way Bobby squeezed her, but it was nothing - he was nobody.

"I will kill him," James said softly.

"You don't mean that. You don't, James. Look at me... you do not mean that," she reiterated.

"I do mean it. If he comes near you again..."

She could work with the new qualifying statement, because she and Bobby wouldn't come near each other: not ever again. She'd make certain of that. Now that she knew what kind of person he was, she would've needed no encouragement to stay clear of him anyway.

"He won't come near me, ever," she said firmly. "What's important is that you and your family don't talk like that here. You're good people - you don't say ugly things that could have devastating consequences."

"When someone threatens an innocent person, not to mention someone we care a heck of a lot about, the Parkers can get pretty ugly," James retorted.

Cashell swallowed. She wanted to steer the conversation further away from murder, but she didn't want to squash the opportunity for him to share whatever it was that had happened such a long time ago. She waited a bit longer, and soon he spoke.

"Something happened a while ago. Something bad, that I can't get over."

"I want to know," she said.

James winced. "Even I don't want to know, and I was there."

Cashell didn't laugh: this wasn't the time for some silly punch line. Although she hoped it wasn't as major as it sounded, she was mad at herself that whatever revelation was coming was way too late as far as her heart was concerned. Every time she'd even looked at him today, her heart beat a little faster - but she had no idea where his was at.

"I'll get some ice. Be right back. Sit down."

She nodded absently, lost in her own thoughts. Despite the feelings he sparked inside her, she didn't ever want to be one of those women who look past a glaring red flag early on only to be made painfully aware of her mistake later in the relationship, after personal investment and at great risk to her heart.

"I think only Cole and Allontis are eating in the dining room with the girls. Jacoby, Dexter and Leedra have all turned in for the evening. I was thinking I'd drive you home now and pick you up early for breakfast tomorrow. What do you think about that?"

It sounded great, but now Cashell wasn't sure she could come back at all.

"Are you going to tell me what happened, years ago?" she persisted.

James sat down with a sigh and she took a seat next to him. She felt a small flicker of renewed hope.

"Now, hold this onto your arm." He handed her an ice pack.

"It's cold," she said, wincing.

James gave a small laugh, but she saw that his eyes were still sad. "Um, it's supposed to be cold." He stood up and moved to the closet.

After such ominous words, his extended silence made her increasingly uncomfortable - but she remained seated through the silence. Eventually, though, that absence of sound got loud in her ears. Being the chatty Cathy that she was, Cashell couldn't help but express what was weighing on her heart and mind.

"I want you to know that I can handle anything you want to tell me," she told him quietly. "If you've got some deep dark secret, it's best for me to know it, like, right now. Something is obviously eating away at you and I can tell it's something heartbreaking. You punched someone's lights out today. Even though h-he deserved it, I watched you drag your own brother out of here like you were taking out the trash. On a regular day, you seem like a really good person. But somewhere underneath all that, either certain things set you off or you really are just another bad boy in disguise. Which is it? What I can't stand is not knowing before I get more involved."

Cashell didn't realize she was breathing hard until she stopped talking.

"I don't take kindly to threats against people I care about," James said stonily. "He was a threat to you and he was mean to Hannah. It was time for him to go."

"Okay, sure... but do you always overreact that way? You

forget how strong you are: you're athletic. You could really hurt someone."

"When you don't protect the people you care about, they can suffer the consequences," James said enigmatically, studying her.

"It's a silly bruise," Cashell assured him.

"And it could have been much worse."

When she didn't reply, James stood up abruptly and went to a closet. When he turned on its small light, she could see that there wasn't much in it other than a few more boxes stacked on the shelves. He reached to the top shelf and retrieved a shoe box, which he carried over to the sofa and sat back down next to her. Opening the lid, he pulled out an older-model cell phone. He held the phone in a vice-like grip and pressed the button but it didn't turn on, so he dug through the box for the charger and plugged it in.

"I get upset easily because, uh, I've witnessed what happens when you get upset much too late," he said as he dug. "The people you care about pay dearly." The tears returned to his eyes, and her own stung just from seeing his.

James's left leg bobbed up and down as he stared at the phone. Together they were quiet as he waited a few moments before trying again to turn it on. This time, it winked to life fairly quickly. He flicked impatiently through a number of photos with his thumb until suddenly he stopped at one. Cashell looked at the photo, her arm brushing his as he held the phone up for her. Her eyes were riveted to the image of a beautiful girl with long thick black hair and big bright eyes, smiling at the guy standing next to James. Though it was obvious from this image that he and Macy hadn't been together, she couldn't help feel a twinge of jealousy even across all the years that separated them. The feelings surprised and annoyed her. She had to focus, couldn't think like that now.

"This is a girl I knew. Her name is Macy. I liked her. She wasn't my girlfriend or anything like that, but we were close. Friends, I mean. She was going to be a model - she studied fashion. She was dating this other guy at the time." His finger pointed to the other figure in the picture.

Cashell looked closer at the image of a young, smiling James with the pretty young woman, who wore a pair of cutoff Daisy Dukes and a crop top that showed a sliver of her belly. It looked like the photo had been taken quite a few years ago: maybe late high school or early college if she had to guess.

Before she had really finished looking, James's thumb hovered over the phone, scrolling through images in a blur. Occasionally he held the phone closer to inspect certain images, obviously searching for something else. She steeled herself for whatever tragic thing he might share.

He held the phone up again. The video was old and grainy, like security footage, but she could make out Macy and some other guy. Even with the muffled sound, it was evident that they were arguing. Then she spied James at the edge of the picture. He appeared to push the man away from Macy and the man lunged back, shoving them both out of the frame. A few moments later, the young man reappeared, grabbed Macy's head and slammed it into a table. All at once, the video became graphically violent. James proceeded to viciously beat up the guy that had assaulted Macy. Her feet were now all that could be seen of her in the shot, as if she'd fallen unconscious. Suddenly, the frame was empty, with only distant commotion and yells before another figure could be seen rushing to Macy's side.

Cashell covered her mouth with her hand. James tore the phone cord wordlessly from the wall, tossed the items back into the shoebox and stood again to replace the container in the closet where he'd gotten it. When he returned, he simply stood there, his hands in his pockets, looking like a hunted animal.

"Did she live?"

"Yes."

"But – I mean, is she...?" He knew what she was trying to say.

"Her face is permanently disfigured and she suffered a traumatic brain injury."

Cashell closed her eyes. She should have known there were complications. Life was never simple. As if in a trance, James continued:

"Her brother, Kirk, killed the man that did that to her. I wanted to kill him myself. I was going with them to do it, but I - I couldn't go through with it. Kirk's in jail now. Macy lives in North Carolina, still in a tiny house with her Mom..."

Cashell stood up. The anger he still carried obviously stemmed from long ago. Perhaps he'd loved Macy more than he desired to admit. Maybe pretending he hadn't loved her helped him to distance himself, kept him from feeling the rawest pain: the guilt of not having been quick enough to act, then stopping short of the murder that he felt was just. That was so much to carry.

"I didn't protect her then, and today I didn't protect you. I'm sorry."

Cashell's head spun. The realization dawned on her that since they'd met, every single instance in which he'd reacted with anger or smoldering hate had in fact stemmed from these haunting memories of his experience with Macy. In that moment, she understood everything even more than he could know. He was obsessed with protecting people he cared about because he'd witnessed what happened when you did nothing.

"Why are you hanging out with me?" James asked her without preamble. I'm what you call passive-aggressive."

"I love you." She wasn't worried when he didn't respond. It was okay, for now. She knew he was afraid. His expression told her he doubted the very words she spoke.

"You are not passive-aggressive. But you do have one little flaw," she told him.

"What's that?"

"You can't see the woods for the trees. This happened a long time ago: it was an accident that you had no control over. You're not responsible for this. Sure, you could have gone with her brother that night, but in your heart you knew there would be consequences."

James's head was in his hands. "The guy she liked was bad news. He wasn't nice, but we all hung out together... who would hang out with such a monster? I was clueless, naïve, stupidly thinking that everyone is good. They are not. And now we know I obviously come from a seedy group of folks myself. My real folks, my blood brother..."

"Means nothing," she cut him off firmly. "Hear this. Young people do silly things. Some get themselves killed. Some do dangerously stupid stunts, thinking they're invincible: that whatever they do, they'll somehow come out unscathed. I believe you are a great person. I believe that, at your core, you're a stand-up guy."

"I want to hurt him for putting his hands on you."

"But you didn't hurt him. You just bruised his ego a little. For some reason he thinks he can have whatever he wants. Plus, I think he was..." Cashell hesitated to complete her guess.

"A little high?" James offered.

Cashell nodded. She'd only noticed Bobby's condition when she'd gotten really close to him: when his foul breath had pierced her nostrils. She wouldn't know what pot or any other wrongfully ingested drugs smelled like, but that acrid stench had turned her stomach.

"I should never have let him near you guys," James said, pacing the room. "I would never let anyone hurt you. I'd die before someone hurt you," he added gravely.

Her fears allayed now, she nodded her understanding. "I know." James wasn't a bad guy, he was just extremely protective. There was a difference. Somehow, she knew now that he had nothing else left to hold back. As she moved closer to him, she took his hands and gently unclenched his tight fist before placing his hands on her waist. She embraced him, standing on the tips of her toes, and when she lifted her mouth to his she didn't have to wait long before his lips met hers.

"Can I meet Macy?" She waited a beat, sensing his surprise

at her request, but eventually he nodded.

Before he could change his mind, Cashell headed for the door. "I'm going to change, eat my veggie burger, then go home."

"Will you come tomorrow, please?" he asked.

She nodded. "I have to. Cole and I are having a grits cook-off: sugar versus cheesy," she smiled. She was gratified to see the relief on his face at the promise of her returning for the last day of the family weekend.

"Tell me which one you make and I'll vote for yours."

"That's cheating," she admonished, privately thrilled.

"I'd cheat for you any day of the week. Cole has half a football team behind him." He flashed her a small smile.

"I've got some recruits, thank you. Kira and I are getting pretty tight, and Hannah is warming up to me too," Cashell bragged.

"I'm gonna have to speak to them about that. I can see the three of you ganging up on me."

"Well, I guess you better not get on our bad side," she replied with a playful wink. The gloom had lifted now but she had one more request, one that she already knew he wouldn't like. "I do want you to do something else for me."

"Anything," he replied.

She stood closer to him. "I want you to pray for the strength to forgive yourself. To let go of what happened to Macy, and to pray for your brother."

James's nose wrinkled and she saw a brief storm pass behind his pupils, but she could tell he was thinking about it. At least he hadn't dismissed her request right away.

"Okay."

She was so surprised at his acquiescence that she actually put a hand to his forehead, frowning. She didn't dare say anything else lest he change his mind for some reason, so she kissed him again and he hugged her tight, mindful of her sore arm. He was the best hugger. She lingered in his arms just a little while longer.

Eventually they parted and he handed her the travel bag, giving her one last kiss before leaving her alone with her many thoughts. One day had seemed to last a week, but at least everything was now out in the open.

28
Endings and Beginnings

"I TOLD YOU. I ASKED AND he don't seem too inclined to help."

The smoke hung thick in the dimly lit living room, more pungent than just cigarette smoke. A big burly figure sat on the couch as if that were his usual spot. He held a cigarette between his fingers, but he wasn't really smoking it. His pleasure lay with the variety of amber and clear liquids in the bottles crowding the table. He took a deep breath and, resisting the urge to gag from the encroaching fumes, turned up the thick bottle he held, resolving to stay just a little longer. He could drink more freely here. Alcohol was his thing, not drugs: there was a difference, he felt. Impatiently, he spoke.

"What are you doing, man? - what is the plan already? I'm tired of him, and the season is about to start. I ain't seen you do nothing whatsoever to take him out."

"And I ain't seen you do nothing but drink up my booze," his companion responded tartly.

"I'm paying you for nothing. The least you can do is offer me some good beverages."

The second man shrugged. He sat on the arm of the sofa, eyeing the man across from him. "You never did tell me why it is you have it in for my brother?"

"It don't matter. I got my reasons… what do you care? He ain't done nothing for you or your crazy Momma. Ain't that's why you called me in the first place, Bobby?"

"Watch it. Only I get to call my Momma crazy. You shut up."

"Whatever," the large man returned dismissively.

Bobby straightened as he thought to himself. "I got it, take the kids, then we'll lure him here and... do something with him."

"Do something: either injure him good or kill him. That's the only thing that will do. No comeback kids, you understand?"

"I got it. I'll handle it."

"You better."

"I could go back to jail."

"Yeah, if you get caught, I guess you could. Best not to get caught then, ain't that so?" The big man gave a harsh laugh.

"How much are you talking again?"

"A cool mil – but that's it. I done paid up your Momma's bill for the rest of the year already, but that's it 'til I see some more results."

"Yeah, 'bout that, thanks - appreciate it," the man mumbled.

"You welcome, now make it happen."

"How about his girl? You going after her too?"

"What girl?"

"He got a fine girl – Cashell, something like that?"

"What?" The red-rimmed eyes sparked with interest. "They going together?"

"Looks like it."

The large man looked thoughtful. "Somebody been keeping secrets on me."

"You didn't know?"

The large nostrils flared. "Do I look like I knew?"

"Yo, why you tripping? Just askin'. Shoot. Yeah - they real hot and heavy."

The big man looked as if he was contemplating the new information. He stood up and moved toward the door, then turned back to his associate with a dark grin.

"I don't want her, but there's no hurt in seeing if she likes me."

"Yeah, all right, all right." His ally chuckled knowingly, as if the two shared an inside joke.

"Thanks for the information. But look, hurry up, dude. I got an NFC East championship to clench, then I'm going to the Super Bowl again. Ain't nobody gonna take credit but me – 'specially not some young blood fresh on the scene from Podunk North Carolina. I'ma sober up just for training camp. I don't have time to be second. Anyway, whatever you planning to do, make it look good – got it?"

With that, the man pulled his cap down low and his jacket up closer around his neck before stepping out of the door to the street. He looked around carefully, then got into his rental car and left. He'd been sure to cover his tracks: no-one would ever know he'd been there. He had training camp tomorrow.

This time around, James and Cashell arrived in North Carolina together. Speeding along in their airport rental car, they were now almost to Lenoir, about an hour's drive from Charlotte-Douglass. While James did want to go back once more to ask whether he'd be permitted to visit his mother, they had decided that their first stop this trip would be to meet Macy. They wouldn't be in the area for long, and rather than extend the stay, they'd agreed to pack as much into their time there as possible. As much as they would have enjoyed taking a leisurely road trip together, they knew that there'd be plenty of time for that in the future. Cashell was excited about the upcoming season: she looked forward to supporting the team, and one player in particular.

James didn't need the GPS as he drove the familiar roads, and they didn't talk much. Cashell kept a book open on her lap, practicing keeping herself occupied in the various stretches of silence and occasionally making some lighthearted chatter with him when he was in the mood to talk.

She loved the scenery around her: cute little towns dotted the road. Things were just calmer down that way. She found herself contemplating whether she could ever get used to quiet small-town life, or if the hustle and bustle of a big city was just part of her natural rhythm.

They parked on the street in a quiet cul de sac and walked up to the small house hand in hand. James rang the doorbell. A woman, who looked to be in her late forties except for her completely gray hair, answered it and smiled a wide, friendly greeting of delighted surprise.

"Oh my goodness, Jimmy. How are you?"

"Fine, Mrs. Jennings - how are you?"

Cashell noticed that the bright smile didn't falter as the woman's gaze traveled over to her.

"You must be Cashell?" The woman stepped forward and leant to embrace Cashell, her arms open wide and her hug friendly and warm.

"Yes, hello," Cashell said as she stepped forward, taken aback that the woman knew her by name. She glanced at James, but her attention went quickly back to Mrs. Jennings.

"When James called he told me he was going to bring a very special person. I was ecstatic," said Mrs. Jennings. "Please, come in."

She moved to the kitchen after they sat down and returned swiftly, armed with a pitcher of lemonade and a tray of glasses. She set the things down on the coffee table, pouring each of them a glass. Cashell took one but James declined.

The tiny house was in pristine condition. Cashell noticed a mantelpiece groaning with photos: mostly of Macy before her accident. She noticed one of James and Macy together, in what looked like homecoming attire. Mindful not to stare too hard at the mantel, she sat back as the other woman took a seat opposite them. James spoke up.

"I told Cashell about Macy and she wanted to meet her."

"Oh goodness, that's wonderful. Our Macy doesn't have many friends. I'm glad you've been able to tell someone about it, honey." Mrs. Jennings's eyes were kind.

James nodded. Cashell reached for his hand and he gripped

it. She was somewhat surprised. Mrs. Jennings's choice of words – being glad he'd "been able to tell someone" – seemed to indicate that not even the rest of the Parker family knew about what had happened. She hated to think he'd kept it a secret all this time, but it seemed as though he must have.

"I think you're working on the forgiveness I been trying to tell you about all these years. Takes a special woman to get you to start thinking the right way. I'm so glad. Cashell, dear, what is it that you do?"

"Um, I'm a writer for the team - communications manager type."

"Oh. That sounds really nice." The older lady poured herself some more lemonade. "Are you guys thinking about getting married?"

Cashell almost choked on her drink, as James looked like a deer in the headlights.

"What? – oh no, ma'am." She smiled awkwardly at their inquisitor as she scooted to the edge of the sofa and put her drink down, afraid she'd drop it.

"I don't see why not. He's a good guy, Cashell. Macy always got mixed up with the bad boys: she could never seem to keep her hands off a bad boy when she met him. James was right there in front of her and she just looked right over his tall head so to speak." Mrs. Jennings's laughed ruefully and stood. "I tell you what, if I were twenty years younger, I'd steal James myself. Don't sleep on this man, girl."

Cashell smiled. It was evident that the woman was still hurting over her daughter's decisions, and while James looked embarrassed, he also looked like he felt for her. Regret abounded. The lady smiled sadly.

"Let me see, I'll just call Macy in here. She's out back."

Before Cashell could say anything, she hurried out through the kitchen. There must have been a back door, because a slam reverberated throughout the tiny house.

It was only a few moments before the door slammed again, not as hard this time, and heavy footsteps pounded in through the kitchen. Cashell stood when James did.

"Jimmeee, Jimmeee, hey Jimmeee!" Out of breath, the heavy-set woman barreled into the living room and wheezed as her eyes lit on James. Mrs. Jennings, not far behind her, hugged her arms.

"Hey, girl." James smiled and visibly steeled himself to withstand the vigor of Macy's embrace. She got him in a bear hug, squeezing him so tight that he looked like he was having trouble breathing, and pulled his face down to plant a sloppy kiss on his cheek. After the hug, she backed up and pummeled him with her fists.

"Oh, wow. How ya doing, Macy?" James gave a forced chuckle, trying to be playful with the girl-woman, but Cashell knew it wasn't genuine.

"Great! Ma got cookie?" Macy said, turning to her mother expectantly.

"All right - two cookies, that's it." Mrs. Jennings folded her arms.

No longer interested in James, Macy took off for the kitchen again.

"Ma, Ma, Ma? Ho bout tree?"

"No, not three, two. We'll have lunch soon. I counted the cookies this morning, Macy," Mrs. Jennings called after her daughter in warning. She smiled tightly at the two of them.

"How is she doing?" James put his hands in his pockets and moved over to the mantelpiece that Cashell had been looking at earlier. He pulled down the homecoming picture to stare at the two of them.

"Oh, she's fine, James. The new medication makes her hungry all the time, that's all. She's gaining weight, but she gets so angry when I set limits..."

James nodded. Cashell continued to stand there until Macy returned, holding a crumbling cookie in each hand. She finished off the last bites with a loud chomp, cookie crumbs and chocolate covering her face as the remnants scattered to the floor.

"Ma, one mo pleas..."

"No, Macy - and you were very rude just now. James brought his friend Cashell with him - did you greet her?"

"Castle?" Macy repeated, nonplussed.

Cashell smiled as Macy's face lit up. It could have been much worse: she'd answer to 'Castle' any day. She wondered for a second why James had just moved closer to her - then she remembered the hug Macy had given him earlier. James spoke up: "Macy, wait, Cashell can't be hugged too tight. She – uh – her arm hurts, okay?"

Cashell smiled, grateful that he hadn't mentioned her heart condition. Her arm was actually fine now, but at that moment, with Macy regarding her as if she were the coveted third cookie, Cashell was thankful for any excuse not to be embraced. "Oh, her arm hurt?" Macy spoke up. "She got a booboo?"

"Yes, she has a booboo." Cashell smiled when James looked down at her, conveying with his eyes that the explanation was the best he could muster on the spot.

"Macy, hey, uh, how about a group hug?"

Macy laughed and squealed. "Group hug!" she sang, diving at the two of them. Just in time, James held Cashell in his arms, creating an almost forcefield-like cocoon of protection around her so Macy couldn't squeeze her to death. He was less worried about her bruise than about her heart. Somehow, their innocent group embrace made Cashell sad.

When the three parted, Mrs. Jennings smiled at Cashell before addressing Macy. "Go back outside now, honey. I'll call you when lunch is ready, okay?"

"Kay Ma... bye Castle, bye Jimmeee."

After saying their goodbyes, they all sat again. James was the first to speak.

"Do you need anything, Mrs. Jennings? I just wanted to say hello and let you meet Cashell - see how things are going and all. I'm, uh, I'm sorry I haven't been by since I moved back to Virginia. In college, you guys were like my second family. I appreciated everything. I want to try to stay in touch..."

"Of course we don't need anything," the woman replied, her eyes misting over. "We have everything you've already given us, which is much too much. I mean, if you brought some patience along in that rental car of yours, more of that couldn't ever hurt, but you couldn't bring that, could you?" She gave a slightly sad laugh.

James shook his head gloomily.

"Stop looking so sad, honey. You've got your whole life ahead of you. Try not to take life so serious. Now, I want you to go back to Washington and I want you to do something that makes me proud of you. And I want you to stop sending money each month."

Cashell listened but pretended to study her drink.

"Okay, but, uh…"

"But nothing," Mrs. Jennings said firmly. "You don't owe us anything, James. This is not your fault. Cashell, honey, can you tell him this isn't his fault?"

She turned to look at Cashell, who nodded mutely.

"Were you able to find any good folks from the home health agency for Macy?" James asked.

"I have a couple who come by on rotation, so I can have a little respite and they don't get burnt out," Mrs. Jennings replied. "It's hard to keep them, though. It usually just takes one big Macy tantrum to scare them off. But I think I've found two now that are godsends. I try not to let her overtax them. My sister helps, and some people at our church. The kids in Sunday school are awesome with her…"

She paused. "James, listen to me. I can't tell you forever that this is not your fault. You have to believe it in your heart. You have to believe that you are a good person, and that you did the right thing. I thank you for trying to support us financially but you don't owe us. People make decisions, and more often than not they're the wrong ones. Most of the time that can't be helped, but it's upsetting when those decisions could have been prevented. People just don't know how their choices can impact everyone around them."

"I try to tell him that, Mrs. Jennings," Cashell spoke up.

"Thank you, honey. Now James, I want you to move on with your life. And I'll always be grateful to you for helping us."

"And Kirk?" James uttered.

Mrs. Jennings took a deep breath. "Kirk and I talk once every few weeks. He's doing okay."

James nodded. Mrs. Jennings stood up and moved to embrace him. She hugged Cashell, too, before opening the door.

"Jimmeee, Jimmeee?" Macy ran from the other end of the house and pummeled him again. "Bye Jimmeee."

"Bye, Macy." James hugged her. Macy stood back and when her mother wiped the drool from her mouth, she batted her hand away in annoyance. Then she was off again, headed for some other part of her backyard oasis. Cashell squinted into the sun as she raced away.

"I'll see you." James waved again and bent to kiss Mrs. Jennings on the cheek. As he made his way to the car, the older woman placed an arm around Cashell's shoulder and whispered close to her ear.

"You know the fact that you're here means he's closing this chapter on us, don't you?"

Cashell hadn't known that, but what could she say? It had been her idea to come there, not his.

"Think about what I'm saying, now. He's never brought a single girl here, ever. Not one - not even a Temporary Tiffany at Christmas time."

The two women shared a giggle, but now Cashell was feeling sorry she'd made him come here. As if reading her mind, Mrs. Jennings continued:

"Don't wallow, honey. This was good for him. You are good for him. I don't know you that well, but you seem real special. Be good to him - take care of him, okay?"

"Okay," Cashell nodded. Somehow, she felt like she was enacting a meeting that she would normally have expected to have with James's real mother. This woman before her was almost a surrogate. Mrs. Jennings cared deeply about James, having known him throughout his college life.

"He's ready. Life is fleeting at best," Mrs. Jennings said, squeezing Cashell's hand and giving her a nudge toward the car where James was waiting. He opened the door for her and she climbed inside. He waved one last time and pulled away from the curb.

They drove in silence for a few minutes. At last, Cashell spoke.

"Thank you for allowing me to come here with you."

"Thanks for coming. I just wanted to find some peace in that."

"Sometimes there is no peace: only acceptance."

"Really? Hmm. You have the greatest one liners."

Cashell laughed. "I'm a writer." She wished right then she could've been a time traveler instead, like the creation of her beloved H. G. Wells. She would have warned Macy - and Kirk her brother, for that matter - of their grave error. Only then, she reflected, Macy and James might have had their happy ending after all, and she herself wouldn't have had this chance to know him at all. She watched his profile, pondering.

"Think you can write the happy ending to the story of me and you?" James asked softly.

"I come up with some different ones about us every day."

"How many are you up to?"

"Oh, I don't know…" She tempered her runaway imaginings by saying a lower number. "About four or five?" No need to reveal the extent of her daydreaming pastime.

James gave an enigmatic smile.

29

What's up, Doc?

THE WEEKEND WAS OVER AND Cashell was glad. Waiting in the doctor's office for a routine checkup, she tried to catch up on any work she could do on her phone, but James's numerous dilemmas were consuming her thoughts. She found herself thinking about everything that had happened, from visiting Macy and her mother to the less uplifting time that followed: a second attempt at visiting James's mother. Once again, it had not gone as he had hoped, and she hadn't been sure what to advise. He did get to see her, to talk to her and introduce Cashell, but she surmised that may be all he'd ever be able to do.

Cashell couldn't be certain about whether James wanted more of a relationship with his mother – well, of course he did, but only under the right circumstances. The main reason he didn't pursue the matter, she was sure, was that disrupting the status quo would mean declaration of an all-out legal battle, going toe to toe with his brother. And who in their right mind would want to do a thing like that if they could possibly avoid it?

Just thinking about Bobby made her skin crawl. There was, however, one practical reason that he was still on her mind. When James had asked to pay his mother's nursing home bill, his request had been denied. He'd asked for more details about it, but patient privacy rules meant the only response he got from the administrator was a disapproving look and dismissive wave. They'd simply assured him that everything was fine with her bill, but hadn't explained why, just a week or so after they'd declared non-receipt of payments, everything was suddenly fine. That unnerved James, and Cashell too. They'd spent the entire ride home discussing it, and revisited it again later that day, but the only conclusion they could reach was that Bobby had somehow scared up some money for the tab — that or he'd simply lied about the bill in an attempt to get some hard cash out of James.

She wanted to do something to help, but she remembered dismally that she'd forbidden Brandon to search for any more information about James or his family after the near-disastrous result of her intern's prior research. As their relationship developed, James's past had gradually become sacred territory, not to be messed with.

She would make sure that all details of Macy and her family stayed hidden from public scrutiny. Mrs. Jennings herself found no fault with James, because there was no culpability to be found; but that wouldn't stop the media from turning it into something scandalous if they got their hands on it. She scoured the internet for new coverage but didn't find much. It seemed that most stories didn't last long before natural disasters and political imbroglios swept the media's attention elsewhere.

Cashell set her phone down, her eyes glazing over from all the scrolling. She would protect James with everything in her, right down to her last breath.

If there was one positive aspect of their visit with James's mother, it was that the older woman hadn't exhibited any hint of the violent outburst James had described from his first visit. Mrs. Banks had been docile and quiet this time, but she didn't speak at all. James had tried to feed her some applesauce but she wasn't hungry.

Notwithstanding his sadness about his mother and her steady decline in health, she had to hand it to him: James was a trouper. His ability to mentally put it all aside, separate life from work and do well for his team was just part of his character. She supposed they were alike that way. She had her health issues, but she refused to let them keep her from living and enjoying life. No matter what, she kept giving it her all each and every time God saw fit to wake her up for another day.

Cashell sat on the doctor's examination table in her oh-so-pretty - and drafty - medical gown. She blew out a bored breath. The longer she sat there, the harder it was to resist scratching every patch of sticky residue left on her skin from the telemetry leads the nurse had placed on her chest and abdomen earlier that afternoon. Each of the leads monitored and measured her cardiac rhythm. The sticky pads holding them in place had since been removed, but the itching would continue until she could take a shower. It always annoyed her, although she should really be used to it by now considering all the years she'd been going through this exact same procedure. Some of the little round white stickers even managed to find their way home with her occasionally, ending up on the shower floor.

The door swung open and Cashell resisted the urge to yell 'hallelujah'. Pretending she hadn't been musing about her doctor's lack of punctuality, she mustered a smile, but the cheery look wasn't returned. On the contrary, the look her doctor gave her said the news wasn't good. It wasn't the you're-going-to-die look: it was the what-on-earth-have-you-been-doing-for-the-last-few-days look. The readout from the cardiac monitor, coupled with her blood pressure levels and other stats, likely betrayed more activity than she'd admitted to.

Over-indulging was fun, but over the course of the last two weeks she had been in full Parker mode: the wonderful fried egg Cole placed on top of her veggie burger, all the sweets, the shaved ice, the rich snacks, buttery or cheesy popcorn (take your pick) during movie night, already-sweet grilled peaches with a little brown sugar… If this doctor could just experience Cole's cooking, maybe she'd be a little more sympathetic about Cashell's numbers. Her mouth watered just thinking about hanging around this family for the foreseeable future. How could she pass up those delights? She'd had a most wonderful time with them, and thus had already resolved to suck it up and bear whatever disapproving looks she had to endure from her doctor.

"So," her doctor began. "I assume you know, Cashell, that these numbers are unusual to say the least. Do you have anything to say about it?"

"Not really, doctor." Cashell looked down, playing with the hem of her robe, slightly shamefaced.

"Your heart numbers are impeccable."

Cashell did a double take. "They are?"

She looked up in disbelief and held out her hand to receive the paper with the various readings. They shared a laugh before her doctor became stern.

"Your heart numbers are great, which is obviously surprising. Your other numbers, not so much."

"Oh well, please. I can fix that with my diet," said Cashell, relieved. "I spent some time with friends and one of them is a chef. It was so good…" She trailed off dreamily, continuing to look away. She didn't understand all of her numbers, but she understood enough.

"Really? Just diet, Cashell? You didn't get another puppy, did you?"

Cashell made a face and gave the paper back to the older woman, remaining seated on the bed. The readings simply translated to no sugar or salt for the rest of the week. She'd have to opt for the salad: more veggies, nothing fried and a moratorium on the high calorie dressing she loved to drench her salad in. Oh, and she'd have to get back on her water regimen. Old hat really: all the things she'd been doing so diligently until she'd met James Parker.

"A puppy - really?" Cashell scoffed. "I haven't had a puppy since I was… thirteen."

"Yes, and do you remember why you haven't had a puppy since eighth grade?"

Abashed, Cashell shrugged, somewhat needled at the direction her doctor was taking the conversation. Kira Parker's drama paled in comparison. In Cashell's mind, the food and the falling in love constituted living. So what if she'd had too much sugar and salt, or didn't get quite enough exercise? Be that as it may, she'd been living, and she'd had such an awesome time doing so that she really didn't want anything to mar her fantastic memories. Even the incident with Bobby Banks paled into insignificance when she recalled James's soft, caressing touch, or the feeling of relief when she'd finally heard his emotional disclosure about the past that still haunted him.

"I met someone," she admitted.

"That's great," replied her doctor dryly. "I'm excited for you... but is it the right person?"

Cashell glared. "I'm sorry - did I miss something? When did you trade in your MD credentials for a relationship counselor qualification?"

"I'm just reminding you that your – ah, habits in making unwise choices at certain times have been known to have a direct and often negative impact on your health."

"Well, doctor, I can't protect myself from everything," Cashell retorted. "I've just been living, and you can't expect me to live in the sort of bubble you and my family are suggesting." She folded her arms.

"That's not what I'm saying..."

"Sounds like it to me." Cashell took a deep calming breath. She couldn't don her shirt in front of her doctor, she was too modest for that, but she could at least get off the bed and slide back into her six-inch heels. With the added height came a confidence boost.

She liked her doctor well enough, but the woman was older, her attitude often reminding Cashell of her own father's. Cashell was astounded she hadn't yet retired. She and Cashell's dad were stuck in the same time warp with some very old-fashioned thinking, plus a common tendency to dispense unsolicited advice. Every appointment felt like when you visited a mechanic for a simple oil change and got handed a list of everything else that was wrong with your vehicle to boot. She'd prefer to just let it all fall apart. At least that way she would have lived and had a very fun time en route to her demise, she mused. She did not need this right now. Although her doctor was stern and serious, Cashell decided not to let her project her ideals into her own love life.

"When your dog died, you had a mild heart attack," the doctor reminded her.

"I was starting junior high school - it was a stressful time," Cashell protested. "I'd been homeschooled for many years, in and out of hospitals for most of my childhood, and finally I was getting the chance to go to public school. I'm much better equipped to handle everyday adversity nowadays. I am an adult... Are we seriously having this conversation?"

"I'm just saying, Cashell. Go slow. Take your time. Pace yourself."

"Thanks. Oh, and I'm running low on blood thinners."

"I'll write you a prescription and chat about our visit with Dr. Williams later."

"Sounds good." She was contemplating whether or not to speak to her primary doctor herself, about whether she was required to keep seeing this woman at all. Cashell was a strong adult: a fighter. A rocky relationship and a little broken heartedness would not take her out.

As soon as the doctor left her alone, Cashell removed the stupid drafty gown, balling it up and tossing it into the plastic-lined laundry bin across the room. She dressed again, then hurried to the elevators and out into the bright afternoon sun to fetch her car.

Once outside, she took a deep cleansing breath, squinting in the bright sun. The air was growing cooler, the season beginning to change... and she was in love.

Next thing she knew, she saw James waiting by her car and she wanted to cry. Overjoyed at the sight of him, her pent-up frustration vaporized instantly when a grin split his face. Her own smile took over and she took off running — well, she walked as fast as she could - into his arms. In a single movement he scooped her up, lifting her off her feet.

Cashell and James decided to head to Cole's restaurant. It was located in downtown Alexandria, not far from where Allontis and Leedra worked over at the Anchored Empowerment Center. Cashell was glad to be alone with her thoughts while the two of them drove over in separate cars. She was still surprised that he'd met her after her appointment. The excitement at spotting James there waiting for her still lingered, but it was significantly tempered by the words of her doctor ringing in her ears.

She hated that she was this preoccupied. Why was it so easy to doubt that James was the man for her, when she'd just decided 'for sure' over the previous weekend that he was? The fact was that she hadn't really decided whether he was or was not: she just kind of fell in love. She planned none of it and she also couldn't stop it. Things just happened. Honestly, she believed she'd fallen in love with him while they were dancing on the very first night they'd met.

After being welcomed as old friends and seated at the best table, tucked away from the busy entrance, she focused on her tablemate.

"What are you in the mood for?" he asked.

"Hmmm... probably salad." She perused the menu, pretending she didn't know exactly where her actual favorite item was listed. In fact, she'd met Cole and eaten at his restaurant years ago, when it first opened. Her doctor had said her numbers were wonky just this afternoon, so she'd take this opportunity to practice restraint. She couldn't do a darn thing to reign in her wayward heart, but at least her appetite was one thing she could keep in check. She pushed the menu aside, placing it at the edge of the table before looking up to find James watching her.

"Salad? Are you on a diet?" he asked skeptically.

"I need to be."

The eyebrows shot up. "You're joking, right?"

"Could we talk about something else?"

James put down his own menu and smiled at her.

"Okay... well, your reaction at the hospital today surprised me. I'm grateful you were happy to see me, but what was that all about?"

He grabbed her hand before she could sit back and put them in her lap. He tugged a little and she was forced to lean closer and put her elbow on the table.

"Just my doctor's usual antiquated bedside manner."

"Are you sure?" James looked at her with a searching expression. "Look. Game opener is tomorrow, things will get busy, and you'll have articles to finish. I wanted to make tonight special."

"Really?"

"Yes."

"Why?"

Before James could respond, Cole came out to the table to greet them. Cashell lifted her face to receive his cordial kiss on the cheek, and James shook his hand - but his other hand never let go of hers. A young man followed Cole to set down a pair of drinks: raspberry lemonade for her and root beer for James. It was a simple yet thoughtful welcoming gesture: Cole knew each of his guests well and prided himself on remembering the food and beverage selections which kept them coming back. Cole's place was like a live version of the popular television show Cheers - only she was sure he had way better food. She was impressed that he had remembered her favorite drink from her visit so long ago.

"I'm sorry, can I just have some water?" She extracted her hand from James's grasp and set the drink back firmly at the end of the table.

James's expression dimmed but he didn't say anything.

"Oh. Sure. You feel all right?" Cole asked, surprised.

"Yes, I'm fine, all right?" She tried to keep the hiss out of her voice, but it was there. Cole gazed at her a moment, then looked at James questioningly, but otherwise didn't say anything. He excused himself politely, took their order, and went back into the kitchen.

When Cole left, James reached for her hand again.

"Cash, you have to tell me what's going on. Did something happen in the doctor's office?"

And there she was thinking her first answer had sufficed.

"It's fine, I was just annoyed at my doctor. Her thoughts can be rather primitive sometimes – she's a bit set in her ways."

"About your prognosis?"

"No – actually, she says my heart is doing great. It's getting stronger."

"Really? That's wonderful. I've been in prayer about that."

"You have?" She looked up, feeling suddenly shy and very self-conscious. Where had her own faith gone, and why did his surprise her?

"Don't look so shocked. I do pray for the safety of my family and the people I love, like you."

He had her full attention now. She responded with a nervous chuckle. "Okay."

"Okay? Let me repeat that: I just said 'people I love, like you'. And you said 'okay'? I'm wounded."

"You - you said it in a very roundabout way." What exactly was she testing?

James leaned further across the table and took her hand in his once more, staring meaningfully into her eyes.

"I love you, Cashell Bruer."

"Okay."

James's frown returned. He stood and walked around to sit on her side of the booth. His arm came around her gently, and when she looked at him, he wiped away her tears with the pad of his thumb.

"I can't promise all our days together will be easy, but I've loved having you with me the last few days. I want to get closer to you, be your boyfriend and love you, eventually get married. How's that?"

"Okay." She laughed, because this time she really was at a

loss for words. 'Okay' was the only thing she could think of.

"I see I'll have to get the writer a new thesaurus," James laughed. "See, this is hard for me too. I haven't loved anyone before. I know now that I didn't love Macy. I just felt like I ought to. Thing is, I'm just afraid, Cash."

"I'm afraid, too," she replied softly.

"There you go: some more words. That was good honey - yay."

They shared a laugh and she moved closer to him, her arm reaching over to rest against his chest.

"I want to live as long as I can," she whispered.

"When this heart gives out, we'll do what we gotta do to get you a new one," he assured her.

She wondered if he knew that he'd just named the root of her fear: that she'd give out as soon as life got good. Right then, it was really good. To be perfectly frank, everything had been wonderful since she'd met him. The night of her birthday had marked the first night she had really lived. She didn't want to set that much store by James - she didn't want to omit God's hand in all of this; but life wasn't fair. She just wanted a fighting chance. Perhaps she was just frightened by the awareness of being on the verge of something so wonderful. That would explain the constant push-back her heart gave her. Cashell brought her attention back to James and spoke:

"That's what my doctor says is bad for me."

"What?" James asked, a little wrongfooted.

"A relationship with the wrong person. I had a puppy in the eighth grade. He was already sickly, I knew that when I got him. He died and I was devastated. I went into a coma for a week."

James was quiet for a moment. "Am I the proverbial puppy?" he asked.

"I guess my doctor thinks so, but it's not that way to me."

"Aren't you the only one whose opinion on that matters?"

"Of course, James, but I'm just trying to see reason. I didn't expect to fall in love. It just... happened."

"To me, too," he replied.

She nodded, suddenly realizing that there was nothing to be resolved. She loved him, and he was trying to be real about his feelings - and that was all she cared about. Her heart issues and her doctor's well-meaning yet wrong-direction counsel were just some rain on her parade. She had to stop buying into the devil's lies.

James gripped her hand to keep her attention focused on his words. "Look at me. Nobody is perfect. I love you, and I want you to know that no matter what. The rest of it will play out in the weeks to come."

She nodded. "I love you, too."

She closed her eyes and tilted her head back as he leaned over to her, his lips fastened to hers and he delivered the best kisses she'd ever had.

When Cole came around a second time, she apologized for her sharp words and, ever the gentleman, he assured her there was no need for an apology. In a burst of self-confidence, she ordered grilled chicken on top of her salad. James ordered the same, and this small show of solidarity warmed her heart still more.

When Cole left to prepare their food, James remained on her side of the cozy booth. They barely touched their meals: it was difficult to eat as they held on to one another's hands, talked and made plans. Their future looked like a bright one. She knew that if he could let go of his past and move on, she could deal with her heart condition. Right then and there, she resolved to do right, eat right, and allow herself to dream of whatever God had in store.

30
Game Time

THE PRESEASON RUSHED BY IN a blur. Four weeks of Thursday night games and one on a Saturday night showcased the usual grandstanding and showing off; and while a few rejects had gotten their walking papers, the core of the team remained intact. There was the standard round of minor injuries and petty squabbles on the field, but as the preseason drew to a close, everyone had found their groove and their proper place. In amongst all the other shuffling, Cashell's man - she really liked the sound of that - was chosen as starting quarterback. She was so proud of him. He'd worked particularly hard over the year and had pulled ahead, while Braxton's performance continued to be held back by his drinking. Sadly, he just could not seem to shake the old demons: he was letting them rule him.

Cashell felt a jolt of anxiety every time Braxton and James were around each other. She had even spoken with the management as tactfully as she could about the team dynamics and tried to raise the possibility of a reshuffle, but her recommendations had been summarily dismissed. She also couldn't say too much about either man's character, because when her relationship with James came to light – which couldn't be too much longer now - they would all come to know where her bias lay. While there wasn't an official rule against their dating, she knew her professional objectivity would be compromised as soon as the two of them went public.

Before each game, the team's press room was a loud and crazy frenzy of activity, with pregame interviews and hustle and bustle all around. Cashell watched the journalists, mostly men, nervously adjusting their ties, rehearsing questions and trying not to fawn too much over their favorite players. Naturally, when all geared up, the football guys were by far the biggest and tallest men in the room. Even the shorter running backs looked buff, tall and larger than life next to the newscasters, who likely played sports themselves but hadn't been good enough - or lucky enough - to get a contract. Most of them, it had to be said, lived vicariously through their interview subjects.

Cashell had her own special personnel teams lined up for game day: to corral the press, to control access to the players and to cut off that access whenever it was time to wrap up and let the team get back to the business of playing ball. This room was the domain of the press, but beyond these walls they'd only be allowed onto the edges of the field for few moments before being shepherded back to their posts until halftime. At that point, Cashell would assign permissions to interview the coach and other players, depending on who had made the key plays.

Cashell smiled as she caught sight of her intern Brandon, who was having the time of his life. Brandon's assigned job – if he could find the time to do it in between his countless selfies, she thought wryly - was to upload game-day videos and personal stories to the team's social media outlets. His input would allow their fan base to interact with their favorite players, get to know them on a more personal level and learn about their game day regimen. It all added to the fan-user experience. Watching him, Cashell contemplated with some satisfaction how well the social media strategy she had spent all that effort creating was playing out. It felt good to be good at your job.

Though James and Cashell had managed not to tell anyone about their relationship for the duration of their whirlwind summer romance, it was becoming clear that the need to keep quiet was over. Any and every time she looked his way, she found him staring back at her more and more openly. The constant commotion downstairs faded into white noise whenever they saw each other.

"Guess I missed a golden opportunity, huh?"

A large hand shoved Cashell roughly off balance. She stumbled, grabbing for the all-access badge that dangled around her neck to make sure it was safe, then turned in startled annoyance to see who had bumped her. She had a pretty strong guess in mind. Nevertheless, she stared incredulously as Braxton's face leered back at her. What did he mean by 'golden opportunity'?

"Yo, what's up with you, Braxton? Game hasn't even started yet."

James seemed to teleport himself to her side in a matter of seconds, squaring up to Brax in readiness to defend her.

"I'm gonna go. Good luck," Cashell said, trying to address both of them. She wasn't needed in the press room for quite a while yet, anyway. It would soon be time for the team to run out, for fireworks and the National Anthem. She and James would have plenty of time to talk afterwards.

"You gonna give him a kiss for good luck?" Brax taunted, making wet sloppy kissing sounds as Cashell turned to leave.

James rounded on him. "Grow up, man, would you?"

"Come here, Cash - why you with this loser?" Brax reached out a hand to grab her. Before either of them had time to register what was happening, James hit the extended hand so hard that Braxton reared back, clutching it and howling in pain.

"My hand, man - my throwing hand!"

Cashell was alarmed as the commotion drew the attention of some security personnel, who hurried over flanked by the injury team. The figure of Bill, the team manager, loomed into view behind them.

"In the office, now. You two. Everyone else get out on the field."

Braxton moved first to follow Bill and James followed too, but not before quietly addressing Cashell.

"I'll see you tonight. Tell my family hey, okay?"

She nodded. For some reason she couldn't put her finger on,

her nervousness mounted. She saw the two players walk down the hall alone with Bill. Suddenly feeling very eerie about the whole situation, she started to follow them, keeping a safe distance; but hesitated after a few paces. Maybe she'd just wait for him here. The noise of the press room had died down as the players filed out, and now there was complete quiet: nothing but the distant roar of the crowd. Cashell pulled out her phone and tried to distract herself with checking the team's Twitter feed – Brandon was uploading stats like there was no tomorrow, she noted approvingly – but her mind kept wandering back to what could be going on in the manager's office. The minutes dragged on.

After what felt like an age, Cashell decided that she should really find out how things were going between the players and the manager. This was taking too long, she thought, as she stood and began walking down the lengthy corridor that led from the press room to the administrative offices. The game was just minutes from starting and everyone connected with the team was already up on the field – well, almost everyone – so the hall was dim, lit by only one or two security lights.

As she turned the corner, a familiar figure dressed in gray sweats and a black hoodie stepped out of the shadow of a doorway, blocking her path.

"What are you doing here?" Cashell said, surprising herself with how calm she sounded. She got a sinking feeling as Bobby's cold eyes stared back at her.

"Came to see your boyfriend play," he replied softly.

"W-why?"

"'Wha-wha-why?'" Bobby mimicked mockingly. "You ask a lot of questions, missy." Cashell took a step back as he moved menacingly forward.

"Do I scare you?

"No," she returned evenly. "I'm scared for what James will do to you. I- I tried to be nice inviting you to our family - "

"'Our family', huh?" Bobby interrupted. "Well then. So you and Jay official now or what?

"No. I mean…" She didn't know what she meant. Her brain began to cloud over with panic. She hoped she didn't faint.

"Oh, so this is just wishful thinking, am I right?" Bobby sneered.

Cashell kept her cool. "I'm saying that when you first came to the house, we wanted to try to get to know you, but then…"

"But then…" he repeated. "my own brother dragged me out of the house like I was some dog he found on the street," Bobby finished. "Ain't that a fine way to treat your own brother? Well, guess what? It won't be happening again."

Bobby pulled up his hoodie. It was only a slight move, but effective: it showed all she needed to see. There, tucked into the waistband of his sweatpants, was the butt of a gun.

Cashell's face fell as her concern for James escalated several notches. The danger she herself was currently in didn't even register. Intent on trying warm James about his brother, she tried to turn and run, but strong arms caught her around her neck in a chokehold. Bobby dragged her down the hall into one of the many darkened corridors. She gasped for breath as he muttered awful things in her ear, about what he'd do to James, what he would do to her if she didn't stop struggling against him.

"Please," she managed to get out. With every move, his hold tightened.

"You too good for me, huh, Cash?" he hissed in her ear.

If she could only keep her head, she thought, she could just collapse, a dead weight, play dead… but she was starting to become frightened about the lack of air while getting increasingly worried about what would happen to James. Bobby maintained the chokehold. She wouldn't last much longer. She tried to reach her phone, but it slid from her grasp and clattered to the floor. As her lungs struggled to give her the oxygen she needed, her eyes closed as her vision faded to black. Her heart beat wildly in her chest, and in desperation she felt it slowing before she succumbed to nothingness.

James left the meeting room angrier than when he went in. He couldn't figure out why the coach wanted to talk to him – and right now of all times. They had a game to play, and if it were delayed, their team could be penalized. In short, this was not the way he had wanted to start the official season.

The hall was quiet. There was a chill in the air, and he could hear the distant roar of the crowd as they awaited the start of the great American pastime. Regardless of what was going on in his life, he'd always had football. Through Momma G's cancer, through the revelations about his biological mother's illness, and now through Cashell's heart problems, he always kept coming back to the game. It had been the one constant through all of the turmoil life had thrown at him, he reflected. He loved it, almost as much as he loved Cashell. Imagine that: she'd come and eclipsed everything... even football.

As he walked briskly back along the hall deep in thought, he noticed something on the ground and bent to pick it up. Examining the cell phone in his hand, his heart sank. He knew Cashell's phone. She would never have dropped it: she always kept it with her. Always.

With a belly that felt like it was full of ice, he half-jogged further down the hall until he saw her. She was crumpled on the ground, unmoving.

"Cashell, what – ?"

Numbly, he knelt beside her and felt gingerly for a pulse. He tore off the bulky protective padding he still had on and threw it impatiently aside. Rolling Cashell carefully onto her back, he regarded her pale face. She looked... lifeless.

He bent down. His shaky hands hovered over her chest. He reached for the phone again, dialed Dexter's number and set the phone aside, on speakerphone.

"Dex – Dexter?"

"What? James? Why aren't you playing?" His brother's voice crackled tinnily in the echoing hallway. "They said there's some kind of delay. Are you okay?"

"Cashell's hurt," James croaked. His voice had suddenly deserted him. "I need you in the locker room, now. C-can I do CPR on her?"

"What?" A note of alarm entered Dexter's voice.

"Can I?"

"Of course, of course. Just like normal. You can't worry about it hurting, 'cause it will… but what happened? Why isn't she breathing?"

"I don't know. I don't know. Get down here, please," James begged, fighting tears. "Please hurry."

"Okay. I'm on my way."

James didn't' bother to click off the phone. He eyed his own hands as they shook before threading his fingers together in the CPR position, he prayed. He was afraid of hurting her. His hands shook more still, but he found some hypnotic comfort in the rhythmic pushing and counting of chest compressions. He made himself concentrate on watching for any change in Cashell's face as he pressed down hard. Every single push felt like he was pumping his own heart. As he completed the first round of chest compressions, he muttered the only words that came to mind: the Lord's Prayer. "Our Father" – push – "who art in Heaven" – push…

"What happened to you, babe, please?"

Tears stung his eyes. Football was nothing. He felt like he should take it back, whatever he'd been thinking about it earlier, because it was nothing – nothing compared to her. He couldn't live without her. Tucked away deep in his locker upstairs was a ring in a velvet box. Tonight, after this first game, he had planned to propose at dinner, with his family gathered all around. Now, as he started on the next round of CPR, he wondered whether he'd get that chance.

He saw someone approaching and thought for a moment that it was Dexter, but it wasn't. As he registered who it was, James felt sick with rage, but he managed to shove the feeling aside and just kept his fingers flexing, doing what he'd set out to do: save Cashell's life.

"Shame what happened here," came a familiar voice. "I don't know, Boss, she look dead to me. What you think?"

James didn't need a big reveal to know who spoke from beneath the black hood. He would deal with Bobby in due course, but right then he forced himself to keep working on Cashell, not letting his brother's words stop him. She would live. He would make sure of it. Right then, though, he wasn't so sure about Bobby's mortality. As soon as he was through, he'd see about that.

He placed two fingers under the back of Cashell's neck and breathed air into her mouth while holding her nose closed. Dexter had taught him the method. He pressed her chest again, waited, and repeated, silently pleading with her to wake...

After what seemed like an eternity, Cashell's head rolled to one side and bobbed a little. With a start, she gasped and coughed weakly. Giddy with relief, James pulled her up into his arms, cradling her and murmuring reassurances that she was going to be okay. She looked into his eyes and he smiled. He leaned back and breathed deeply as he gazed down at her.

"Why you scare me like that?" he joked, but he knew this was no joking matter.

Her eyelids flickered. "I – Bobby..."

"Yeah, he's right here."

She looked startled and she tried to turn to see him, but weakness and exhaustion overtook her. "Please get help, James, please leave this. He..."

"He's a coward," James said, cutting her off. "Ain't that right, bruh?" he added, imitating the turn of phrase his brother had used on him.

Bobby stood and so did James.

"You come to take me out?" James asked softly. After the burst of relief that Cashell was all right, the old rage was taking over again. This man had almost killed his beloved and he could barely think straight beyond the knowledge of that fact

In an instant, he fully understood why Macy's brother Kirk

was in jail: why he'd felt he had to kill the person who had rendered his sister unable to care for herself and stolen her hopes, dreams and future. James understood, because at that moment he felt exactly the same way. Part of him wanted to justify the action. That little voice whispered that going to jail would be worth it, if he could just earn some vengeance for the wrongs done to Cashell. He asked God to guide his actions; but it was a halfhearted plea, lacking the conviction he'd put into the prayers about saving Cashell's life.

"James, stop, please. Stop it. Not worth it. He has a gun. Please?"

James looked back at her. She sat there on the cold concrete floor. She was still weak. Her heart couldn't take any extra stress. He turned away from her as what she'd just said registered in his brain. He glanced at the waistband of Bobby's jeans. He had to get Cashell to a doctor. Thankfully, Dexter was on his way, but James had saved her this time. At least this time he'd managed to save someone.

Ignoring Cashell's pleas, he rushed his brother and in a flash he had him by the shirt collar.

"You like choking people? Is that what you did to her, huh? How about I choke the life out of you? You like that, you like how this feels?" James hands wrapped around his brother's neck and squeezed - and his brother, fighting to breathe, had the nerve to smile.

"Yeah, I like it. Feels good," Bobby got out with a leer.

"James - please, please?" Cashell was screaming now.

James relaxed his grip. He had reigned in his emotions once, and he knew he could do it again.

"You're a sicko, you know that? How are we even related?" he said in disgust.

He punched Bobby across his jaw, hoping against hope that he could end this; but when he backed up, Bobby only laughed, touching his jaw gingerly and working it back and forth. With an insane grin, he reached into his pants and to James's horror pulled out the gun.

James heard footsteps running down the hall and he turned to see Braxton headed toward them. He was yelling.

"What are you waiting for? Do it already! You take too long! Security is coming, man!"

Confused, James instinctively kept his hands up. The barrel of the gun stared him in the face for a long beat - then it swung away as Bobby pivoted abruptly and trained the gun on Brax. Braxton's face dropped.

As if in slow motion, James moved forward, his hands outstretched. His horrified voice rang in his own ears as Cashell screamed, ducked low and buried her head in her arms. A shot rang out, and Braxton looked down at his stomach in sheer idiotic surprise. He fell to his knees, touching his gut in disbelief, and let out a frustrated roar when his own red-stained hands quivered in front of his face. He fell to the ground. Cashell's screams reverberated against the dark walls. For a long moment, James's eyes met his brother's… then Bobby let the gun fall to the floor as he took off running.

31
Changing Hearts

CASHELL FELT LIKE SHE WAS going to pass out a second time. When she saw Bobby run like the coward he was, relief cascaded over her like a gallon of water tipped over her head. She'd gladly drown in it if she could.

At long last, Dexter arrived, along with some other men in uniforms who rushed to Braxton's side. They loaded Braxton up on to a gurney and rushed him away to the waiting ambulance.

Dexter got down on the floor and examined Cashell closely, speaking to someone behind her. "... should probably go to the doctor, too," she heard.

She nodded, as if he'd been speaking to her. She didn't want to argue, and she didn't have strength enough to do so now in any case. She wasn't surprised to see her brother out of the corner of her eye: Dexter must have been addressing him.

"Are you okay, Cash? Talk to me." Malcolm's eyes were full of fear.

She nodded, but she knew her brother was not convinced.

Before she could utter another word, the door at the end of the hall burst open and six police officers raced for James.

"Put your hands up," one yelled, reaching for his weapon. She saw James comply with the instruction, as confused about what was happening as she was.

"Did you shoot this man?" The officer kicked the gun on the ground well away from James.

"What? No!" James returned heatedly. As if he hadn't heard the answer, the officer moved forward, frisked James and pro-he bent over her, his lips against her forehead.

"Her skin feels cool, Dexter - what's happening? I think Bobby choked her and she passed out, but I don't know how long she was out," James said in panic. "Cashell? Cashell?"

She opened her eyes to look at him again. "I just wanted to tell you that I love you so much."

"I love you more."

She smiled. "You're my puppy."

He managed a worried smile. "Okay, I'll be your puppy, but just know that I'm not sickly, you understand? I'm doing fine. I'm not blind in one eye, and I didn't get hit by a car and I don't chase cars or trucks or runaway balls that roll into the street without looking both ways first."

She smiled again. He always made her laugh, no matter what.

"Go to the hospital," he continued. "I'll handle this. I want to see you when I get there. Do you understand me?"

"We gotta go," Dexter said.

Cashell smiled, though she wasn't really listening anymore. Then she felt hands on her flesh - people putting different cold instruments on her extremities and something on her index finger. The low evening sun blinded her - she couldn't see James anywhere, and she was jostled as they rolled her along, moving quickly. She heard Dexter's voice in the distance, but after a while she just closed her eyes and concentrated hard on getting better. She prayed with her whole heart that the next time she opened them, James would be there without handcuffs and all would be right with her world once more.

32
Foggy Bottoms

———◆———

JAMES WAS HELD IN QUESTIONING for way too long. Almost four hours later, when he finally got to the Fairfax Hospital, his nerves were out of control. Cole had been with him during the questioning session, which had been more like an interrogation. Cole was driving now, because if James had been at the wheel he'd doubtless get a ticket before they reached the end of the street, which would of course prolong everything.

James still had so much to process, but he hadn't had time to reflect on any of it. He was just operating on pure adrenaline, running on fumes, and all the time his thoughts were consumed by Cashell. He was, however, also all over the news. Every single waiting-room television he hurried past showed some image connected to the League, but he simply kept walking until he saw Dexter down the hall, waiting outside Cashell's room.

"What's happening?"

"She's in a coma," his brother replied.

James knees weakened and he sank to the floor in defeat.

Dexter bent down to pull his brother up and embraced him. Cole was there too and he placed a hand on his back. James closed his eyes. Finally, all that had happened that day caught up with him and at last he let the façade of strength drop, standing there in front of his real brothers: his family. They were only ones that weren't out to kill him or do him harm. This entire thing, he thought sadly, was his entire fault.

He sniffled and managed to step back from Dexter, who

issued him an authoritative command.

"You are going to go in there right now and pray with and for her. Tell her it's going to be okay and that she's going to wake up," he instructed.

James nodded, crossing his arms as he tried to concentrate on what his brother was saying. Cole squeezed his shoulders and pointed him in the direction of Cashell's unit. She lay there with the lights turned down, and as he got closer, he noticed that Malcolm was sitting in the corner. James hadn't initially seen him. As always, the darkness was deepest in the corners.

"Malcolm. I'm sorry."

"You can save it." Her brother's face was stony. "Tell her whatever you got to tell her, then get out."

James tightened his lips and nodded. He'd likely be that way too, he reminded himself, if the two men's positions were reversed.

"Can I uh, talk to her alone, please?" James watched as Malcolm stood up slowly - hesitantly. He wouldn't fault Malcolm for anything he wanted to get off his chest. It was fine, whatever he wanted to call him. Even if the man saw fit to throw a punch, James felt beat down and defeated enough that he would probably just take it.

"You're not worth her dying over," Malcolm growled. "Hurry up. I'll be back."

He exited the room, shoving the curtain so hard he nearly ripped it from its rings. James got a glimpse of Cole and Dexter standing anxiously outside before the curtain swung back into place. He looked back at Cashell and began:

"I don't have much time here, Cashell. Your brother is gonna hurt me, but he don't know how much I'm already hurting. I'm hurting because of what all this has caused you. But I know how strong you are. I believe you're strong, super hero strong, as well as beautiful, and I need you more than anything."

James bent down. The medical machinery seemed to crowd

him, obstructing his ability to get closer to her, to touch her. His wrists still hurt from the handcuffs, but at least they were now free to caress her bruised arms and hands, mindful of the IV taped to her arm. He kissed the side of her face: as close as he could get to her lips with the tube taped to her mouth.

He glanced toward the door, wondering if Malcolm was on his way back. While there was still time, James told her all that was on his heart. He described how he felt, and that he'd never felt that way about anyone before. He told her all about how he planned to marry her as soon as she woke up. When Malcolm did reappear, Mr. Bruer was with him. The older man did not greet James at all. James didn't know whether he felt relieved or sad about this lack of acknowledgment - but he'd deal with that later. Malcolm took a seat in the lone chair by Cashell's side. Neither man told James to leave out loud, but they didn't need to.

James bent down once more to whisper in Cashell's ear, telling her he loved her. As much as he hated to leave her side, James knew it was time for him to go.

———◆———

"Is the wedding postponed again?"

Leedra looked at Kira across the table. The girl's large, sad eyes were wide with disappointment: carbon copies of the eyes of the man Leedra was in love with and would marry at the drop of a hat, if only their family's chaos would subside for long enough.

Leedra took a seat at the kitchen table and patted her lap. Kira Parker was getting taller every day, she noted. By the time Kira hit fourteen - or even twelve, for that matter - she'd probably be near six feet. For now, though, Kira still fit on her lap, her long legs dangling with charming childish innocence. She was getting heavier, that much was undeniable; but Leedra knew she'd never tire of the ability to hold one another when they really needed support. Now was one of those times.

Leedra rested her chin atop the girl's head. The sweet smell of kid's shampoo tickled her nostrils. She touched Kira's head, smoothing down the wayward tendrils of hair, and silently asked God to help her find His perfect words to ease her soon-to-be-daughter's troubled mind.

"I love you so much..." Leedra began.

Kira's tearstained face looked up at her and it was almost Leedra's undoing, but with a great effort she managed to keep her own sobs at bay.

"Honey, listen to me," she continued. "I am going to marry your daddy no matter what, and we're going to be a family. You and your father are all I've ever wanted. I have you now, and I'm not letting you go - do you understand? Now, Uncle James just escaped from... being badly hurt. Cashell is sick and needs to get better. We just gotta wait a little longer, so everyone can be a part of this. You want all of our family to be able to take part, don't you?"

Kira sniffled. "What if she doesn't make...?"

Leedra glared at her in warning. "Don't you dare let those words out of your mouth. Where's all this faith you've had every single one of these hard days? She will be fine," she said firmly. "When she wakes up, she'll get stronger and stronger. I would even hazard a guess that she and James are gonna get married, too," she added. "That means I need you to keep it together for just a little while longer. We gotta be strong for Allontis, too, remember. She's... very sad."

"She's sad all the time," signed Kira. "It's... it's tiring being strong."

Leedra resisted the urge to laugh at how true the child's statement really was. Aloud, she said: "What was our memory verse in Sunday School a couple of weeks ago? 'Be not weary in well-doing, for if you faint not...'"

"In due season..." Kira joined in, repeating the beloved familiar Scripture by heart.

"That's right. I know you're tired, baby. Gimme a kiss. I love you."

"I love you too."

They held each other tight. Leedra was quick to recall another night in her life when it had seemed that all was completely lost. Then, too, in the dark basement where she had been held captive, she'd felt like a scared little girl: like everything she had come to love - this family for one - would be taken away from her forever. But Dexter had come for her then, she reminded herself; plus, she herself had fought back.

Her heart hurt for James. She'd known him less than a year, but she could tell he was as kind as Dexter and just as tough. They really were all so much alike a real family, despite their means of coming together. She knew this was all just a test in her life - her wonderful life. Sure, it remained fraught with adversity, she considered, but it was a good life all the same.

They both started when they heard the jangle of keys in the lock and turned to see a weary Dexter trudge in through the kitchen door. After Dexter gave Kira a tight hug and kiss goodnight, Leedra ushered the girl to her room, promising to come back and tuck her in as soon as she'd made her father a little snack. Dexter was strangely quiet as he took the seat she'd vacated at the table.

As it was almost morning, Leedra quickly made coffee and covered all her freshly-baked goodies with foil to warm them in the toaster oven. She'd made blueberry and lemon scones, muffins, and a big loaf of soft raisin-cranberry bread with a sugary top. She fetched her pre-prepared icing and zapped it for a few seconds in the microwave to soften it, then poured it into an exquisitely patterned gravy boat normally reserved for the holidays. With a flourish, she placed the delectable spread on the table before him.

As soon as she finished, Dexter pulled her to him, clasping his hands around her hips and nuzzling into her neck. "Are you all right?" he asked.

"Of course, I'm fine," she returned. "How are you? And James - where is he?"

"He's staying at the hospital. Cole is there with him, just in case he and Malcolm decide to duke it out - or Mr. Bruer, come to think of it. I'm going to return in a few hours, get some sleep. We're gonna take shifts. Kira okay?"

Leedra nodded. "She guessed that the wedding is postponed a while longer. I told her it was, but not indefinitely."

"As much as I'd rather do it the proper way, I say we go to a Justice of the Peace," Dexter said. "At least we'll be married then: we can have a reception later, when everyone is better. But we can't let all this keep us from… getting on with things."

Leedra nodded. "I want to do whatever you want to do," she answered fervently.

He smiled at her. "What if I just want to hold you forever?"

"Well, then I must want that too," she smiled. Their arms entwined as they moved closer and just held on.

33

Crowd Pleaser

AS CASHELL DRIFTED INTO THAT strange liminal state between sleeping and waking, her first thought was that she must have arrived in heaven. Wherever she was, it didn't worry her, because James's voice was somewhere nearby. She couldn't see him, but she could hear him. She smiled as she listened to his soothing words, but when she tried to formulate words of her own to respond, it was as if her throat was blocked. Nothing came out.

Forcing her eyes open for just a moment with a tremendous effort, she squinted at the bright lights overhead, realizing her mouth was also open. Worriedly, she registered that her tongue and mouth felt like she'd been sucking on cotton balls. She couldn't be in heaven, she reasoned, because she couldn't speak. She tried to jolt her memory into action. She knew that the last time she'd seen James, he was being led away in handcuffs by armed police. James didn't seem to have a mark on him then, as far as she could tell. He was beautiful... but something bad had evidently happened. What?

She wanted to panic, to cry... It should have been impossible to cry when she couldn't talk, surely, but she managed it. She tried to move her hand, but she noticed that it was restricted. Her heart beat sped up rapidly and the digital monitors surrounding her started up a shrill chorus of bleeps and buzzes to alert the doctors.

"Cashell - baby, baby, it's all going to be fine. Look at me: I'm fine, do you hear? I need you to breathe - let the machine breathe for you... Calm down. Be still."

Moments passed as she focused, then Cashell registered that Dexter was in the room with them. Her blood pressure went down, but only slightly. She was worn out. Most of all she wanted to talk to James, but she remembered that Dexter was here because he could help her. He wasn't her doctor, but he was a doctor. Just then, her own primary doctor did appear: first the iron-gray hair, then the rest of him.

"Cashell, welcome. Blink if you understand me, yes?"

"J, let's go," she heard Dexter say quietly to James. "We gotta leave so the doctors can tend to her."

Cashell wanted to protest. She shook her head. James looked at Dexter and nodded. He stared deep into her eyes. "I love you. I love you."

She blinked and felt his hand grab hers... but she wanted to touch his face. She wanted to rip the device from her throat, but that was likely why the restraints were in place: to prevent her from doing so. As she strove to be calm, she saw James leaving and other nurses rushing in. He was all right. He was all right. She was immeasurably relieved.

He would be back to see her. She clung to the hope supplied by that thought. She closed her eyes tight while the doctor asked her more questions, to which she agreed or otherwise by moving her head as much as the machines permitted. She focused as much as she could, knowing that any display of anxiety would only prolong her separation from James.

She was okay; everything was going to be okay. Now that she was conscious, she answered their too-numerous and too-stupid questions about pain and feelings and tried her best to be okay.

The next day, James was back at Cashell's side. She was able to speak again now: her voice came out only in a whisper, but this time he heard every word. She could not go home until her heart rate went down, and while that was admittedly annoying, at least most of the machines had been wheeled away. The few that remained included a pulse monitor and her ever-present electrocardiograph machine, with its ugly gray box and itchy telemetry pads dotting her chest. She desperately wanted a shower, but James was there and she wanted time with him more than anything. They watched mindless television, favorite channels like HGTV and the Food network, and talked about everything. For obvious reasons, they avoided channels that showed any news - cable or certainly local.

James sipped a cup of coffee and gave her hand his familiar reassuring squeeze. Cashell looked skeptically at the cold, rubbery pancakes in front her and pushed them away. She longed for Cole's cooking, or even James's. Heck, she knew a pair of preteen girls who could both cook just about anything better than what was set before her. The memory of Kira and Hannah, and the thought of seeing them again really soon, brought an instant smile to her face.

"They found Bobby," James informed her. "He's gonna be arraigned in a week or two, then I guess he'll go to trial."

"And Braxton?"

"Rehabilitation after surgery. They couldn't get the bullet out of his spine. Rumor has it that he's lost some use of his legs. I don't know how much. It's just internet gossip and press speculation at this point."

Cashell was silent, looking at the television. She was saddened by it all.

"You'll need to press charges," James continued. "I'm going to."

Cashell shrugged. "You go ahead, but I won't be doing that," she replied simply.

"Cashell?"

"I won't, James. I prayed really hard that God would change your brother's heart to you and look what happened. Do you think that wasn't all God? How could Bobby get all the way in there, choke me out, then not ultimately shoot you?" Tears ran down her face and James reached over to wipe them away.

"All that does not change what he did to you." James leaned

onto her bed, his face hovering near hers.

"It changed everything - every outcome. It spared your life and that is the only thing I wanted. Now, I'd rather not dwell on this subject. I have a wedding to plan." Cashell picked up her phone and began scrolling through her Pinterest boards.

James looked at the pictures as they flashed by. "Our wedding?"

"What?" Her thumb hovered above the cellphone touchscreen and she turned to James.

"Our wedding?" he repeated, smiling.

"I'm sorry, but I don't recall a proper proposal. If you popped the question while I was in a coma, Mister, that doesn't count." She shrugged, smiling and pretending to dismiss him.

"How's this?"

Before she could register what was happening, he got down on one knee and reached into his pocket. Her phone fell from her fingers, Leedra and the other wedding instantly forgotten, as she watched James open the small velvet box.

"Cashell Bruer, will you marry me?"

Rendered speechless once again, she simply nodded. He reached for her, pulling her up so he could hug her tight.

34
Finally, I Thee Wed

"I'M ALMOST READY. ARE YOU?" called Leedra.

James nodded. He'd just entered his house, hiding from all the noisy camaraderie going on outside, and she had heard him come in. He was relieved to have found a quiet space to wait for the bride-to-be in peace. He hoped no-one else discovered him for a while.

It had been a hectic morning, but in just a few hours Dexter and Leedra would be married at last. Somehow, he and Cashell had ended up in charge of the entire thing. She'd gotten him to agree to it by way of a dupe, a set-up of epic proportions; but he'd do anything to make her happy. Since she'd been discharged from the hospital, she was back to her old take-charge self, full steam ahead. True, they saw each other almost every day, but his weekly and weekend football schedule plus her fast-accelerating freelance work meant that their days were full. He guessed that helping to plan this wedding was as close as he would get to a run-through for his own nuptials.

Cashell had everyone on their toes, with endless lists and military-grade organization. Her ability to bounce back astounded everyone, especially her doctors and her family – well, almost everyone. James had always known she'd be back as her old self eventually, even though the thought of another relapse or setback occurring again was a constant weight on his mind. Over the last couple of days, he reflected, it seemed like everything was catching up with him.

"Hello."

James looked up as Leedra placed a hand on his shoulder.

He sat up and had to catch his breath as he looked up at her. She was beautiful. Her simple, classic white dress was long, billowy and elegant: perfectly understated, just like her.

"Did you hear me?" she asked, with a twinkle in her eye.

"Uh, no. Sorry. What did you say?" James fidgeted with the bow tie Cashell had helped him put on. He felt suffocated by it, and couldn't wait until the wedding was over so he could lose it altogether.

"I said, I've been watching you this entire morning, and one thing you are not going to do on my special day is to sit around here feeling sorry for yourself," Leedra admonished, only half playfully.

"I'm not," James protested. "I've just been thinking a lot. Wedding prep kind of gives you, uh, a fresh perspective."

Leedra narrowed her eyes at him. "This doesn't have anything to do with news of your mom, does it?"

"I suppose." James shrugged his shoulders. He and Cashell had been to see his mother almost every other weekend. She wasn't much better, but a few subtle signs that she was finally starting to recognize them made the visits that much better. On their last visit, Cashell had downloaded a midi piano keyboard app on her phone, and pressing the pixelated keys had actually made his Mom smile. Buoyed by this breakthrough, James was in talks with the facility about hiring a musician to come in and lead music therapy. That, too, had been Cashell's idea.

James smiled. Surely just for today he could manage to put aside all that had been happening in his life, both on and off the field. He'd had a very difficult time forgiving his brother, but in the end he had to.

"I don't want to be a Debbie Downer on your special day," he smiled. "I'm'a get it together."

"You are not a Debbie Downer, whoever Debbie was..." Leedra replied thoughtfully, and James laughed. She continued: "Nothing can ruin my day. We all need time to process our lives, and you've had a lot happen in the last few months.

When are you and Cashell getting married?"

"Um, we haven't set a date yet."

The scrutiny of Leedra's gaze caught him once more. "Are you the holdup on that?" she asked knowingly.

James shrugged. He wasn't the hold up, or at least he didn't think he was. He'd marry Cashell in a heartbeat, but so much had been going on that he really couldn't even remember if she'd expressed a preference for a particular time of year. "I – uh…" he stuttered.

"You do want to get married, don't you?" Leedra asked.

"Of course," he said without hesitation.

"That's what I thought."

James stood up. "So, we ready? I mean, I'm not exactly worthy to walk you down this aisle… I don't know why Dexter would ask me, of all people."

"And why not? I couldn't think of anyone else I'd want to do it," Leedra smiled. "Plus, you gotta get some kind of practice in before you and Cashell tie the knot. Ye of so little faith, consider this your rehearsal."

Leedra took a deep audible breath that had James concerned. "What is it?" he questioned. "That kind of sigh should not come out of a woman about to be married."

James waited. It looked as if Leedra was struggling against herself.

"I'm… going to take a risk and sound like Allontis," she rushed out in one breath. "I'm not sure you need this pep talk – you should really talk to your intended instead of me – but I just want to say that I'm here for you. You are worthy of all the love. See, when I moved back to town – after Allontis and I got to know each other again and I started to have feelings for Dexter – Allontis was real keen to give me all this unsolicited love advice. It felt a little like a romantic novel. I started to think it might be normal for people just to melt about all over the place, falling in love with whoever happens to be nearby. It's contagious, I suppose."

"Well, Lonnie is hard to argue with," James agreed. "When

you look at your own family... well, no matter how it came together, it is together, and it's just beautiful. She and Cole make it look so easy. That said, we all know that for every situation that seems picture-perfect, there's almost always a back story: a hard road to get there. You know, like your road to love with Dex: both your pasts, Flora and all that jazz."

"Yes, absolutely. Anyway, you're hovering, not committing... there's no-one else, is there?" She made a plane with her fingers and circled it around as if about to land. James shook his head no. Leedra continued:

"Ever since Allontis gave me that talk more than, what, a year ago now, I've begun to understand how important it was for me to hear what she said. It plants the seed of hope in your heart - even when your mind refuses to believe it, as yours is now. It's easy to just go through the motions, but I want you to be really invested in it."

"I'm invested in Cashell's happiness," James replied.

"And I'm saying I want you to be invested in your own, too. You deserve it," Leedra returned firmly.

James smiled. He was trying to force himself to accept that as the truth. When he'd first met Cashell, he hadn't foreseen her being anything more than a friend. Then he fell in love, then all hell broke loose... but he'd survived, and so had she.

"And you're not that special, by the way," Leedra added with a smirk. "Dexter just didn't want me to feel alone today. The wedding is so small as it is, and with Cole playing the piano you were the only brother available. But seriously, I don't care who walks me down the aisle as long as I eventually get to the man waiting for me at the front. You feel me?"

"I got you," said James.

"Let's go, then. Oh, and thanks for letting us use your beautiful backyard."

"You're welcome."

The two of them walked slowly out of the house and around to the backyard, where just thirty or so people were seated. James took her hand in the crook of his arm, and as he prepared to give her away to his brother in marriage, he also prepared his heart to receive still more of the many blessings God had in store.

It couldn't have been a more perfect day, Cashell thought, when she finally saw the bride and her escort appear at the terrace doors beyond the pool. Her heart fluttered with happiness at the sight of Leedra wearing a dress that was clearly made for her. She looked exquisite. The bodice was deceptively conservative, yet incredibly elegant: sleeveless to accentuate her Michelle Obama arms, and fitted to show off her beautiful height. Despite her beauty and the striking good looks of the man who walked beside her, neither of them were looking at one another. Leedra clearly had eyes for Dexter alone – and Cashell couldn't tear her eyes away from James. She smiled to herself - everyone was smiling, all around the backyard, and it was just infectious.

The music cued. Cole struck up a wedding march on the rented keyboard, duetting with the violinist he'd hired to produce gorgeous, melodious sounds that filtered through the portable speakers dotted strategically around the garden.

James gave her a wink as he passed her. With an effort, she refocused her dreamy smile away from him: the man who, she reminded herself, would be waiting for her at the other end of an aisle one wonderful day. Right now, though, she wanted to be fully present to hear Dexter and Leedra utter their vows – their words.

Allontis moved to take the bridal bouquet from Leedra so she and Dexter could join hands, and Cashell bent to arrange the modest train perfectly behind Leedra before stepping back into the bridal party formation. Her heels kept sinking into the soft grass beneath her feet.

The Pastor began to speak. "Ladies and gentlemen, married couples and future married couples..."

On hearing that phrase, Cashell looked up at the Pastor. She was sure he gave her a meaningful look. James took her hand and smiled down at her, mouthing the words, "I love you." She smiled, returning his sentiment before focusing again on the service. The prayer began, then Leedra and Dexter lit their unity candle just a few feet away. In a whirl of words, more prayers and the final kiss, it was done. The minister pronounced them man and wife, and Cashell let her tears fall. She loved weddings.

Now that the happy deed was completed, everyone got up from their seats and began to mingle, gradually wandering up onto the special wooden dance platform that James had ensured was built to suit in his garden. As the reception was being held at James's house, all the guests would be staying the night. The cooling evening air was already infused with light, up-tempo jazzy sounds: elegant yet low-key, perfectly befitting the happy couple.

Watching the revelry begin, Cashell remembered that she needed to go and help Leedra change out of her wedding dress into the shorter sheath she'd helped her pick out... but right then she just wanted to enjoy the joyous afterglow and gaze at the sun as it moved down behind the mountains.

"Are you doing all right?"

Turning, Cashell noticed James approaching her with a glass of water. The ice clinked as she gulped it thirstily through the straw. "Thank you. Yes, I'm doing great." James took out a handkerchief and dabbed at her forehead. Cashell regarded him with a dreamy smile.

"How do you know just what I need?" she wondered aloud.

He smiled. "It's my mission in life." He took the now-empty glass from her hand and placed it on the chair. "Are you hungry?"

Cashell grinned. "Hunger is beside the point. I helped Leedra pick out every item on tonight's menu, and I'm not leaving until I've sampled every single dish. It's a matter of principle." Her attempt at humor didn't draw a laugh. If she was so excited about eating, he wondered, why did she have tears in her eyes?

Cashell blinked fast, seeing that he'd noticed her misty eyes and trying to banish the evidence. "Today was perfect, you know."

"Not as perfect as you," James said.

"I'm not perfect. You of all people should know that. OK, your turn. What are you thinking about?"

"All I can think about is all the stuff that's happened over the last few months. My brother, Mom… I just feel like I've been a little stuck."

Cashell shook her head. "You've got a lot on your mind: your brother and your Mom, as you say."

James's face became serious. "If I would just keep you on my mind, I wouldn't be bogged down by all that. Be honest: have I been holding us up with the date?"

Cashell was surprised by the sudden earnestness. "No, I just thought you wanted to wait for things to wrap up with your brother and Leedra first - and I know you've wanted to take the kids off their hands on one of your bye-weeks."

"That's no excuse," he said resolutely.

"You know I don't fault you for anything. You take your time."

"Said no bride-to-be ever," James retorted sardonically.

Cashell chuckled. James was still distant, it was true; but no longer in a way that implied he wasn't invested in their relationship. They were together often, and that in itself was a comfort. In the past few weeks, they'd been getting even closer than before. Meanwhile, her contract with the team had actually come to an end, but she was doing some freelance writing that kept her busy enough.

"I want to pick a date right now, but I've got something else to tell you, too. I got a book deal."

"You did?" Cashell hugged him in delight. "I thought they'd start calling you one of these days, but this is so quick! Who with?"

"One of the big five you're always talking about."

"That's nuts. How much?"

Cashell was genuinely excited, although to tell the truth she was a little disappointed at the same time. She had been entertaining the idea of writing his story herself and pitching it to the very publishers that had likely offered him this deal.

"Oh, two million."

Cashell caught her breath. "Oh my goodness! Wow! Are you gonna take it?"

"I'm still thinking about it," he replied cautiously. "It's a big investment for me: a lot of personal stuff to share about myself. I'm just not sure I'm ready to divulge all that to everybody."

Cashell kept her arms around his neck and spoke carefully. "Sure, it's a lot to share – but it's also a grand narrative that would inspire others. It'll show the level of adversity you've overcome, as well as helping others to see the paths not to take. Your story is an amazing illustration of God's hand over your life, even in the midst of all the mistakes so many others around you have made."

"Yeah," James admitted. "Actually, I was thinking there was this one writer in particular I want to work with."

"Oh, okay," she replied softly. She wished she worked for whatever publishing house had offered him the deal, so she could be the one to help him tell it. She was slightly crestfallen not to be more involved, but she told herself it would be awesome for him to get his story out there regardless of who wrote it.

James studied her face. "Are you disappointed?"

"Of course not," she fibbed. "We're in this together. I'd just love to read over the drafts – you know, to make sure your voice is coming through, make sure there's no slant, all that sort of thing."

"Well, you better start writing so you can read those drafts, then," James said, poker-faced. "That's a lot of work."

Cashell did a double take. "What?"

"I told them I would only work with this fantastic writer I know right here in Virginia. Cashell Bruer."

Cashell shook her head in disbelief before laughing a little hysterically. "I'm sure they told you to forget it."

"Nope. They said they would draw something up and overnight it to me and my advisor – who also goes by the name of Cashell Bruer - and my lawyer to look over." James beamed at her.

Cashell couldn't believe it. The opportunity of a lifetime and the man of a lifetime had both fallen into her lap within the same week.

"You'd do that for me?"

"I'd do anything for you," he responded. "Now, we'll talk about all that some more later. We can't stay out here all night: we have eating and lots of dancing to do. There's just one thing that I want resolved before we go back to join the party."

"Okay, but I'm not sure I can handle much more," Cashell said apprehensively.

"It's about us getting married. How about on the anniversary of the day we met? That way I'll never forget it."

"Oh, on my birthday? In March, right?" she clarified.

James laughed. "You forget your own birthday?"

"I'm just making sure. Only one date to remember - very funny." She smiled again. "I think that would be wonderful." She felt a surge of energy.He bent to hug her tight and she returned his embrace.

"Never let me go," she whispered into his ear. "I won't," he promised, before sealing his pledge with a kiss.

The End

ABOUT THE AUTHOR

TRACEE LYDIA GARNER IS A bestselling, award-winning author whose stories feature complex relationships and characters experiencing tough but realistic challenges in their quests for love. Born and raised in a Virginia suburb of the DC metro area, Tracee has a degree in Communications, works in health and human services by day and is a speaker-advocate for people with disabilities.

Tracee is a member of the Romance Writers Association (RWA); the Washington Romance Writers DC Chapter; Faith, Hope and Love, an online-only chapter of RWA; and the Association of Christian Fiction Writers (ACFW) Virginia chapter, for which she serves as secretary. Visit Tracee at www.Teegarner.com